'I know what it is you want

'Something you've never been offered, something deep inside you waiting to be used. It's called passion.

'I heard it in your voice when you sang,' Sir Chase Boston continued, 'and I can see it in your eyes. I felt it as we drove together, wildly. You were breathless with it, and guilty with it, too. You are angry with men, your father, your brother, those pathetic creatures who offered for you, and me in particular, because you're interested, for once, and you dare not say so because you're insulted by the urgency of it all.'

His arm lay along the back of the couch. One forefinger touched the bare skin of her upper arm just below the petalled sleeve, sending a shock through Caterina's body that instantly washed away the snub she would have liked to deliver. The finger bent, caressed, and withdrew, leaving its memory behind to linger upon her arm.

Juliet Landon's keen interest in art and history, both of which she used to teach, combined with a fertile imagination, make writing historical novels a favourite occupation. She is particularly interested in researching the early medieval period and the problems encountered by women in a man's world. Her heart's home is in her native North Yorkshire, but now she lives happily in a Hampshire village close to her family. Her first books, which were on embroidery and design, were published under her own name of Jan Messent.

Dishonour and Desire is a sequel to *A Scandalous Mistress.* They feature descendants of characters you will have met in *One Night in Paradise.*

Recent novels by the same author:

A SCANDALOUS MISTRESS
THE WARLORD'S MISTRESS
HIS DUTY, HER DESTINY
THE BOUGHT BRIDE
THE WIDOW'S BARGAIN
ONE NIGHT IN PARADISE

Look for Seton's story.
Coming soon.

DISHONOUR AND DESIRE

Juliet Landon

First published in Great Britain 2007
Paperback edition 2007
Harlequin Mills & Boon Limited,
Eton House, 18-24 Paradise Road, Richmond, Surrey TW9 1SR

ISBN: 978 0 263 85182 3

Set in Times Roman 10½ on 12 pt.
04-0707-84368

Printed and bound in Spain
by Litografia Rosés S.A., Barcelona

DISHONOUR AND DESIRE

Chapter One

1812—Richmond, Surrey

Still smiling at some absurdity, Miss Caterina Chester and her sister rode into the stable yard behind Number 18 Paradise Road, patting the damp glossy necks before them and fully expecting the usual smiles of welcome from the grooms eager to help them dismount. This sunny morning, with steam rising from the tiled rooftops, the stable yard was busy with lads sluicing mud off the wheels of a coffee-and-cream-coloured crane-neck phaeton while another groom in an unfamiliar green livery held the bridle of a large grey hunter in the shade of the covered walkway. No one came running to meet them.

'Father has a visitor,' said Sara.

'That's Aunt Amelie's phaeton,' said Caterina, coming to a halt. 'Why is it covered in mud? Joseph,' she called, 'what's all this?'

Joseph lowered his dripping broom and turned, shading his eyes. 'Sorry, Miss Chester. I didn't hear you coming,' he said, wiping his hands down his apron.

He came forward to take the bridles, but Caterina threw one leg over the pommel and slid to the ground before he could reach her. 'Help Miss Sara,' she told him. 'I can manage. Who's been out in the phaeton?'

'Master Harry,' said Joseph, leading Sara's horse. 'He borrowed it last evening and—'

'*Borrowed* it? Without asking?' Angrily, she looked up at her sister. 'Did you know of this, Sara?'

'Certainly not. Aunt Amelie lent it to you, not to Harry.'

'So why didn't you mention this to me when you brought the horses round this morning, Joseph?'

The groom stared apologetically at the grimy phaeton, blinking in surprise at the sudden deep waters. 'Well, because I thought you knew, Miss Chester. Master Harry told me he'd had permission to use it, and to be quick and get it ready.'

'Ready for what?'

'He didn't say for what, miss. But whatever it was, I don't think Lady Elyot would've liked it much. Just look at it, caked with mud and splashed all over. We're having to scrub every last inch of it.' He scowled at the shining areas of panelling just showing through runnels of water. 'It only came back a half hour ago.'

Pretty Sara did not intend to dismount by herself as long as there was an attractive groom to help. Bouncing lightly onto the cobbles, she removed her hands from Joseph's shoulders but, even then, was not able to get her question in before her sister's. 'Back from where?'

The stable yard grew quiet at Caterina's razor-sharp tone.

Joseph let out a breath. 'It's been over at Mortlake all night, Miss Chester. In Sir Chase Boston's stables.

That's Sir Chase's groom over there. They brought it back this morning. Shall I ask him…?'

'No, I'll find out the rest for myself.' The hem of Caterina's dove-grey riding habit skimmed over the wet cobbles as she strode away to the steps that led up to the house, her slender back curved like a bow, both hands raised to unpin her veiled hat. Before her sister had reached her level, a mass of dark copper curls came loose with the net, tumbling onto her shoulders like a fox-fur cape, glinting with red highlights in the sun. Her slender figure appeared to pour through the door with a fluidity that typified all her movements.

'So that's her,' said Sir Chase Boston's groom, smirking.

'Aye, that's her,' said Joseph, leading the two horses away. 'Now for some fireworks.'

The man grinned. 'Should be interesting, then.'

Joseph glanced at the big grey. 'I shouldn't bother unsaddling him. Your master'll be out in five minutes with his ears afire.'

'Want a bet?' the man said, settling himself onto the mounting-block.

In the elegant white-and-gold hallway, Caterina paused only long enough to glance at the table where a beaver hat, a pair of pale leather gloves and a silver-banded riding whip lay where the butler had placed them. A row of calling-cards marked the exact centre of the silver tray, and the reflection in the ormolu mirror above received not even a cursory acknowledgement in passing. From the upper landing came the slam of doors, a woman's faintly commanding voice, the siren-wail of infants, nurses cooing and strains of a distant lullaby. Wincing at the cacophany, Caterina just failed to hide the grimace before she opened the study door.

Not usually minding her interruptions, her father stopped his conversation abruptly, sensing the arrival of a minor whirlwind. 'Ah, there you are,' he said, turning to face her. 'You received my message?' Middle-aged and lean with the look of a harassed greyhound, Stephen Chester did his best to smile, though it did not come naturally to him.

'No, Father. There appears to be a breakdown in the system somewhere. I received no message about the phaeton, either.'

'So you've seen it. Well, Sir Chase has ridden over from Mortlake to explain the situation. I don't believe you've met. Sir Chase Boston. My eldest daughter, sir.'

There was a movement behind her and, to her discomfort, Caterina realised that her father's guest had been lurking behind the door, watching her without being noticed. Well, perhaps not exactly lurking, but one could not help thinking that he had positioned himself there on purpose.

Like her father, Caterina was tall and there were relatively few men who came near to dwarfing her so that she had to lift her chin to see their faces. This man was not only tall, but broad and deep-chested, too, which she did not think was due to padding. She had heard of him; everyone in society had heard of Sir Chase Boston's on-off *affaires,* his nonsensical wagers, which he always seemed to win, his amazing exploits in the hunting field and his phenomenal driving skills. There was little, apparently, that this man had not attempted at some time. Except marriage.

She had expected to put a more ravaged face to a man with such an intemperate reputation—deep creases, muddy complexion, that kind of thing. What she saw instead was a pair of very intense hazel eyes that held hers with an alarming frankness, a well-groomed craggy face with a firm dimpled chin, and thick black hair raked back untidily off a broad forehead and curling down the front of his ears.

Yes, she thought, even his looks were excessive, though his dress was correct in every detail, spotless and well fitting. Looking down at the toes of his shining black-and-tan top-boots, she felt herself blushing like a schoolgirl, having seen in his eyes something more than mere politeness. The bow of her head was accompanied by the tiniest curtsy. 'Sir Chase,' she said, 'may I ask how you come to be returning my aunt's phaeton in such a condition?' Her eyes, golden-brown and very angry, were not having the effect upon him that she had intended.

'I won it,' he said. 'The horses, too. From your brother.' His voice was deep, as one might have expected from such a well-built man.

'My aunt's dapple-greys? Harry took those?'

'A good colour. Goes well with the brown.'

She suspected he was not talking about the phaeton and pair. 'Father,' she said, stripping off her gloves, 'will you tell me what's going on, please? Aunt Amelie lent them to me, you know, and—'

'Yes,' said Mr Chester, 'and young Harry's returned to Liverpool on the early mail this morning without saying a word about this ridiculous wager. It appears that Sir Chase and he had a race round Richmond Park last night and Harry lost. Hadn't you better sit down, my dear?'

'Harry lost with property that was not his to lose. I see,' snapped Caterina. 'No, I *don't* see. Sir Chase, if you knew it was not my brother's, why did you—?'

'I didn't,' interrupted their guest, pushing himself off the wall and going to stand by his host's side from where he could see her better. 'He led me to believe it was his when he made the bet. And I won. He was obliged to leave the phaeton at Mortlake. When I looked, I found this tucked into a corner of the seat.' His hand delved into his waistcoat pocket as he spoke, then pulled out a very delicate lace-edged handkerchief, which he handed to Caterina. 'The initials A.C. in the corner suggested the young man's aunt, the former Lady Amelie Chester, now Lady Elyot. And in case she particularly wants the phaeton back, I have offered your father the chance to redeem it. I dare say it's worth about two hundred or so. One of the great Felton's, I believe. Five years old, one owner, patent cylinder axle-trees, and the horses...well...they're worth—'

'And my brother walked back from Mortlake, did he? Or did you offer him a lift?'

His eyes sparked with scorn. 'Your brother owes me money, Miss Chester. I don't offer lifts to people in my debt. Do you?'

'The point is, my dear,' said Caterina's troubled father, 'that Sir Chase has every right to expect his winnings to be paid promptly. It's extraordinarily decent of him to return the phaeton and horses, but a wager is a wager, and—'

'And it would be even more extraordinarily decent if Sir Chase were to draw a line under this silly nonsense and write his loss down to experience, wouldn't it, Father? After all, I don't suppose Sir Chase is lacking horses, or phaetons, is he? Harry is twenty, not yet earning, and tends to be a little irresponsible at times.' Her heart beat a rhythm into her throat, and she could not quite define the singular hostility she felt towards this man. Was it simply his claims? His uncompromising directness? Was it his attitude towards her father? Or to her? Was it that she had heard of his many and varied love affairs?

'Your brother's lack of funds, Miss Chester, is his own problem, not mine,' Sir Chase said. 'If he makes a wager, he should have the resources to back it without embarrassing anyone else. His irresponsibility is farcical, but when I win a wager I tend not to draw lines under the debt until it's paid. Nor do I pretend that I've lost. I'm not a charitable institution, and it's time young Mr Chester learned a thing or two about honour.'

'I would have thought, sir,' said Caterina, 'that in a case of this kind, a phaeton and *pair,* for heaven's sake, you might have waived the inattention to honour. I realise that my brother is at fault for gambling with something he doesn't own, but surely—' She stopped, suddenly aware that there was something yet to be spoken of.

Stephen Chester had never been good at concealing his thoughts, and now his long face registered real alarm, with a hasty doleful glance at Sir Chase that spoke volumes and a twist of his mouth before he spoke. 'Er...ahem! It's not...oh, my goodness!' He sighed, casting a longing glance at the two glasses of brandy, just poured.

'Father, what is it? There's something else, isn't there?'

He nodded, abjectly. 'Harry owes money, too,' he whispered. 'Sir Chase was just about to tell me as you came in, but I really don't think you should be hearing this, my dear. I didn't know all this when I sent a message for you to come. Perhaps you should—'

'How much?' Caterina said, flatly. 'Come, Father. Sit down here and tell me about it. You cannot keep this to yourself.'

'I don't know how much,' he said, weakly. 'Sir Chase?'

'He owes me twenty thousand, sir.'

Mr Chester's head sunk slowly into his hands, but Caterina stared with her lips parted. She thought she saw stars until she blinked them away. 'Twenty *thousand?*' she whispered. 'Pounds?'

'Guineas.'

She gasped. 'And how in heaven's name did he…oh… Good grief! And he's left you to repay a debt like that? How could he…how *could* he do that, Father?'

Sir Chase seemed remarkably composed, as if they were talking of pennies rather than guineas. 'I have your brother's IOU for that amount, for which I gave him twenty-four hours' grace. He assured me he would bring the money to me yesterday morning, but when he arrived at my house in London, he proposed that we should race a team round Richmond Park, the debt to be written off if he won. I would not normally accept such a wager, but he begged me for one more chance and I could see he was in Queer Street. Even so, I saw no reason why I should entirely forfeit the blunt for his sake. As I said—'

'Yes, we heard what you said, Sir Chase. Did my brother say how he would get the money? Money-lenders?'

'It's not my business to ask, Miss Chester, but I don't think he'd found a way of raising the wind, otherwise I would not be telling your father about it.'

'So you came here this morning expecting to find him?'

'As you say. And to return Lady Elyot's phaeton.'

Mr Chester's hand groped blindly across the table for his glass of brandy, and Caterina pushed it towards him, then went round to support it as he sipped and sighed noisily, her anger at her brother's lack of principles combining with sympathy at the shock of such a crippling debt.

Her father had done nothing to deserve this. Twenty thousand guineas was a vast sum of money for which he would almost certainly have to sell this house here in Richmond as well as the one he owned in Buxton, for the income from his late brother's estate which he had inherited was already being stretched to its limits, and he was not allowed to raise capital by selling anything that had been entailed on him. That would all go to Harry, eventually.

Her father's second and much younger wife, Hannah, had presented him with two pairs of twins in six years, and now their handsome house on Paradise Road, which had once been Lady Elyot's, was bursting at the seams. For the sake of comfort, Harry's month-long holiday had been spent mostly in London, about two hours' drive away. And Sir Chase had clearly come here for full recompense, not to negotiate.

Hoping to put him out of countenance, Caterina went in with both barrels blazing. 'Do you then live off your earnings, Sir Chase?' she asked.

'Caterina!' he father spluttered. 'My dear, you may not ask a man questions of that nature. Please, it's time you went. Sir Chase and I will discuss this and find a way, somehow. The debt will be paid. You had better go and see how Hannah does. She's been asking for you.'

Sir Chase reached the door ahead of her and, with one hand on the brass knob, would have opened it but for

Caterina's hand placed firmly over the join. 'One moment, if you please,' she said, tilting her head to look scathingly into his eyes. 'I understand the meaning of honour as well as any man, Sir Chase, but if I may not ask you about your winnings, then perhaps I may ask if you truly believed it was honourable to challenge my brother to a race you must have known he could not win when he already owed you money he could not pay? What exactly was your purpose in encouraging him into such folly that could only end in my father's embarrassment?'

Her heart-shaped face was held up to the light, showing him the full opulence of her loveliness, the luxuriant waving chestnut hair touching the silken-sheened skin, amazing golden-brown eyes framed by sweeping lashes, a straight nose and wide lips full of sensuous beauty. Her eyes blazed with the kind of passion that would respond instantly and without inhibition to any situation, and Sir Chase doubted very much that she would have obeyed her father if she had not already decided to do so. Perhaps she wanted him to see her as submissive, but he could see in her eyes, in her very bearing, that it was not so. This one would do as she pleased.

Mischievously, he incensed her further by allowing his eyes to roam briefly inside the frilled collar of her habit-shirt and then over her firm high breasts. 'But I have already told you, Miss Chester,' he said, unsmiling, 'it was your brother who challenged me, not the other way round. So if you understand honour as well as you say you do, you'll not need any further explanation, will you?'

Though she sensed there was more to be said on the subject, there was a limit to the time she wished to spend in the company of this arrogant man, so she took her hand away from the door and waited for him to turn the knob. When he did not, she looked up to find him regarding her from between half-closed eyes that were difficult to read, and it was being made to wait until he was ready that made her realise he was telling her something about her manner. When he *did* open it, very… very…slowly, she was not allowed to whirl out as she had whirled in.

Out in the hall, she found that her heart was beating a hollow thud between her shoulder-blades, and the desire to sweep his accessories off the table on to the floor was only curbed by the sound of a high-pitched infant tantrum. With a sigh, she turned and went upstairs.

The same sound reached Stephen Chester's ears before the door closed behind his daughter, making him look up, ruefully. 'Sorry about that,' he murmured.

Assuming he meant the noise, Sir Chase took the seat opposite, sampling his glass of brandy while looking round him at the beautiful Wedgwood-blue room overlooking a large garden at the back of the house. A well-executed painting of a ship under sail against a background of some distant harbour hung on the wall behind Mr Chester's desk. Through the new green of the trees, he could see the distant sparkle of the River Thames, alive with wherries and their passengers. There were no signs of poverty to be seen, but the discrepancy in the ages of his host's family was intriguing, and obviously a cause of expense. And although Sir Chase had not come here intending to negotiate, there was now a new factor in the equation that had not been there when he arrived: Miss Caterina Chester.

'You have an interesting family, Mr Chester,' he said,

replacing his glass on the table. He rested one boot across his knee and held it there. 'I understand Mrs Chester is your second wife.'

Stephen smoothed a hand over his thinning dark red hair from the back of his head to the front, nodding. 'My wife is one of the Elwicks of Mortlake,' he said. 'You will probably know them. Been married almost six years.'

Sir Chase's dark brows moved. 'Oh, indeed I do, sir. Near neighbours of my parents. I believe the eldest son died a couple of years ago.'

'Mrs Chester's brother Chad. Yes. I lost the first Mrs Chester ten years ago, and with three grown children of my own I didn't quite expect so large a second family so soon. If I'd known there were going to be nine of us instead of five, I'd not have moved from Buxton. My Derbyshire home is a good deal larger than this one, plenty of rooms, woodland and paddocks, and orchards. But my wife is a Surrey woman, and Caterina and her sister wanted to stay near London.' He smiled at last, softening with fatherly pride. 'Caterina lived here with her aunt, Lady Elyot, who was still Lady Chester at that time. It was perfect for the two of them then.'

'Ah, your daughter. May I ask her age, sir?'

'Twenty-three, Sir Chase.' Suddenly, Stephen's hand slapped the table as he stood up, shimmering the remaining brandy in his glass. 'Twenty bloody three, and not married. And not likely to be, if she can't be more agreeable than that.' He strode to the window, staring out into the distance. 'I hope you'll excuse her forthright manner, sir,' he said, more quietly. 'She can be quite difficult to handle at times, but we've all been under a bit of a strain, one way or another, and unfortunately Caterina has a mind of her own. My other daughter,' he said, lightening his tone, 'Sara , is just the opp—'

'Tell me, if you will, about Miss Caterina Chester, sir.'

'Eh?' Startled, he turned to look. 'I thought you'd have heard by now.'

Sir Chase smiled, but made no reply.

Stephen sauntered to the table, studied the remaining brandy and gulped it down in one go. Then, moving from one piece of furniture to the next and sliding his fingertips over the surfaces, he hopped through what he saw as the main events of Caterina's twenty-three years in a verbal hotchpotch that reflected his own needs more than hers. 'Well, I allowed her to come down here from Derbyshire to live with my brother's widow. Caterina and her aunt are very close. She lives up at Sheen Court now, since she became Lady Elyot.'

'Yes, I know Lord and Lady Elyot and his brother Lord Rayne well.'

'Oh, of course. Well, Caterina was seventeen when she came out. Made quite a stir at the time. Very much sought after. You can imagine.'

'I can indeed, sir. Offers of marriage?'

'Oh, Lord, yes. Plenty. She accepted the Earl of Loddon first.'

'Then what?'

'She cried off at the last minute, the minx. Heaven knows what the real cause was. And what a fuss that provoked!' He stroked his hair again. 'Second engagement to Viscount Hadstoke. We told her she was fortunate to have an offer after that, title, wealth, big…er… well, anyway, she ducked out of that one with just two days to go. I was sure that would be the end of her chances. High risk, you know. A non-starter. She didn't seem to care, but I did, and so did her sister.'

'Why is that, sir?'

Stephen stopped pacing to spread his hands, helplessly, though he did not answer the question regarding Sara. 'Well, how does it *look,* I ask you? Talk...gossip...plenty of offers of *carte blanche,* but no more offers of marriage after that. Well, that's not quite correct. The Earl of St Helen's offered for her last week, but she won't even look at him. It's her last chance. I've told her so, but she refuses to set her cap at any man, and that's that. An *earl!*' He glared at the ceiling.

'I see. And she doesn't give you any particular reason?'

With a snort of derision, Stephen's retort was predictable. 'Oh, girlish dreams of love and all that silly stuff. No doubt her reasons make sense to her, but really, Sir Chase, who can afford to pass up offers of that sort? Her sister is ready for marriage right now, but until Caterina is off my hands she'll be disappointed. No self-respecting father would allow the younger one to marry before the elder one. That's the way round it should be. That's the way it's always been.'

'I've known it to happen.'

'Maybe. But not in my family.'

'Then the pressure on Miss Chester to marry must be quite intense.'

'It is. Well...er...what I mean is...yes. To be quite fair, I don't suppose I've helped much by filling the house with four squalling bairns. Don't get me wrong, Sir Chase, I'm fond of my family, all of them, but four infants in a house this size is enough to put any young woman off unless she's the motherly sort. And I don't think that Caterina is. She wants to practise her piano and her singing. Did I tell you she has a fine voice?' Not stopping to notice the expression on his guest's face, he continued. 'Oh, yes, she's invited to sing in all the great houses, you know. Takes it very seriously. Yes, indeed.'

'And your son, Harry? You mentioned he'd returned to Liverpool.'

'This morning on the early mail, back to his uncle. He's learning banking. My late brother's business, you know. Lady Elyot's first husband.'

'That's not quite what he told me when we met in London, sir.'

Stephen Chester's expression sharpened, his eyes suddenly wary. 'Oh? What did he tell you?' he said, coughing between sips of brandy.

'That he owned two banks in Liverpool. Money no object.'

Stephen stopped his pacing and slammed down his glass. 'Wait till I get my hands on him,' he muttered. 'He's determined to see me on the rocks. As if I didn't have problems enough.'

There was an uncomfortable silence during which both men saw these problems from rather different angles, Sir Chase concentrating more on Caterina than on her siblings. She kept rejecting totally unsuitable marriage proposals, yet was desperate to regain the peace she had once known in which she could develop her talents. This was no place for a woman of her sort.

Her father, in his blinkered state, had done less than justice to her talents by not explaining how, in her years of living in Richmond, her voice had been trained by the finest singing teacher in the country, the Italian Signor Rauzzini, until his death last year. That had been a terrible blow to Caterina, for he had nurtured her voice, proclaiming it to be the finest mezzo-soprano he'd heard in one so young. She still had singing lessons and was greatly in demand, but the pressure of having to find a husband to please her parents and sister was having a noticeable effect on her. Her Aunt Amelie had offered to lend her the prized phaeton so that Caterina could escape more often from the domestic pandemonium.

Sir Chase Boston doubted very much that young Harry Chester would be the ruin of his father, but he did not intend to let Chester off the hook when the debt was so substantial, for debt-collecting was what he had come for, not to offer sympathy. The father would deal with his son as he thought fit and the fright of it might help to knock some sense into both their heads. But he himself was beginning to see that there was perhaps more to be gained from Chester's misfortune than twenty thousand guineas plus the price of the phaeton and pair. 'Well, then, sir,' he said, glancing at the inferior brandy, 'shall we do a few sums to begin with? For the carriage, I would say about…'

'Er…' Stephen Chester put out a hand as if to ward off the sound of debt '…do you think…er?'

Impassively, Sir Chase waited. He had learned how to be patient, how not to show his hand too soon, as this man did.

'Er…that there might be another way? An alternative?' It was as if he was talking to himself. 'I simply don't have that kind of blunt, any more than my bird-witted son does. The Buxton house would not sell for anything like enough. To be honest, it's far more than I would have *believed.*' He looked around him, anxiously chewing at the side of his finger. 'And I'm not sure what I can do about it. Let me think. The dowry, Caterina's dowry. Well, it looks as if that may not be needed after all, although I shall need something for Sara—but then, if the dowry is reduced, her chances will be even less, won't they? In fact, they may even disappear altogether,' he added, habitually accepting the darker side.

'This dowry. Is it substantial, sir?'

'Hah! Anything *but* substantial,' said Mr Chester, gloomily. 'So far, Caterina's face and family have been her fortune, but that won't always be the case, will it? I'd say *her* chances have all but slipped away unless she finds somebody to fit her exacting requirements.' There was more than a hint of sarcasm in his voice.

'And you would not consider making an exception by allowing your younger daughter to marry first, simply to take the cost of her off your hands? You must admit, sir, it would make a difference.'

'No, Sir Chase. I could not do that. It would not be proper. Besides, it would acknowledge that I have given up hope of marrying the elder one off, wouldn't it? She'd be well and truly stuck on the shelf *then.*'

'At twenty-three, sir? Surely not.'

'At twenty-three, my first wife had a family of three,' he replied, sharply. 'No, if Caterina is going to be so difficult to please, I may be obliged to make up her mind for her. She could do worse than accept St Helen's, if he's still interested. But he may not be, without a dowry, and I can hardly bear to think what Caterina herself would have to say about it, though I might be able to hazard a guess. She might be persuaded to see it as her duty, but I dare say it would go ill with her to see her sister marry a man of her choice when *she* was not allowed to. Still…' he sighed '…a duty is a duty, though that won't find me all of twenty thousand guineas, will it? Do you know, I could *kill* that son of mine. He must know that a man cannot turn his back on a gambling debt. His tailor is a different kettle of fish, but never a man who wins his wager.' Then he rallied. 'Oh, do forgive me. I should not be talking to you like this, Sir Chase. Not the done thing at all, is it?'

'And would your wife's family not—?'

'Help?' Mr Chester yelped. 'Good grief, man, no! I would never let Mrs Chester hear a *whisper* about all this, or I'd never hear the last of it. Besides, she has enough troubles with four of her own bairns. Absolutely not!'

'So Miss Chester would not tell her?'

'That my son has got me under the hatches and cleared off to Liverpool?' Stephen Chester looked at Sir Chase as if he'd taken leave of his senses. 'I should think not. His stepmother has little enough good opinion of him as it is. And I can't say I blame her. This would only add fuel to her sentiment that he should have been packed off into the navy.'

'There are liabilities in every family, sir.'

'Hum! Glad to hear it. However, the problem is mine and I must be left to deal with it as best I may. Leave it with me, Sir Chase, if you will be so good. I shall call on you tomorrow with my proposals. Are you staying at Mortlake?'

'I wonder…' said Sir Chase, glancing out of the window.

'Eh?'

'I wonder if you would care to hear my suggestion, sir.'

'If it's about borrowing from some cent-per-cent you know, forget it. I never borrow anything.'

'It's not that.' Sir Chase stood on the opposite side of the table with his arms spread like buttresses, drawing the older man's attention to him by the force of his considerable presence. 'You want your daughter married, and you believe her chances are dwindling. Well, I may be able to help you there.'

'You know somebody, do you?' said Stephen Chester, despondently.

Sir Chase thought his host was the dourest of men, though his excuse was certainly a valid one. Not for one moment did he himself think that Miss Caterina Chester's case was as serious as her father appeared to believe. At the age of twenty-three, many débutantes were already married, that much was true, but this one was obviously looking for something not on her father's list and was prepared to wait for it. Nor did he believe that she was on the shelf. Not even approaching it. She was, in fact, the most prime article he'd ever clapped eyes on, but even a Johnny-Raw could see that her father and stepmother between them were handling her more like a child than a grown woman with a mind of her own. That being so, Chester might jump at his offer, and he himself would have to take a different route to achieve his aim. 'Yes,' he said. 'I know somebody. Me, sir. Myself.'

'Eh?' Mr Chester said with a quick frown. From what he'd heard, bang-up coves like Sir Chase Boston did not marry, they took mistresses. His face immediately registered distrust. 'Oh, I could not agree to that, Sir Chase. She's had offers to be a man's mistress before, you know. Only last month, the Duke of—'

'No, not as a mistress, sir. As a wife. I'm talking about marriage. If I can persuade her to marry me, I am prepared to give you the IOU to tear up, and the cost of the phaeton and pair, too. You'll be in the clear again.'

'And what if you can't? She doesn't *want* to marry, Sir Chase. And you could see for yourself that she would never accept *you* as a husband. Not even as a friend,' he added, sharpening the barb.

'Well, then,' said Sir Chase, straightening up. 'It was simply a proposal. No offence meant. I'll expect you at Mortlake tomorrow morning, sir.'

Mr Chester waved a hand, unfurling himself from the chair. 'No...er, don't rush off. Have another...oh, you haven't...well. Now, may I try to understand you correctly? You're making me an offer for my eldest daughter. Of marriage. Is that correct?'

'Correct.'

'And I get the debts written off. That's part of the deal?'

'Correct.'

'There must be something else, surely? What do I lose?'

'Nothing, unless I am unable to win Miss Chester, after all. Then we shall be back to square one.'

'Then she must be *told* that's what she's going to do. But...' he searched the shining tabletop as if for information '...I know very little about you, you see, and although I'm very tempted, and...er...gratified by your offer, I would like to know that Caterina would be—how shall I put it?'

'Well cared for?'

'Yes. In short, well cared for. But if you'll forgive me, Sir Chase, there are some fathers, you see, who would look a little askance at your reputation in that department.' And in plenty of other departments, too, he thought. There were some fathers who would not see this man as a suitable husband for their daughters under any circumstances, though their daughters might harbour sweet fantasies about it. However, the temptation to solve two major problems in one fell swoop was too great to be dismissed on the spot. 'And if you don't manage to persuade her?' he said, still negative.

'Then I'm afraid, as I said, the debt will stand. You fear I might not?'

'Sir Chase, I cannot see how *anybody* could recommend himself to her as she is at the moment. Well, you've seen, haven't you? Nevertheless, if you can recommend yourself to *me,* I shall do everything in my power as a respected parent to show her where her duty lies. I still have that authority, although I have not so far exercised it. Perhaps I should have done.'

'I would rather take my own time, sir. In my experience, a lady like your daughter would not take kindly to being rushed over her fences.'

Neither man saw anything inappropriate in the analogy.

'In your experience. Yes, you've had quite a bit of that, haven't you?'

'I'm thirty-two years old, sir. What man hasn't, at that age?'

Stephen Chester hadn't, for one, though his elder brother had. 'And your parents are at Mortlake?' he said, avoiding the question.

'Boston Lodge. Sir Reginald and Lady FitzSimmon. Sir Reginald is my stepfather, and I am their only son. My own dwelling is on Halfmoon Street in London, sir. I've lived there for the last few years, and sometimes in my other properties in the north.'

Mr Chester had no need to ask what he'd been doing over the last few years, with pockets as deep as his, his parents swimming in lard, houses scattered all over the country, friend of the Prince Regent, nothing to do but win more money this way and that. He'd heard as much from Lord Elyot and his brother, who appeared to like him. They had also told him that Sir Chase belonged to the Four Horse Club, which he wished his son Harry had known before he took him on a wild-goose chase round Richmond Park.

'Your name, Sir Chase? Is it an abbreviation of something?'

'A childhood name that stuck, sir. My father and uncles used to call me Chase Anything after my first adventures in the hunting field. That became just Chase. My mother always calls me Charles, quite properly.'

Chase Anything, Mr Chester thought, would properly describe what he himself had heard about the man. 'Any light-o'-loves on the go?' he asked, looking to catch any confusion.

There was none. 'No one who matters,' said Sir Chase, callously.

'Any side-slips?'

Again, not a flicker of embarrassment. 'Absolutely not, sir.'

'And where would you expect my daughter to live, if you managed this miracle?'

As far away from her family as possible, would have been Sir Chase's reply if he'd been less diplomatic. 'That would not cause any kind of problem, Mr Chester. I can purchase a place somewhere if Miss Chester doesn't like the ones I have.'

'Well, that's a juicy carrot if ever I saw one. If I've learnt one thing about women it's that they have likes and dislikes about where they want to live. Still, you're an unconventional kind of chap, are you not?'

'I would have thought,' said Sir Chase, borrowing Miss Chester's own phrase, 'that your daughter would be very little interested in the sober, plodding, narrow-minded kind of man as husband-material. She strikes me as being a high-spirited kind of woman who needs a man who can keep up with her. You need not fear that I shall drag her into gaming-hells or be unfaithful. Nor would I allow her to fall into any kind of trouble. When I make the effort to win something, sir, I don't mistreat it. As for my age, how old are the men she was engaged to marry? Loddon is a middle-aged ninny tied to his mother's apron-strings in deepest Cornwall. Hadstoke is fifty, if he's a day, with a grown family at each other's throats. And as for St Helen's...well, a woman would have to be desperate to accept that old tup.'

'Wealth and titles. That's important for any woman.'

'For any father, sir, if I may say so. I have a baronetcy which my heir, when I get one, will inherit with my estate. And I have youth and vigour on my side, also. And if, as I believe, Miss Chester enjoys driving that crane-neck phaeton out there, my kind of life might suit her very well.'

'Oh, I wish Lady Elyot had not lent it to her. It's far too dangerous.'

'For your taste, perhaps. Now, have I put your mind at ease?'

If Stephen Chester's mind was not completely at ease concerning this overpowering man's suitability to be his son-in-law, he did not let the fact stand in the way of his decision, which he had already made well before the cross-examination. That had been a mere formality for the sake of appearances. Caterina must be married, come what may. 'You've never been married, I take it?' he said, trying not to appear too eager.

'Never offered for a woman until today.'

'Then it's a great risk you're taking. You'll need luck on such an impulsive gamble. But then, you have nothing much to lose, do you?'

The man's crassness, Sir Chase thought, was astounding. 'It's a risk, sir, I agree. But I stand to lose *what I want,* as do we both. I shall need your full cooperation, and that of Mrs Chester.'

'Oh, of course. You can rely on that, if nothing else. Caterina's stepmother will use every persuasion to—'

'No, sir. I would rather be the one to use persuasion, if you please. Mrs Chester will have to approve of me, naturally, but if you could leave the means to me I would be more than grateful. I imagine Miss Chester could dig her heels in if she felt she was being pressured.'

Miss Chester had done nothing *but* dig her heels in, of late. What was more, it was going to be difficult, if not impossible, to keep Hannah calm about the glad tidings that Caterina's hand was being sought yet again, after so many disappointments. 'You may depend on it, Sir Chase,' he said.

'Then I shall leave you to tell Miss Chester that I have made an offer for her. There can be no harm in that.'

'No harm at—oh…wait a moment.' Mr Chester's hand went to his forehead. 'Might it…?' he said, whispering his thoughts.

'Might it what, sir?'

'Well, this weekend she'll be away at Lord and Lady Ensdale's house party. She won't be back till Tuesday. Might it be better if I were to delay speaking of this until after her return? She'll be singing, you see, and apparently her voice doesn't work too well when she's angry…upset…you know?'

A lesser mortal would have quaked against such a prophecy, but Sir Chase had begun to expect any kind of tactlessness from this man. At least he'd had the grace to consider the timing. 'I understand perfectly,' Sir Chase replied, wondering if she needed to be told at all, in view of the most unusual circumstances. Perhaps they could judge the situation better after this coming weekend, though he was inclined to disagree with Chester that the lady's voice would not work well once the idea was put to her. He believed it would work very well indeed, with himself in the firing-line. 'One more detail,' he said, bracing himself. 'You mentioned Miss Chester's dowry. I believe, sir, now that my suit is being considered, that I have the right to know what to expect in dowry, settlements and jointures.' He did not intend the man to escape without feeling the sting.

Holding his long jaw in a tight fist as though it might otherwise dislocate, Stephen Chester sighed through his nose, preparing himself for the next few uncomfortable minutes. He did not enjoy giving money away any more than he liked borrowing it. 'Shall we sit, Sir Chase?' he said.

Inevitably, the question of a time limit was raised, though Mr Chester was in favour of a delayed deadline that would assist Sir Chase's success. The suitor preferred more of a challenge. With what he had in mind, six weeks might be unrealistic, but it sounded better than six months. In the end, it was agreed that Sir Chase would need all summer, the situation to be reviewed at the autumnal equinox.

Soon afterwards, the two men walked to the stable yard to look at the phaeton from where Mr Chester was called to attend his wife rather urgently. Returning to the house, he had just enough time to gulp down the remainder of his guest's brandy before picking up the gold-edged calling-card, putting it in his waistcoat pocket, smoothing his hair and, adopting an expression of false cheer, going upstairs to Hannah.

Waiting until her father had disappeared into the noisy baby-scented nursery, Caterina tripped quietly downstairs to the back of the house from where a path led to the door in the high brick wall between the garden and the stable yard. Here, she hoped to take another look at the cleaned phaeton and to examine Aunt Amelie's dapple-greys. If Harry had damaged them, there would indeed be trouble.

To her surprise and irritation, the grey hunter and its green-liveried groom were still there. Worse still, Joseph and Sir Chase Boston were sauntering through the double door of the carriage house from where they could see her easily, standing in the full glare of the sun. The temptation was to return to the house, but the snub to her father's guest would have been unforgivable when he was already walking to meet her. 'I came to see my aunt's horses,' she said, wondering why she needed to explain herself. 'They're my responsibility,' she added unnecessarily, hearing the sharp tone of her voice.

Sir Chase's soft laugh reached his eyes. 'So they are, Miss Chester,' he said as he reached the bottom of the steps. 'Your groom and I have been saying the very same thing.'

'They'll need to be hosed down,' she said, avoiding his eyes, 'if you brought them back in the same state as the phaeton.'

'I didn't,' he said, holding out his hand as she reached the bottom step.

Obliged to accept his courtesy, she felt the instant warm grip of his fingers and the unresisting strength of his arm that reminded her of what she'd heard of his legendary fencing skills, his boxing and horsemanship. She was also reminded of the enormous debt he had lured her brother into. If the tales that circulated about him were to be believed, this man was dangerous to both men and women.

She reached the cobbles, removing her hand from his without thanks. 'You had them washed down?' she said.

He appeared to find her question and manner amusing. 'It's one thing to return a carriage in a filthy state, Miss Chester, to show how it's been misused, but quite another to leave horses like that. It took my grooms hours to get the muck off them last night. If I were you, I'd lock them up next time your brother comes to stay, or you may have a broken leg or two.'

'Thank you for your advice,' she replied, icily. 'Next time my brother comes to stay, we shall probably lock *him* up, away from men who accept his childish wagers.'

'Then you might also teach him how to be more accurate with the truth while you're about it. It doesn't help matters to spin yarns about one's circumstances.' He kept pace with her as she walked quickly towards the stable, his strides worth two of hers.

'So you've never spun yarns about yours, Sir Chase?'

'Never had any need to. Others might have, but not me. Shall we go and take a look?' He stopped by the door, holding out an arm to usher her in.

This was not at all what she had intended, nor could she contain the feeling that Sir Chase had the knack of manoeuvring people into situations they would not have chosen for themselves. He had obviously done the same to her foolish brother.

Well lit by tall windows, the stable's oak stalls were topped by black-painted grilles, each black post topped by a golden ball. Layers of straw muffled the stamps from a forest of legs, and glossy rumps shone like satin, swished by silken tails. The aroma of hay and leather warmed Caterina's nostrils, and the occasional whicker of greeting combined with the scrunch of hay held in racks on the walls.

The two dapple-greys belonging to Lady Elyot were draped with pale grey rugs monogrammed in one corner, spotlessly clean, their charcoal manes rippling, hooves shining with oil. No effort had been spared to remedy the effects of their bruising drive last evening, yet Caterina withheld the thanks that were overdue.

Without comment, she went alongside the nearest horse, ducking under the cord that roped it off, peeping under the rug and stooping beneath its neck to return along the other side, patting the smooth back as she passed. 'Good,' she said, fanning the long tail.

'It was the least I could do,' he replied.

'No, Sir Chase. The least you could do would be to spare my father the distress of having to find the money to pay my brother's debt. Twenty thousand may be a trifling sum to you, but I can assure you that my father's circumstances do not accord with the way it looks. He will not have told you how difficult his finances are at the moment. He's too proud for that. But I'm not, sir. Believe me, he cannot afford it.'

'By no means is it a trifling sum, Miss Chester. If it had been, I would not be taking the trouble to claim it. Apart from that, your feckless brother should be made to learn that a man does not walk away from a debt of honour without serious consequences. I would have preferred it if he had been hurt a little more. As it is, only his pride will suffer.'

'As it is, sir, my father is the one to suffer. And me, too, I expect.' Immediately, she wished she had not allowed him to push her into a snappy retort, for now she would be asked to explain what she meant by that.

'You, Miss Chester? How does the debt affect you?'

'Oh, indirectly,' she waffled. 'Nothing that need be spoken of. Indeed, I should not have said as much.

Please, forget it.' She began to move away, but Sir Chase's long stride took him ahead of her and she was stopped by his arm resting on the next golden ball. Frowning, she scowled at the perfect white folds of his neckcloth, aware that this time she had backed herself into a corner.

'I am intrigued,' he said, looking down at her with those half-closed eyes that held more challenge than persuasion. 'What is it about this business, exactly, that affects you personally? Are we talking of dowries?'

Her eyes blazed darkly in the shadowy recess, a small movement of her body telling him how she chafed at being held to account, unable to avoid a confrontation as she had before. 'That is something I cannot discuss with you, sir. Indeed, it is a subject that will *never* be discussed with you, thank heaven.'

'Ah, so we *are* talking of dowries, and of yours being lessened quite considerably if your father decides to use it to pay me what he owes. Well, that's too bad, Miss Chester. How he chooses to pay—'

'He doesn't have a *choice!*' she snarled. 'Now let me pass, if you please. This conversation is most indelicate.'

'Come on, woman!' he scoffed. 'Don't tell me your delicate sensibilities are more important than your father's so-called distress. I'll not believe you can be so missish, after what I've seen. Talk about the problem, for pity's sake.'

'I cannot, Sir Chase. You are a stranger to me.'

'I am the one to whom the money is *owed,*' he said, leaning his head towards her, 'so if you can't discuss it with me, who *can* you discuss it with? Do you have need of your dowry in the near future?'

'No. Not in the near or the distant future,' she whispered. 'There, now, you have your answer. Let me pass.'

He did not pretend to misunderstand her, nor did he immediately respond, but stood looking at her while the soft sounds of munching and the jingle of chains passed them by without recognition. Then he broke the silence. 'Why not?' he said, quietly.

With a noticeable effort to keep her voice level, she replied. 'If my father and stepmother find it difficult to understand my reasons, Sir Chase, I can hardly expect you to do any better.'

'Do *you* understand them?' he whispered.

The staggering intake of her breath told him that he had found the weakness in her defence, and that she had no ready answer except a sob that wavered behind one hand. 'Oh!' she gasped.

The barrier of his arm dropped as she bounded away, half-walking, half-running out of the stable yard and up the steps leading to the garden door. It closed with a bang behind her. In the stable, Sir Chase leaned against one of the posts, his hand smoothing the dapple-grey coat beside him. 'Well,' he said, 'that makes an interesting change from the usual run of things, my beauty. How long have we got? Five months, is it?'

Caterina stood with her back pressed against the door in the high wall until the beating of her heart slowed to a more comfortable pace and her breathing eased. Cursing herself for allowing the dreadful man to catch her off guard so soon, she listened to the sounds from the stable yard, a deep voice, the clatter of hooves and Joseph's whistle as he went on with his polishing. Angrily, she had to admit that Sir Chase was more perceptive than a stranger had any business to be, for he had been right to ask if she understood her own reasons when they were so contradictory, so fatalistic and uncompromising.

She was not by nature as pessimistic as her father had become, nor was she anything like her two siblings, who cantered through life certain that the future would smooth itself out reasonably enough if they didn't think too deeply about it. But Caterina did think deeply and with passion about what life was offering and whether she had the right to satisfy her own needs or put them aside in order to please her parents. In recent years, the two viewpoints had become more incompatible, the conflict over her future creating more of a barrier than any of them could have foreseen when her father married Hannah Elwick.

Caterina and Hannah had been on friendly terms well before her father first came down to Richmond from Derbyshire. With an age difference of only six years between the two women and only a few miles across the Great Park to separate them, Caterina had been pleased when the gentle Hannah had accepted Stephen Chester's offer of marriage, seeing years of friendship ahead for herself and Sara. None of them, not even Hannah herself, had expected such an explosion of productiveness and the ensuing need to rearrange the town house on Paradise Road into nurseries and day-rooms, extra bedrooms and a study for the head of the family. No longer was there a music room or a work-room-cum-library or anywhere for a guest to sleep. No longer did she have a room of her own.

Caterina did not dislike the children. Far from it; she was happy that Hannah's parenting skills had been employed so promptly and that Mr Chester had the companionship he had craved for years. What she had found increasingly hard to bear was the way that Hannah's mothering had engulfed the smooth workings of the whole household from morning till night and beyond, for Hannah was not one to hand over her duties completely, as some did. Nurses dealt with the peripheral chores, but Hannah's constant rota of breast-feeding seemed to take over their lives and, although she invited the interest of Caterina and Sara on the basis that it was excellent grounding for them, neither was ready for maternalism on that scale.

Sara would rather have been visiting friends and learning her dance steps, and Caterina would rather have been practising her singing. Now she practised at Sheen Court in Aunt Amelie's music room where she and her teacher could work in an atmosphere of understanding. Aunt Amelie herself had given birth to three delightful children, but Sheen Court was substantially larger than Number 18 Paradise Road, and there Caterina could escape the stifling environment she had grown to dislike.

She had not tried to dissuade Harry from spending his month's holiday in London, and she saw now that, as the eldest, she was partly responsible for what had happened. She had been thinking more of her own and her sister's comfort instead of encouraging him to sample the delights of Richmond. The truth remained, however, that Hannah's brand of domesticity had not sent Caterina hurtling into the arms of the first man to offer for her. If anything, it had the opposite effect by creating a scene of such discomfort, Hannah looking ill, distressed and tired, her father short of sleep and temper, that might well be Caterina's lot within a year or two.

The Earl of Loddon had made it clear, *after* their engagement had been announced, that his future wife would live in Cornwall with his aged mother while he spent his time in the city. Viscount Hadstoke had also damned himself after his first attempt at a kiss, for the idea of spending her nights in bed with *that* was worse than life in her incommodious home. Title or not, she could not do it.

It had been of little use to explain to her parents about needing to feel love when they both insisted that such emotions grew *after* marriage, not before. Caterina knew otherwise, though unfortunately the examples she quoted were thc cxception rather than the rule and therefore carried little weight. Aunt Amelie and her husband, Lord Nicholas Elyot, had been lovers before their marriage, and Nick's brother Seton, Lord Rayne, had been the object of Caterina's infatuation six years ago. She had recovered, after a fashion, but six years was barely long enough for her to forget the elation and the anguish of that time, the wanting and the madness. And the foolishness. She had discovered what she thought were the depths of her ability to love, and she wanted it again. Anything else would be second-best, a compromise, and that would be far worse than no marriage at all.

Nevertheless, as she leaned against the garden door, she wondered why her heart was beating to an old familiar rhythm, and why that man's image was impressing itself so forcefully upon her mind. She saw his thickly waving black hair, his wicked roving eyes, the impressively wide shoulders and narrow hips. No detail had escaped her, though she had not wanted to be seen observing. How ironic that a man of his repute, a man so dangerous to know, should have been the only man to ask her about her reasons for not wanting to marry. After such a brief acquaintance, what could it possibly matter to him?

Stephen Chester, Caterina's father, was not entirely without a conscience, though it might have appeared that way during the wager with his daughter's future that morning. But it was rarely that a man was brought bad news *and* a way of righting it in the same visit, and Stephen had wrestled with the problem of his eldest daughter for years now, falling deeper into despondency. Surely he could be forgiven for snatching at this solution with so little soul-searching and so few qualms. And at no cost, either.

It was true he had aimed high, at first perhaps too high. Dukes, earls, viscounts and lords had all shown an interest, to Caterina's amusement and very little cooperation. They had retired, licking their wounds, and he had begun to wonder whether it was her bright sparkling beauty they wanted or her dowry which, if not exactly prodigious, might have lured some of the more threadbare titles. But this man, Sir Chase Boston, had been less interested in the dowry than the idea of a challenge. It was strange, Stephen thought, that there were men who did not mind losing twenty thousand guineas.

Conscience *did* smite Mr Chester, but not very hard and not where it hurt. He knew Sir Chase to be a notorious roué, a womaniser, a gambler, a hard-living hard-playing gallant: one could hardly ignore any of that. But he also had a title, of sorts, and wealth, and had offered to care for Caterina correctly, hitting the nail on the head when he'd suggested that a conventional husband might not be to her taste.

It was hard to know, these days, what would be to her taste, but since she could not bring herself to marry an upright run-of-the-mill duke, then perhaps she might be won over by an extrovert baronet.

Fingering the pattern on the crystal decanter, he sighed deeply. As for not putting any pressure on his wilful daughter to do her duty, well, Caterina knew all about the debt, and if she could be made to regard her future with Sir Chase as a duty to her family, then she might be persuaded to enter into the spirit of the affair with more seriousness than she had previously shown. Compared to an unhealthy IOU hanging over one's head, what was a little fatherly pressure?

Holding up the decanter by its neck, he tilted it this way and that against the light, wishing that Hannah had not, for once, watered his brandy down. No wonder Sir Chase had not been impressed. Nevertheless, he poured himself another tumblerful and carried it over to his magnificent burr-walnut desk, bought only recently at great expense.

Chapter Two

Turning the coffee-coloured phaeton through the massive wrought-iron gates of Sheen Court, Caterina held the dapple-greys to a steady trot into the avenue of elms, bracing her feet against the footboard and seeing, from the corner of her eye, how Sara clutched at her bonnet. 'Take it off,' she laughed. 'Nobody will mind. Let the wind blow through your curls, as I do.'

Good-naturedly, Sara grinned. 'If I looked like you when it does, I would,' she said. 'Unfortunately, I'd only look as if I should have worn a bonnet.'

'Rubbish. They know how pretty you are, windblown or not.'

At nineteen, Sara was very conscious of looking her best at all times while striving to emulate the poise and individuality that had radiated through her elder sister's formative years. To Sara's eternal chagrin, her own blonde prettiness was of the fragile kind that did not respond as it ought to attempts at the wind-blown look or to bold styles that showed off voluptuous curves, for Sara's curves were not voluptuous. If anything, they required some assistance from handkerchiefs stuffed down the front of bodices.

There were plenty of young men who preferred Sara's delicate frame above anything, especially when it gave them opportunities to bestow those small courtesies men have in store for such females. Bestowing them on Miss Caterina Chester did not bring quite the same satisfaction, for there was always the impression that she found them amusing rather than touching, unnecessary rather than helpful. To the fair and fairy-like Sara, romance was like a minuet, slow, studied and graceful, with everyone knowing what to expect. It gave her time to think. To Caterina, romance was more like a rite than a dance, in which *being* was more important than thinking. She was waiting for it to happen to her again, but this time with a man who could hear the same primitive beat.

Ahead of them, shining and silvery in the sun, the neo-classical stone façade of Sheen Court watched their approach through unadorned windows and a central portico that soared above both storeys on Corinthian columns. Three flights of wide steps rippled down to the drive between gigantic urns where Caterina brought her aunt's phaeton to a perfect standstill. Footmen in grey livery ran to take the horses' heads as a tall figure strolled towards them at a more leisurely pace, two brindled greyhounds loping at his heels. He was smiling.

'It's Lord Elyot,' Sara whispered. 'I never know what to say to him.'

'It's not Lord Elyot,' said Caterina, 'it's his younger brother, Lord Rayne. Lord Seton Rayne.'

There was something in the urgency of her sister's contradiction that opened Sara's blue eyes even wider. 'You mean...Seton? The one you—?'

'Shh! That was years ago. I didn't know he was back home.'

'Where from?'

'The army.' Caterina called to him as he came alongside and held a hand up to her in greeting. 'Lord Rayne. What are you doing here?'

'I lived here once. Remember?' He laughed back at her with a flash of white teeth.

'Heavens, so you did. I'd almost forgotten.'

He was not meant to believe her. Nor did he. Holding up his other hand, he invited her down. 'Come down here, Miss Caterina Chester, and let me remind you, then. And introduce me to your lovely companion, if you will. Or have you forgotten your manners, too?' He caught her, returning her hug like a favourite brother, almost lifting her off her feet and whooping like a child.

She had often wondered in what ways they would have changed since their last meeting. Then, she had said the same inadequate farewell as everyone else as he went off to join his regiment, the one in which his brother had served some years earlier. Then, she had vowed to shed no more tears for a man, and she had kept her word through the pain of rejection, and through the healing.

It had been very civilised and well arranged. He had been as understanding and sorry at twenty-five as she had been at seventeen, and perhaps more kindly. He had explained that she was too young for him, that he was about to leave for a long spell of duty and that he was not the kind of man she deserved. He had been abroad, visiting seldom, and then only briefly. She had not believed then, nor did she now, that love had much to do with deserving, but she had accepted his explanation because it was sensitively given and because she had little alternative.

Both Lord Rayne and his elder brother had had mistresses and clearly she was not his style, gauche and innocent and, though pretty, nothing like the raving beauty she was now. There had never been any kind of intimacy between them and she had no reason to reproach him except for not wanting her, for his behaviour had been utterly correct, if sometimes maddeningly confusing. For the last few weeks of their friendship, when matters had been resolved between them, they had been more like brother and sister than before, where affectionate bickering was a comfortable substitute for one-sided adoration.

For Caterina, it had been the hardest and most emotional lesson of her life, learned with Aunt Amelie's help in lieu of a mother's. Her dignity had won her aunt's admiration, for this had all come at a time when her astonishing singing voice had just been discovered, her little feet placed on the first rung of stardom and her launch into the best society. It was for that very reason her widowed father had asked her widowed Aunt Amelie to be her chaperon.

With her feet now firmly on the same level as Lord Rayne's, she realised that her heart was not all a-flutter as she had thought it might be, and that, although she was delighted to see him again, he was even more like the adopted brother than the one she'd left behind all those years ago. Full of curiosity about what those years had done to him, she watched as he handed Sara down from the phaeton and was introduced to her.

To anyone less familiar with every detail, the slight loss of weight would have gone unnoticed with the new soldierly bearing, the bronzed skin stretched more tautly over perfect cheekbones, the skin around the eyes rather more lined, weathered more than suffered. From what she'd heard, life in the Prince Regent's own regiment, the 10th Light Dragoons, was never to be suffered, even at the worst of times, their reputation less for fighting than for just about every other masculine activity.

Lord Rayne had changed physically less than Caterina, but he was still as handsome as he had been before, still as immaculately dressed, dark hair as carefully disordered, neckcloth simply tied and spotless. Lord Elyot and his brother were probably the handsomest pair in the *beau monde;* no one had ever contradicted that in Caterina's hearing.

Sara had already turned a pretty shade of pink as they mounted the steps with their arms tucked through Lord Rayne's, and it was Caterina who fired the first salvo of questions. 'How long have you been home? Have you sold out now? Have you been offered a position?'

He squeezed her arm against him, looking down at the mass of deep chestnut curls as rebellious as their owner, at the flawless skin and the sun-kissed cheeks, the sweep of thick lashes and the marvellous arch of her brows. How she had changed; her movements now every bit as graceful as her aunt's, her manner assured and confident. 'Only a couple of days,' he said, smiling into her eyes. 'But never mind that. Tell me about all these improper offers you've had, Cat. I thought you'd have had a clutch of bairns by now.'

'Oh, how vulgar you are,' she scolded. 'And don't fib. You didn't think of me at all, did you?'

'Yes, I did. Once or twice. But I didn't imagine… well…'

'Well what?'

'That you'd have blossomed so. We have some

catching up to do. And does Miss Chester sing?' He looked down at Sara's bonnet.

'Only a little, my lord,' Sara said. 'I mostly play the harp when Cat sings. It's easier.'

Lord Rayne smiled indulgently at her, thinking how very different the two sister were and how agreeable their relationship. He did not believe it would be as easy as all that to accompany Caterina when she sang, knowing what he did of her high standards. 'Signor Cantoni is already here,' he said. 'Would you like an audience for your lesson?'

'As long as you don't disturb us with your snoring,' Caterina replied.

Always welcoming, Lady Elyot greeted her nieces more like sisters, embracing them and keeping hold of their hands, noticing her brother-in-law's obvious delight. 'Now, you've met again at last. Any changes, Seton?'

'Plenty,' he said, with a teasing glance. 'Thank heaven.'

'Still ungentlemanly,' Caterina snapped. 'No change there. Don't expect any compliments, Sara dear. Lord Rayne has even forgotten the one he knew.'

Sara giggled, understanding but unable to match her sister's wit. 'We've brought the phaeton back, Aunt Amelie,' she said. 'Cat thought it best because we're away to Wiltshire tomorrow and it won't be used for a few days. And Hannah won't be coming with us after all, because the baby twins are coming down with something.'

'Oh, my dear, I'm sorry to hear that. Has Dr Beale been?' Lady Elyot's dark almond-shaped eyes filled with concern. She was an inch smaller than Caterina, heart-stoppingly lovely and, at thirty, still the kind of woman men hungered for, with warm brown curls falling through bands of ribbon and spiralling down her long neck. Her figure was firm and slender, even after bearing three children, showing off to perfection the blue sleeveless pelisse worn over a blue-bordered white muslin day dress. A Kashmir shawl was draped over one shoulder, which Sara would never have thought of doing. Lady Elyot was responsible for Caterina's transformation to assured womanhood, and a special bond had grown between them of the kind that Sara and Hannah had not quite managed to forge.

'Doctor Beale was arriving just as we left. Hannah is going to ask Aunt Dorna if she'll take on the duties as chaperon. She was going, anyway,' said Sara without a trace of regret.

'Dorna as chaperon,' said Lady Elyot with a lift of her fine brows. 'Well, I'm sure she'll agree, my dear, in principle if not in fact.'

Lady Adorna Elwick was not only the widow of Hannah's late brother, but she was also Lord Elyot and Lord Rayne's sister. The sudden loss of her husband, however, had been a tragedy only in that it obliged Dorna to wear black, which she would not otherwise have done.

'As long as you don't expect the onerous duty of chaperon to make the slightest difference to Dorna's own enjoyment,' said Lord Rayne. 'Perhaps it's as well that I was invited along to partner her, for I'm sure she has no intention of being saddled with her brother, and I was all set to find myself a couple of innocent young sisters to pass the time with. You two should fill the bill quite nicely.'

'Thank you,' said Caterina, taking her music case from the footman with a smile, 'but we have no intention of filling your bill. We are not nearly innocent enough for you. Anyway, I didn't know you'd been invited.'

'Not invited to Sevrington Hall? The Ensdales would never have a house party without me. I'm one of the standard eligible males.'

'Good. Then you'll know your own way around the place, won't you? Sara and I have been invited to perform.'

'Oh, Lord,' he groaned in mock despair.

'And we must not keep Signor Cantoni waiting any longer. Aunt Amelie, thank you *so* much for lending us your phaeton. It was polished only this morning. We had such fun with it.'

'Then you shall borrow it again, love, at any time. Go through to the gallery, both of you. May we peep in later on?'

'Of course. We're rehearsing our songs for the weekend.'

A lengthy glass-covered corridor led into one of the first-floor side wings where a previous Lord Elyot had added a long gallery, centuries after the fashion had disappeared, in which to house his collection of *objets d'art* and ancestral portraits. Lit by ceiling-to-floor windows on two sides, the room was often used for dancing and concerts; now, as the sisters entered, Signor Cantoni was already playing to himself on the small Beckers grand pianoforte, his eyes scanning the ornate plasterwork ceiling with its riot of foliage, swags and shells.

'Are you all right, Cat?' Sara whispered. 'After seeing him again?'

Caterina was more than all right. There had been a time, years ago, when she had dreaded seeing Lord

Rayne with a beautiful and sophisticated woman on his arm, looking down the length of a ballroom at her with pity in his eyes. It had not happened. Instead, he had picked up the old familiar sparring, the mild insults, the banter that was more acceptable than that awful pretence at politeness, a cover for regret. She had changed since then, realising for perhaps the first time that he must have known she would, that her needs would grow well beyond the dreams of a seventeen-year-old. She was grateful to him for telling her what she had not wanted to believe, that there were other men for her than him.

Placing an arm around her sister's shoulders, she hugged her as they walked towards the piano, almost laughing with relief. 'Yes, oh, yes,' she whispered. 'It's gone now. Really. I mean it. I'm quite free, and we shall get on well together, the three of us.'

Greeting her singing teacher with a kiss to both cheeks, she helped Sara to uncover the harp and sift through the music sheets, settling into the seriously enjoyable music-making that had been her lifeline during the last problematical years. From the start, she had been sought to add glamour and talent to the most select house parties, soirées and private charity concerts, sometimes with Sara, sometimes with her teacher, and often with an orchestra. It was not a voice, they told her father, that one kept to oneself.

Before long, the family at Sheen Court began to gravitate towards the door that only grown-ups knew how to open silently. In a slow trickle with fingers to lips, they went to sit on the window-seat at the far end, or took up positions on the pale upholstered chairs against the cream panelling. Lured by Caterina's rich mezzo-soprano voice, they listened entranced to the music of Mozart, Gluck and Handel and to some by her late mentor himself, who'd had a piece written for him, a castrato, by Joseph Haydn.

Standing to face the harp and the piano so that she could watch her teacher's expressions, Caterina was hardly aware of the growing audience until Sara whispered to her during a pause, 'Lord Elyot's here.'

'Don't look, then,' Caterina whispered back. 'Shall we go from bar fourteen, *signor?* That trill needs polishing, doesn't it?' Taking a pencil, she made a note on her music, glancing towards the little crowd gathered in the distance. Lord Elyot was indeed there with his brother, and wife, and a guest, a man as tall as himself who she had seen only that morning at Paradise Road in circumstances very different from this.

She had never suffered unduly from nervousness while performing, but now she felt an uncomfortable churning sensation beneath her lungs, and when the piano accompaniment began on bar fourteen, her voice was not prepared for it. 'Sorry, *signor.* Again, if you please?'

Watching his head lift as he counted her in, she began again, this time coming in on the beat, facing the room in a conscious effort to show that, this time, she was totally in control as she had not been earlier, when she had last spoken to Sir Chase.

She would rather have avoided another meeting with him, but it was not possible, for Lord and Lady Elyot were interested to hear from him that he and Miss Chester had already been introduced and that he would be happy to meet her again. If they had expected Caterina to share this eagerness, they soon saw that the opposite was the case when she replied to his congratulations with chilling courtesy. Taking the hand of five-year-old

Adrian, Caterina led him to the piano stool for a quick two-finger duet. The last thing she wanted was a display of ill humour, for that would have raised too many questions, but nor did she wish to engage any man's attentions who was coolly relieving her father of twenty thousand guineas for so little return.

On the way back to the green drawing room, however, it was clear that Lady Elyot had noticed. 'What is it, Cat dear?' she said as they walked a little way ahead of the rest. 'You didn't mind us bringing Sir Chase in, did you? He was very keen to hear you.'

'It's not that. I don't mind who hears me. I don't like the man, that's all.'

'But he tells me you only met this morning. What is it you don't like?'

'Oh, only what's generally known, I suppose. He sets my bristles up. I know some think he's all the crack, but dressing well doesn't excuse a profligate.'

'Cat! What are you saying? That's coming it a bit strong, my dear. My lord would not have invited him to the house if he was as bad as all that.'

'Lord Elyot invited him?'

'Yes, love. They've been to the stables. Sir Chase was a captain in the same regiment as Nick and Seton, and they've been friends for years. You won't have seen him until now because he spends most of his time in London and his other properties, when he's not at Mortlake. Of course these men get up to all kinds of tricks, but I find it's best not to enquire too closely about that. Even Nick won't tell me about the pranks they played in the Dragoons, occasionally.'

'Well, I'm sure you're right about that part, but the less I see of him the better I shall like it.'

Lady Elyot had been watching Sir Chase while Caterina was singing and she was quite sure that his thoughts were running along different lines. It would be interesting to see, she thought, how long it would take him to win her to his side, for by all accounts Sir Chase was not a man to give up when he met opposition. And she was sure he'd set his sights on her niece. Was that why he'd been to see Stephen?

Caterina's brush with Sir Chase was not yet over, however, for when Signor Cantoni had taken his leave of them to visit another pupil, Sara wished to delay her departure to practise her harp pieces on her own. 'Then perhaps I could persuade you to drive me home?' said Caterina to Lord Rayne with a smile, making a show of linking her arm through his.

'Can't you walk?' he said, rudely.

'Seton!' said his sister-in-law. 'How *very* discourteous.'

'It's all right, Aunt,' Caterina assured her. 'He's only teasing.'

'No, I'm not!' he said, innocently.

Then it went slightly askew, for although Sir Chase understood the squabble well enough, he saw his chance to be alone with the unwilling lady again. 'Allow me,' he said, stepping forward. 'My curricle is waiting outside, ready to go. I would be happy to drive Miss Chester back to Paradise Road.'

'No…er, no, thank you,' Caterina said, holding tighter to Lord Rayne's arm. 'There's really no need. Really.'

'There you are, then,' said Lord Rayne. 'Problem solved. He's not a bad hand with the ribbons, Cat. You'll be quite safe. Friend of the family, and all that.'

Angered by the way this had gone wrong, she pulled her arm from Lord Rayne's without another word, for there was no more to be said without making a fuss which only Aunt Amelie and Sir Chase himself would understand. At the same time, the thought of sitting close to him in a curricle was both disturbing and vaguely exciting for reasons she chose not to investigate. Suffice it to say that she would rather have walked than accept a lift from Sir Chase Boston, after their earlier encounter.

Unfortunately, no choice was left to her but to accept his offer in silence, leaving Lord Rayne in no doubt that he had let her down badly. Taking her leave fondly of Lord and Lady Elyot, and of the children, she left Seton out.

'Cutting me already, Cat?' he said as she walked past him into the sunshine.

'Yes,' she said, throwing her shawl around her shoulders, 'but I never did care much for your amateur style of driving, anyway.'

She heard sharp whistles at her insult, then laughter from Lord Elyot at his brother's expense. '*Brava,* Cat!' he said. 'Serves the ungallant wretch right.'

But now she was being escorted towards a flashy sporting curricle, the small body of which was on a level with the top of the wheels, the cushioned seat well above the horses' backs as it was in her aunt's vehicle. But whereas the phaeton had four wheels, this one had only two, and instead of the usual pair of horses, Sir Chase drove four matched chestnuts as alike as peas in a pod. Her failed attempt to be unimpressed must have showed on her face for, as she stopped to stare, he watched to see her eyes widen before resuming their flinty annoyance.

Climbing up to such heights held no fears for Caterina. With one lift from Sir Chase's steady hand, she was on the seat and already squeezing herself into the corner, suddenly remembering something to be returned. 'Lord Rayne,' she called down, fumbling inside her reticule, 'would you try to be a little more obliging and pass this to Aunt Amelie for me, please? I found it in the phaeton.'

The tiny scrap of lace handkerchief fluttered down into his hand. 'Blowing hot and cold, Cat?' He laughed. 'One minute the cut, next minute dropping the handkerchief? What's a man to believe these days?'

The curricle tipped a little as Sir Chase climbed up beside her, pressing himself into the space with a closeness she had no choice but to suffer. 'Believe what you like, whelp!' he called to his friend. 'You've missed your chance.' He glanced at Caterina with a half-smile at her rigid posture, her grip on the edge of the hood, her feet tucked away to avoid his black boots spread into her space. 'Ready?' he said.

It would have made little difference, she thought, if she'd said no, when he was taking up the long whip with a quick flip, his nod to the groom coinciding with his command to the wheelers, the move-away so smooth as to be hardly noticeable. For the first few minutes, Caterina was engrossed in the business of driving a four-in-hand, and with his skill, keeping the team in perfect unison down the elm drive through flickering shadows, swinging out of the gates onto the gritty mud track leading to Paradise Road. She was impressed, though she would never have paid him the slightest compliment, nor would she have hinted at the considerable thrill she was deriving from the experience.

But it was she who broke the silence in an effort to

score a point. 'What happened to your policy, Sir Chase?' she said, watching how he looped the reins.

'Which policy, Miss Chester? I have several.'

'The one that forbids you to offer lifts to your debtors.'

'But I am not offering a lift to a debtor. Your father and I have settled the problem very amicably. And anyway, it was not you who owed me, was it?'

'Settled? Already?'

'Yes. Why? Isn't that what you wanted?'

'Yes…but…how did you do it so soon? Have you given him more time, or has he sold you something?'

'Neither. We've come to an agreement. That's all there is to it.'

'But that can't be all there is to it,' she persisted. 'He could not possibly have raised that kind of money immediately. I know he couldn't. What has he sold you, exactly? The house?'

'Ask him,' he said, knowing it would get her nowhere.

'I will.'

'Good. Now, perhaps we can talk about pleasanter matters.'

'Pleasanter than the sound of wagers being paid? Why, sir,' she said, acidly, 'what could be sweeter than that?'

'The sound of your singing, Miss Chester, for one thing.'

She could not bring herself to snub him again while accepting his protection, so, rather than bite back, she bit her tongue instead.

It was not far from Sheen Court to Paradise Road and, as they skirted the edge of Richmond Park with a stretch of open road before them, Sir Chase drew the horses to a standstill beneath an old oak whose branches were barely in leaf. Keeping the reins in his hand, he slewed round on the seat, placing one foot on the top of the footboard, looking into her angry eyes.

For a few conflicting moments, her antagonism flared. She had never taken kindly to being placed in a situation against her will but, while she would like to have asked him why they had stopped, she would not give him the satisfaction of doing what he would expect of her. Her wait gave her another chance to glare at him and to notice again his penetrating arrogant eyes narrowed against the sun, seeming to read the language of her silence like an expert, and it was *her* eyes that swung away to avoid any further reading. Even then, she felt his scrutiny as she had done during her performance earlier; she felt his long legs much too close for her comfort, and she was aware of his deep chest and disconcertingly powerful physique. She gulped, suddenly breathless.

'Well, now, madam,' he said, softly, 'tell me how well acquainted you are with Rayne. Is that bickering you do a cover for something deeper between you, or is it a brother-sister affair?'

Even from a friend, she might have found this question impertinent. From him, it was brazen interference. 'Sir Chase,' she said, as sweetly as her anger would allow, 'being my father's creditor does not allow you free access into my affairs, however much you may wish to the contrary. When I begin to show an interest in how many *affaires you've* had in the past year, then you may ask me again about my private life. Is that agreed?'

His mouth, firm and well shaped, broke into a wide smile just short of a laugh, his eyes widening at her bold set-down. 'Hah!' he yelped, throwing back his head. 'How I love it when you bite so. How many *affaires* have I had? Is that what bothers you then, madam? Eh? Do you really want to know?'

'No,' she snapped. 'I do not.'

'I thought not. Do you often use that kind of language?'

'I rarely have the need to speak to people of your sort.'

'My sort? What is my sort?' His voice was intimately teasing, unlike the brotherly teasing of Lord Rayne.

'This is a ridiculous conversation. Please drive on.'

He lowered his head a little to look into her face, where a slow surge of colour had almost reached her ears. 'Well, then, let me tell you, Miss Chester, since you raise the question, that I never seduce chits, jades, tabbies or dowdies. There, now, that should put your mind at rest. Any other concerns?'

'Please…' she whispered, looking away. 'Take me home.'

'Have you ever handled a team of four?'

She shook her head.

'Would you like to try?'

She would, but it would give him pleasure to teach her, and she did not want to encourage his friendship, even at her own cost. She had always wanted the chance to drive a four-in-hand, and now she looked lovingly down the reins at the beautiful restless chestnuts, at the track ahead leading to Paradise Road, to Red Lion Street, along King Street and on round The Green where strollers would see Miss Caterina Chester driving a curricle and four. They would not see a sight like that too often. Damn the man. Why must it be him, of all people?

Her too-long hesitation was her answer. Without another word, he took her left hand and placed it on top of his own. 'Now,' he told her, 'take the reins up from my fingers, off-wheel between these two, near-wheel and off-lead between those two, and near-lead on top. That's it. Now, just do as you'd do with a pair and we'll walk them, then we'll turn them. Use your right hand to loop the reins up when you turn, as usual. Start up the wheelers first when you've given the command to walk on, or the leaders will pull them off their feet. Don't worry, I'll take over when you start to tire.'

Talking her through each move, he murmured encouragement and instructions as the horses responded to her light contact with their mouths, walking until they reached the first bend, then turning as she drew up the reins with a roll of her hand. One hand, never with two. 'You're good,' he said. 'Very good. Are you getting tired?'

'No, not yet.'

'Keep going. Another right turn ahead. Keep well to the left…well done.'

As if by mutual consent, they passed Number 18 Paradise Road without a glance, following the route into the town along a series of right turns to bring them along the side of the large Green, bordered by houses, where she had to admit that her arm was aching from the strain. Drawing the curricle up, she handed the reins back to Sir Chase with some reluctance, thankful that he had not insisted on changing places, but when they turned on to Hill Street instead of heading for home, she understood that he had not finished showing her the joys of driving a curricle and four.

'Where are we going?' she asked, quietly.

He put the horses to a brisk trot up the hill. 'They

need exercise,' he said, 'so I thought we'd take them across the park. And you look as if you enjoy having the wind in your hair.'

'Do I?'

He turned to smile at her before giving his attention to the horses, as if he knew how she would have protested if she had not so wanted to fly up the hill in the sunshine behind a matched team with an expert whip at her side. She did not return his smile, but her glance told him he was not wrong, and that although she was nowhere near liking him, she would put up with him for such an adventure.

Caterina was thinking that she had never seen such skill, that the thrill of hurtling along in an over-powered light curricle was rather like being shot from a bow, flying, soaring on the breeze. Past the Roebuck they went, past the workhouse, the Wick and the Queen's until Sir Chase slowed down to pass through Richmond Park Gate.

Then he pulled up. 'Now you,' he said. 'First a trot, then we can try a turn or two.'

She took the reins, searching her mind for a middle way between a show of enthusiasm and her former disapproval. The park road was open to them, the horses responsive and keen, and she would have liked to let them go. But Sir Chase knew. 'Keep them to a trot,' he warned her. 'They don't break that rhythm until you tell them to. You're in charge, not them.'

Her arm began to ache again, but it was exhilarating, exciting and completely engrossing, not allowing her mind to wander or to think over the disturbing events that had led to this, or about what might follow.

After a mile or so, Sir Chase took over once more to gallop the team at top speed through the park where other drivers and riders stopped to watch. He was recognised by a group of the militia from the barracks at Kew who called and waved, while ladies out walking watched in admiration the lovely young woman with the flying red hair. He had no need to warn her to hold on when she swung and swayed into every turn, careering like a comet towards some distant target, bracing one foot between his on the footboard, the other on the top edge, not quite ladylike but alert, filled with a vitality so intense that it caught at her breath and tried to make her laugh. This was freedom. Escape. Sun, wind and speed. This was even better than the applause after a recital. Uncaring that she leaned on him as they took bends like a Roman chariot in the arena, or that her knee pressed his thigh, her enjoyment was heightened by his sheer skill, for not once did she feel the slightest danger with him in control.

He knew the tracks well, bringing them full circle back to the gate on top of Richmond Hill where he walked the team as far as the Terrace. From there, the view across the town and the wide silver-blue stretch of the Thames spread below them, a giant counterpane of new spring greens, and for some time they sat in silence like two eagles on a cliff, ready to take flight again whenever they pleased. Caterina felt no need to talk, and Sir Chase had no need to ask if she had enjoyed her liberty, having only to look at her to see the sparkle in her eyes, the pink in her cheeks, the wildly tumbling hair like dark fire.

'Better move,' he said. 'They're sweating.'

'Yes.'

Without a smile, he looked intently at her. 'Do you need to tuck your hair up before I take you home?'

There was something alarmingly conspiratorial

about the question in that deep gravelly voice that implied his awareness of her parents' censure if they were to see her wind-blown state. Once more, she found herself wondering whether he had said similar things to the women he had known. With her shawl, she made a hood to cover her hair, wrapping the ends around her neck, tucking her feet neatly into one spot, pressing her knees together, sitting primly to await his approval.

Leaning his whip against his thigh, he pulled off one kid glove with his teeth and held it in his lips while brushing a speck of dust off her nose with his thumb, catching her eyes with the merest hint of amusement.

'Thank you,' she whispered, shocked by the tenderness of his skin, by the contact she had allowed, as if she'd taken a first step without moving.

Replacing his glove, he took up the whip and moved off at a walk down the hill. 'That was more or less the route your brother and I took yesterday,' he said. 'But then it was muddy.'

Caterina frowned at him. 'Four-in-hand against his pair?'

'No! Of course not. We both had a pair, but we drove them in tandem.'

'But Harry's never driven tandem before. And how could he ever have passed you on that narrow track?'

'He could if he'd been a better whip and if his team had been as good as mine. But he isn't, and it wasn't.'

'I still don't think you should have accepted his wager.'

'And how do you think that would have been interpreted?'

'Does it matter?'

'It does to me. Look what I'd have missed by refusing it.'

It would have been easy enough to pursue that line, to be told how her brother's stupidity had been turned to Sir Chase's advantage in two ways, by money and association. But she preferred not to hear anything from him except regret for his relentless pursual of the debt, which she was quite sure he would never give up.

The drive had not only blown away her cobwebs, but it had also given her a glimpse of the fearlessness and sheer proficiency that had earned him his reputation for heroics. Yet she had felt something more significant than blind courage or audacity, more than daredevil antics or the masculine urge to impress a woman. She had felt completely safe and understood, and there had been moments when her dislike and resentment of him had dissolved in their silences, intensifying her awareness of him as a companion quite unlike any other man. She could never like him, of course, but nor could she suppress the regret that they could never truly be friends. She would tell those who had seen her driving his curricle and four that he was just an acquaintance. A friend of her father's.

Stephen Chester was understandably taken aback to hear that Sir Chase Boston had already driven his daughter around Richmond without actually abducting her. Naturally, he did not expect to see her return full of smiles and approval; she certainly did not do that. But nor did she have much to say, either good or bad, about the experience, only about the means her father had used to pay back the debt.

Closing the study door quietly behind her, she took her father by the hand and sat him beside her on the window-seat in view of the garden. 'He told me to ask you,' she said, 'obviously not thinking you'd tell me. But I think you should, because I know what the debt amounts to and any demand for that kind of money is going to affect us all, not only you. We shall all have to share in any hardships it's going to cause. Is it the house, Father? Have you decided to sell it? The other one, too?'

'I'd like a little brandy, my dear, if you wouldn't mind.'

'You've already had one, Father. You know Hannah doesn't like it.'

Father had had three, to be precise, and what Hannah didn't know would hardly concern her. 'Yes, dear, I know. Just a small one.'

Caterina obliged, sure that this would loosen his tongue, but dreading what she was about to hear. She had developed a love for this house on Paradise Road as great as that for their much larger home in Derbyshire, and the thought of losing them would be like losing two beloved friends. Gently, she removed the glass from his grasp and replaced it on the table. 'Now, tell me the worst,' she said. 'I can bear it. We're all in this together, remember, and we shall all have to do whatever is necessary to help. Harry will have to be recalled from Liverpool to start earning some money, and I shall go and see the manager at Covent Garden. He's told me more than once that there's a place for me with the company whenever—'

'Caterina…stop! That's not it. It's not the house.'

'*Not* the house?' she said, blinking. 'Well, what else *is* there?'

'We…Sir Chase and I agreed not to say anything until your return from wherever you're going this weekend.'

'From Sevrington Hall? Why ever not? You mean,

before you know how much you can raise.... Father...what is it? What have you agreed to? What is it you don't want me to hear immediately?'

His hand had retaken hers upon his thigh where his nervous fingers were dragging at her skin with an ungentle caress, too unfamiliar to be soothing. She drew her hand away, full of sudden misgivings and an awareness that the matter concerned her personally more than all of them, that her offers of help were about to fall with a thud at her feet. And as her father struggled to find a way of explaining, her own realisation grew that his long talk with Sir Chase, the latter's air of satisfaction and his flippant 'ask him,' his interest in her reasons not to marry, his questions about dowries, his assurance that the debt had been settled 'very amicably' were all to do with her. Only her.

'What have you done, Father?' she said, breathless with foreboding. 'This concerns me, doesn't it? Tell me?'

'Such a lot of money,' he whispered. 'I could never repay it, but it was not *my* suggestion, my dear, it came from—'

'*Tell* me, Father,' she snapped. 'This agreement. What is it?'

'You, Caterina. He wants you. He's made me an offer for you.'

Like a sudden mountain mist, cold anger swirled around her, prickling every hair with a freezing, numbing indignation. 'No, tell me the truth. It was a wager...a *wager,* wasn't it? That's not quite the same thing as a straightforward offer, is it, Father? He's agreed to release you from Harry's debt *in return for Harry's sister,* hasn't he? And if he doesn't manage to get Harry's sister, you're going to have to pay up, aren't you? That's the top and bottom of it, and that's not an offer, but a wager. You see, I'm not the green girl I used to be; I do understand these things. But what *you* don't appear to understand is that I shall not be marrying *anybody,* and if I ever changed my mind, that hell-rake of a man would be the very last person I would consider.' Panting with fury and the torrent of words, she felt his betrayal as keenly as a sword wound. 'How could you do this, Father?' she said, standing upright before him. 'Will you never see that I am a woman, not a thing to be bargained with? I can go out any day and earn a good living whenever I choose. In fact, when I return from Wiltshire next week, I shall make the necessary arrangements. Any father who can rid himself so easily of a daughter doesn't deserve to have one.'

'You said you'd do whatever you could to help, Caterina.'

'So I did. But I didn't offer myself in exchange, did I? *All I can do to help* doesn't mean forfeiting my entire happiness single-handed so that Harry can carry on gambling with money he doesn't have. Surely you can see that?'

'That's an exaggeration. If I had disapproved of Sir Chase, I would not have agreed to his generous offer.'

'Nevertheless, since it didn't occur to either of you to consult me about something that affects me so closely, you will now be obliged to refuse Sir Chase's wager, and tell him that your daughter would rather be an opera singer than marry him.'

'No…no! You cannot do that.'

'Yes, I can, Father. That way, I get to choose who I go to bed with.'

The gasp of shock was audible, but the words that followed were cut off by the slam of the door and a loud crash as the brass knob bounced across the polished oak floor like a pomegranate.

The door reopened with a grating sound, and there she stood, holding its partner in her hand with an extension protruding from it like a dagger. 'I've had an idea,' she said in a voice too sweet to be anything but sarcasm. 'Why not sell Harry to the highest bidder? The problem is of his making, after all. It certainly isn't mine.' Placing the weapon carefully on the polished table, she turned away quickly before he could see how her eyes were flooding with tears. 'Better have that repaired before you sell the house,' she whispered.

Early on the next day, the journey to Sevrington Hall was undertaken in two stout travelling coaches, one of which belonged to Lady Dorna Elwick, Hannah's sister-in-law, and the other to Lord Rayne's elder brother. And since that one had the Elyot cypher and crest upon the doors, spaces for two large trunks, Venetian blinds with tassels, fringed cushions, carpets, straps to hold and pockets to put things in, that was the one occupied by Lady Dorna, Caterina and Sara, and Lord Seton Rayne, Lady Dorna's younger brother. The two maids and one valet rode in the second carriage with two brindled greyhounds lying across their feet, and more luggage. Strapped to the fourth seat of that coach sat a harp in its leather cover, rocking gently over each bump in the road.

It was not long before both Lady Dorna and her brother noticed that Caterina had spoken only to answer questions, and then briefly, and that Sara was casting sympathetic glances at her sister as if she were ailing. Caterina was usually more than happy to accept invitations to sing when it provided a way of meeting established friends and making new ones. Even better was the prospect of escaping for a few days from her harassed father and Hannah's eternal carping about the duties of marriageable daughters.

Today, however, appeared to be an exception, for Caterina had not had time to recover from her father's drastic solution to his problem, despite what she had said about sharing it. In her view, this was not sharing it but landing it on her, and her resentment had burned all night. Not that she had any intention of complying with his intolerable agreement, but there was no escaping the fact that she could expect some stormy weeks ahead before either her father or Sir Chase would acknowledge defeat. Since yesterday's unhappy interview, she had not spoken to her father, all her meals having been taken in the room she shared with Sara. Surprisingly, Hannah had not tried to make contact with her, though she must by now have been told of the offer.

'Headache, love?' said Lady Dorna, laying her cream kid-gloved fingers upon Caterina's knee. 'Are you not looking forward to this weekend?'

'More than ever,' said Caterina. 'No, not a headache. You know how it is at home these days. Even our dear Sara is glad to get away.'

Sara's smile agreed with this, although her reasons were not quite what her sister had implied. Lord and Lady Ensdale had two very handsome and eligible sons.

'You're not still blue-devilled about yesterday, are you, Cat?' said Lord Rayne. 'I could see you didn't much like Boston's offer of a lift, but by that time there was not much I could do about it. Amelie tells me you've taken a dislike to him. If I'd known…'

'I dislike what I've *heard,*' she agreed, finding it impossible not to smile at the pretty face opposite her. Except in their remarkably good looks, the brother and sister were not otherwise much alike. Whereas Seton's dark and strikingly masculine features were strong, Dorna's were feminine in the extreme, fair and blue-eyed and very lovely. Complete to a shade in the most daring modes, she was used to showing off her physical attributes with a candour that some of the older generation thought was taking things a little too far. 'And I certainly didn't care to be seen,' said Caterina, 'with a man of his repute. Not in Richmond, anyway. You know how people talk.' Immediately, she was aware of her feminine hypocrisy. To be seen in his curricle had been the greatest excitement.

'Only too well,' said Lady Dorna, squeezing her hand in sympathy. 'Sir Chase told Seton that he'd called on your father and that you'd already been introduced. So Mr Chester approves of him, does he?'

'I suppose so. What do you know about him, Lady Dorna? You and his parents are neighbours, are you not?'

'Know about him, my dear?' The wide blue eyes were almost violet in the shady coach, gleaming with laughter. She would have liked to have known much more than she did about the man her brothers admired, but the opportunity had never presented itself. Her mouth pouted, prettily. 'Ooh, only that half the women in England would like to have driven home with him, even if it was only half a mile. That's all.'

'And the other half probably *have* been, and that's *not* all,' drawled Lord Rayne to himself, glancing out of the window. 'No.' He revised the caustic remark. 'That's doing it too brown. Boston's bang-up to the mark. A real out-and-outer. He and I were together for a while in the Dragoons and all the men admired him then, and probably still do.'

'Wasn't he a captain, like you and Nick?' said Lady Dorna.

'He was. Prinny still thinks the sun shines out of him. Did you know he belongs to the Four Horse Club, Cat?'

'It doesn't surprise me,' she said. 'He certainly is a master with the ribbons, isn't he? But you must know more than most about his other side, the gambling, the adventures. The *affaires,*' she added, unable to hold back the word.

Lord Rayne was dismissive. 'Oh, Cat! He does everything more than most men. He's that kind of cove. Larger than life. Rides like the devil, but as good with horses as anyone I know. He's an amazing athlete, fencing, boxing, beats the rest of us hollow every time, wins his wagers, yet is as generous as the day. And he's extremely wealthy, too.'

'And women? Is he as generous to them?'

'Is that what's bothering you?' he said, peering at her.

'It's not *bothering* me at all,' she replied. 'I merely mention it as an addition to his long list of accomplishments. Or do I mean *activities?*'

'Oh! So that's what it's all about? He's put out a line for you, has he? And you don't want to be reeled in.'

'Seton,' said his sister, 'will you please try not to be so vulgar? Cat has been angled for quite enough while you've been away. She must be getting tired of it. You surely cannot expect her to welcome his advances, after all that.'

'Is Boston making advances, Cat?' Lord Rayne persisted.

'Answer my question first. It makes no difference who makes advances, I'm not interested. I'm simply curious to know whether the reputation is deserved or just gossip. I don't see why I should like a man simply because everyone else does.'

'Your father, you mean.'

'Anyone.'

'Well, then, if you really want to know, he's probably had more women than I've had suppers, and I shall not say another word on that subject while Miss Chester's cheeks are so flushed. So there.'

'I don't think there's any more I need to know, thank you. Shall we change the subject then? How well do you know Lord and Lady Ensdale?'

'Well enough to know that their house parties are never dull. They used to entertain the regiment at Brighton, you know. Kept open house there. Look, Cat…' Lord Rayne said, leaning forward a little from the buttoned velvet seat, 'if you're concerned about Boston, about him…you know…calling on you, you send for me, eh? I'm at home for a while and we can always ride out, or drive, and if you need an escort I shall more than likely be available. If you need an excuse, use me.'

'Thank you,' Caterina said. 'That's very thoughtful. I may well do that. It will only be temporary.'

'Yes, of course.'

'In that case,' said Lady Dorna, jauntily, 'send Sir Chase on to me at River Court and I'll do my best to take his mind off you.'

Privately, Lord Rayne did not believe his lovely widowed sister would succeed in diverting Chase Boston from anything he had set his mind to. But if Caterina was as unhappy with the possibility as she appeared to be, he himself would gladly help her out, for they had once been good friends and he had not made a promising start of their second phase. Besides that, he would not mind being seen with her on his arm.

With that offer in mind, a certain peace was established for the first time in twenty-four hours and, because she did not want to put a damper on a weekend so much looked forward to, Caterina brightened up. The five days ahead would surely be enough time to displace thoughts of Sir Chase Boston and her father from her mind. She wished Hannah's youngest twins no harm, but their high temperatures had been a godsend in forcing their mother to relinquish her duties as chaperon, duties she took far too seriously for most people's enjoyment. Lady Dorna, known to her friends as The Merry Widow, had quite different ideas about what a chaperon ought (and ought not) to do, and the two sisters had no doubts who was most in need of a duenna.

The journey through the rolling countryside of Hampshire and Wiltshire, however, provided ample opportunity for memories of Sir Chase's unforgettable presence to intrude upon Caterina's peace, whether she wanted them or not. In the light of Lord Rayne's high opinion of him, heard at first-hand, it was hardly surprising that he should have taken it for granted that a woman would jump at the chance of being driven behind his team of chestnuts in a *curricle,* of all things.

Not surprisingly, Lady Dorna had noted only Sir Chase's most memorable features, but then, she had not suddenly discovered herself to be indebted to him by twenty thousand guineas. She might have looked upon matters less facetiously if she had not been proposed by her father as the means of paying him off, simply because her brother was not in a position to do so.

Caterina and Sara had visited Sevrington Hall once before, but that had been two years ago when snow had prevented their return home on the appointed day, and the delayed house-guests had made good use of the new plaything by arranging snowball fights, sledging on trays, snowman-building and skating on the lake. Now it was early May, with pink and white blossom lying thickly on the roads instead of snow, whitening the hedges and flying behind the wheels. With two rests and a change of horses along the way at Farnham and Winchester, it was almost dinnertime when they came in sight of Sevrington Hall near Salisbury, gleaming like a golden ingot on the blossomed hillside.

Turning through a solid Renaissance gatehouse, they drove through herds of deer in the parkland towards the Elizabethan house whose many window-panes flashed apricot in the late sun. They were neither the first nor the last guests to arrive, but to judge from the ecstatic welcome of their ebullient hostess, they might have been the first people she had seen for a year.

Lady Ensdale was one of those rare aristocrats about whom no one spoke unkindly except, on occasion, about her voice, which any regimental captain would have been proud to own. One also had to accept her slight tendency to overdress, though there was no hint of cheapness in the finery. Her quiet husband and two charming sons adored her as, it seemed, did everyone else. Still blooming well into middle age, she possessed an enviable energy and zest for life, and now her welcome rang through the Great Hall, where the odd mixture of Tudor minstrels' gallery and Georgian staircase epitomised the whole house and its eclectic contents.

'You'll know almost everybody,' she called over her shoulder as she led them up the wide white staircase. 'Only a small gathering this time. I've put all the ladies in the west wing and you, Seton dear, are in the east wing with the other men. Now don't pull a face like that, wicked boy. What you get up to in the middle of the night is your business, but don't trip over your hounds and wake us all up, that's all I ask.' Her laughter was infectious; even when they had closed the doors of their rooms, it could still be heard over the barking of dogs.

Millie, the sisters' maid, opened one of the small casement windows to see a flight of honking swans with peachy wings on their way towards the lake, the rippling V-shaped ribbon dropping lower and lower until it shattered the mirror of water with a splash and a flurry of feathers. Caterina and Sara leaned out to watch. 'Only a small gathering this time,' Sara murmured, smiling.

Dressing for dinner as a guest in someone else's house was always more fun than dressing for one's own family, and Millie's expertise was such that she could easily attend to both her charges at the same time, having once been a dressmaker's talented apprentice. There was nothing she didn't know about the latest fashions, accessories and hairstyles, or the art of wearing them with panache, nor was there ever any argument about what the sisters should wear when their tastes were so different.

Before the long cheval mirror, Sara observed the swing of her pale blue gown with borders of fine gold beading. Her silk stockings were embellished with clocks of gold thread which she hoped to be able to show off discreetly during the evening. 'The sapphire earrings?' she asked Millie.

'The small pearl drops, Miss Sara,' said the maid, without explanation.

There had been a time when Caterina had needed advice, too, but now she needed her sister and maid for little else but approval, the twitch of a seam or the lift of a curl from one side to the other. In the half-gown of figured silver silk worn over a grey silk under-dress, low-cut at front and back and with tiny petal sleeves that barely covered her shoulders, the warm peach blush of her skin set off the cool colours, as did the rich tones of her hair. Bound with narrow silver braids, it had been piled into a high chignon from which curls fell provocatively down her long neck, not quite hiding her diamond earrings, like frozen tear-drops.

Draping a snowy silk shawl over her arms and shaking out its long fringe, she smiled at Millie. 'Thank you. Ready, Sara? You look enchanting, love. Which one are we aiming for this time? Constantine, or Titus?'

Sara giggled. 'Either will do nicely, thank you.'

Although Caterina had dismissed Lord Rayne's first offer to keep them both company that weekend, she had appreciated the spirit, if not the casual delivery. As she walked with her sister and Lady Dorna along the open landing above the Great Hall, her quick peep over the beautiful white balustrade was intended to find him. There were, as expected, far more than the estimated small gathering, bearing in mind their hostess's distorted perception of the world, so they were not too surprised to find that the hall was almost filled with guests, some of whom were well known to them. Her eyes, however, continued to scan even after she had identified Lord Rayne's black long-tailed coat amongst all the others, for although she was accustomed to having so many eyes turned upon her when she sang, she felt that something down there in the assembly was compelling her attention with an unresistable force, like a magnet.

Her gaze swung and stopped and, instead of feeling surprise, alarm or even irritation, a strange sense of inevitablity stared back at her from the face she had not managed to banish from her mind. Sir Chase Boston.

Someone was talking to him, but he was paying no attention.

Someone was speaking to her, someone else calling her name, but she heard nothing except the hollow thud behind her ribs, reaching her throat. And of all the eyes that watched each of her slow steps down to their level, the only ones she was aware of were his.

Chapter Three

He came to meet them, weaving his way through the crowded room ahead of Lord Rayne, bowing to all three ladies with faultless grace. 'Lady Adorna, Miss Chester, and Miss Sara. Were you expecting a small gathering, too? Or has our hostess ceased to surprise you?'

Sure that Caterina would wish her to divert Sir Chase's attention, in view of her dislike, Lady Dorna Elwick was happy to oblige, drawing Sara into the conversation, then by some meaningless chatter about the guests, and finally by an alluring flutter of long eyelashes that Caterina took as a signal of her availability.

For some reason that eluded her, she felt a twinge of annoyance, as if the matter of her dislike had so soon been dealt with, which she knew it had not. Sir Chase was expecting a greeting from her, although from a distance their eyes had already greeted. The bow of her head was perfunctory, her words lacking welcome. 'Sir Chase,' she said, looking beyond him. 'You brought a partner, did you?'

You know I did not, his eyes told her. 'I followed

her,' he said, quietly. 'Ah, Rayne. Fortunate fellow to have three ladies at your elbow.'

Lord Rayne made a jesting kind of reply meant to sound as if they might curb his enjoyment, but Caterina was hardly listening, faced once more with the man she now knew had offered for her, however she had chosen to interpret the arrangement earlier. He would certainly respond to Lady Dorna's flirting, but he would be obliged to pursue *her,* nevertheless, and all his attempts to ingratiate himself would be no more than an effort to win his wager.

His brief reply to her question had been understood by them all, but it was Sara's large sympathetic eyes that rested longest upon her sister. In Sara's experience, one either wanted a man or one didn't. Caterina could do both at the same time. As the two men stood side by side before her, she was able to compare them, to note their similar build and powerful physique, the upright graceful carriage and Lord Rayne's nonchalance that had once taken her heart by storm. She set this beside the overpowering force of the other man's controlled energy and the sheer magnetism that had drawn her halfway across the room, unwillingly. She felt it now, and was still unsettled by it, disturbed not around the heart as she had been six years ago, but deeper down into her roots where her passions lay.

Recognising the source of her interest, she knew that he also would be familiar with the purely physical response and that this would surely have been why he'd made his spontaneous and absurd offer for her. That, and his love of gambling.

According to Lord Rayne, he was a man with large appetites, though a glance at the lean, square, dimpled chin showed no extra folds overlying the white cravat, but tanned healthy skin with a faint blue shadow reaching up to the long sideburns of black hair. He had raked his mop back with his fingers, probably without a mirror, she thought, for some strands had fallen forward over his broad forehead in a casual disarray that others took hours to achieve. His mouth was wide and firm, not at all red like that of the awful suitor who had kissed her.

Her observation of his mouth was caught before she could withdraw it, but she felt his hazel eyes lazily examining her lips as she had been doing to his, and she was glad when Lord Rayne stepped smartly to her side, intending a more efficient display of protection this time. As dinner was announced, he offered her his arm with a wink. 'Miss Chester, you *will* partner me, I hope?'

Smiling, she accepted his offer just as her sister's hand was being drawn through the arm of the Honourable Constantine Ensdale, eldest son of their host, while Lady Dorna was attaching herself like a pretty limpet to Sir Chase, who had little choice but to put a happy face on it. Caterina was well satisfied with Lord Rayne's gallantry, but she wished that Lady Dorna had not thrown herself with quite so much relish into the business of steering Sir Chase's thoughts away from its intended course. A little reticence would have done very well, at this early stage of the game.

Watching carefully for precedence as they shuffled into the dining room, Caterina whispered to her escort, 'Did you know he'd been invited?'

'He said nothing about it yesterday, but then, I didn't mention it either. Could your father have told him you'd be here?'

'Well, I certainly didn't.'

'You dislike him as much as that, do you?'

'Yes. Don't ask me why.'

'Well, then, stay close. He'll get the message. Anyway, once Dorna's taken him in hand, he'll be kept busy.'

With her natural liveliness and good nature, Lady Dorna wore her desires with the same transparency as her gown, the minuscule bodice of which was the focal point for everyone within range. Caterina had no doubt that Sir Chase's attention would be securely held for the rest of the evening, and perhaps beyond.

Yet for all the formality of the dining room and the impressively decorated tableware, the silver candelabra and fruity centrepieces, the crested cutlery and snow-white napery, there was a contrasting gaiety and leg-pulling about who should go in with whom, about the proper seating, and Lady Ensdale's loudly boisterous admission that she hadn't given it a moment's thought, dears.

'Sit ye down where ye will,' she bellowed across the table, waving her arms about. 'Loughborough, over there by Perdita...no, over *there,* dear. What? Oh, that's Barbara, is it? Well, of course I knew. Now, Chase, my boy.... Oh, you're with Dorna, are you? Right. So who's got our little songbird? Ah, Seton! There you are. Do sit down...I'm famished.' She looked round for the butler. 'Sanderson, get on with it, man!'

Sanderson had seen it all before.

From experience, Caterina knew it would be a lengthy affair, testing both her social skills and her stamina, for it was not going to be easy for her to relax and enjoy herself with Sir Chase and Lady Dorna sitting almost opposite with an uninterrupted view between two enormous epergne.

But with six years of news to exchange, Caterina and Lord Rayne suffered no shortage of conversation, and although they could not indulge themselves completely so soon, it might have been thought by some of the guests that their interest in each other signified the rekindling of an old *tendre.* He was assiduous in his attentions, and she responded accordingly with smiles and private jests that belonged to an earlier time, which seemed to be the easiest way for her to avoid a certain pair of eyes that watched from between a pineapple and a large yellow peony.

Even so, with the lax rules at Lady Ensdale's merry table, there were times when the conversation flowed in all directions, when Caterina was obliged to reply to Sir Chase's questions from across the table to which a simple yes or no would have been impossible. She could not help her feelings of surprise at his own part in the general conversation, which showed a seriousness quite different from the Banbury stories recounted by some Tulips and would-be beaux with whom she had sometimes been obliged to dine. He did not regale them with bragging accounts of his daring exploits, even when Lord Rayne offered him the chance, nor did he talk about himself at all except in the most amusing and self-effacing terms that seemed to imply a genuine boredom with the subject. This not only made his listeners laugh, but it showed Caterina a side of him she had not suspected. Whatever reasons she might give to refuse his offer of marriage, she would never be able to say that he pitched the gammon too far, or that he had maggots in his head, for he certainly did not.

But nor did he pay Lady Dorna the kind of attention that lady had hoped for, providing no foundation of flirtatiousness upon which she could build something deeper. She was not so addle-pated, though, that she could ignore the way he took every opportunity to glance across the table to where Caterina and Lord Rayne chattered, seemingly absorbed in each other. On the other hand, Lady Dorna could not have known how Caterina and Sir Chase were more aware of each other than of anyone else in the room or that, although their eyes rarely met, Caterina's danced and flitted like a moth around a candle flame, more than once coming perilously close to being singed.

By the time the covers had been removed to reveal the glorious satinwood table and a new experience of reflections, Caterina had at last begun to enjoy herself. Lady Dorna's efforts to keep Sir Chase's attention had become an amusing charade that was only partly for her sake, the other part being a sensual woman's natural reaction to a physically attractive male. For her own part, Caterina thought how fortunate it was that Lord Rayne had returned home at this opportune moment to offer his services, and how satisfying it was to know that their friendship had so soon been questioned by Sir Chase. That, at least, was going according to plan.

Dabbling her fingertips in the glass bowl, she took up the small napkin to wipe them, raising her eyes to find that Lord Rayne was watching her with an expression of tenderness and a smile hovering around the corners of his mouth. 'My lord?' she whispered, dimpling.

'You've become a very beautiful woman, Cat,' he replied, softly. 'I'm not the only one who can't keep his eyes off you.'

'I'm obliged to you, my lord. Can you keep up the pretence a while longer?'

'It isn't pretence. You know how poor I am at pretending.'

'Now that's a pity, because we may be obliged to play at charades later. I shall make sure you're not in my troupe.'

'Never mind that. Tell me why Boston has suddenly offered for you.'

'Keep your voice down. I didn't say he'd offered.'

'Well, he has, hasn't he?'

'The whys and wherefores are neither here nor there, but he'll soon find out that I don't intend to accept any man of my father's choosing. Would you mind passing that little dish of olives, please? Thank you.'

Lord Rayne's handsome face could not conceal a fleeting expression of deep scepticism. 'Is it only his reputation, or is there something else you've taken a dislike to?'

She nibbled around the olive, studying her teeth-marks. 'You know my thoughts on the subject,' she said in a low voice. 'When I marry, it will be to a man of my own choice, not one who bounces up to my father's front door and declares his interest. I've seen too many unhappy women caught in that manner, and I've seen the ways they devise to make life tolerable. Look at your sister, for example.'

'Dorna? Unhappy? What nonsense, Cat. It was not an unsatisfactory first marriage that made her the way she is. She'd have gone her own way no matter who she was shackled to. She's her mother's daughter.' Lord Rayne chuckled. 'So, the proud Miss Caterina Chester rejects all suitors unless they've been personally hand-picked by her. So where do I come in, my passionate Cat? Am I to be hand-picked?'

'No, my lord. Not again,' she said with a rueful smile.

'I see. And what about Boston?'

'Certainly not. One could never be sure of a man like that.'

'That, my dear child,' he said, 'is just about the daftest thing you've ever said to me. If you can't be sure of a man like Boston, you may as well stop looking. He's the most dependable man I know, bar none. Now, I'm here to be obstructive, not to sing his praises. Drink up. It's almost time for the ladies to withdraw.'

Tilting her glass, she peeped through the mouthful of pale wine and the distorting pattern at the handsome face and challenging eyes she had studiously tried to avoid for the last two hours. Warped though her view was, there was no avoiding the determination written upon every line of his face, in his unflinching regard of her, in his bold and upright posture and the tender caress of his long fingers upon the stem of his glass. Holding her eyes with his own, he lifted it and paused before touching the rim to his lips like the slow ritual of a dance and, without a word to indicate who they were toasting, they drank to each other, both silently picking up the other's gauntlet.

The company stood as the ladies left the room, Caterina's mind darting off-course down its own dark track where two unyielding arms caught her, hard thighs pressed shamefully close and warm lips...no! *God in heaven...what foolishness!* Hauling her mind back up from the depths, she sought Sara's hand for safety. 'Cup of tea, dear one?' she said. 'Shall we go and talk to Lady Caroline over there?'

'Caroline Lamb? Do we know her?'

'Not yet, but we soon will.' Pulling the white shawl around her shoulders, she could not suppress a shiver as the hair on her scalp prickled, settling her thoughts back into place and making her aware yet again of the dangers of owning a too-romantic imagination.

The two sisters soon discovered, however, that no woman of their acquaintance possessed the imaginings of Lady Caroline Lamb, who had expected to find her beloved Lord Byron as one of the party. He had not turned up, and now the otherwise intelligent and interesting young woman could speak of nothing except what might have happened to him, short of being swallowed by an earthquake.

Sara was made so uncomfortable by it that she drew her sister gently away rather than listen to any more of the hysterics. 'You won't find me revealing my heart in that fashion,' she said, once out of earshot. 'If the man I want doesn't turn up, I shall do what Lady Dorna does and find another. Such a silly fuss. Who is this Byron man, anyway?'

'Oh, Sara... You must have heard of him. He's all the rage. He's the one who wrote that book of poems when you were fourteen, called *Hours of Idleness*—don't you remember? Everyone's started to take notice of him now.'

'Oh, him. I thought that was by an old man.'

'No, he's young and handsome, and highly immoral, and all the ladies are in love with him, except us.'

'Well, I hope for her sake he turns up or she'll be a wreck in twenty-four hours. Perhaps Sir Chase will stand in for him, if he doesn't.'

'What do you mean by that?'

'Mr Constantine Ensdale says that Sir Chase arrived unannounced, as he often does. They don't mind, because he's an old family friend. There's always a room ready for him, Constantine says.'

'How convenient,' said Caterina.

It was not long before they realised that Sir Chase, not Lord Byron, was to be the main topic of conversation among the ladies, and that few details of either his character or appearance had escaped their attention. Almost without exception, they wished he would bestow upon them one of his cool lingering looks from those bold hazel eyes, and most had noticed Lady Dorna's particular good fortune with the beau. 'What's he like?' the newly married Mrs Bannerman wanted to know, eager for comparisons. 'He looks so severe. I'm sure I'd swoon if he looked at me like that.'

Lady Dorna agreed, with an inappropriate cheerfulness, 'Yes, dear, you probably would, but I think Sir Chase would expect more from a woman than a well-placed swoon. He would not do for you, Mrs Bannerman.'

'Oh,' said the young lady.

Caterina came to her aid. 'From what I've heard, Sir Chase would not do for any of us except as a temporary diversion. His reputation puts him well beyond our reach.'

'Don't rely on reputations,' said a quiet voice coming from one end of the striped sofa. All eyes turned to the elderly dowager, Lady Inchall, whose frail lace-covered figure belied a mind as sharp as a razor. 'I believe it's better to make your own mind up about people rather than rely on hearsay. By their very nature, reputations are biased, you know.'

'Forgive me, my lady. I stand corrected,' said Caterina.

'You are young.' The old lady smiled. 'That's all there is to forgive.'

'Do you know Sir Chase well?'

'Since he was a young lad, Miss Chester. He was full

of spirit and adventure even then, the bane of his father's life and the idol of his mama's. He's learnt discipline over the years, but the energy is still very much there.'

'Discipline, my lady? That's not what I've heard.'

'Reputations again? We all have them. Lady Dorna has. So have you. And so have I, for that matter, but only we know the reasons for them.'

'I have? A *reputation?*'

'Indeed. After two broken engagements, why would you not?'

'Oh, dear. I had not thought—'

'That it could be of interest to anyone else? That only goes to prove my point, that what we get up to is not essentially to amuse others, but to fulfil a need inside us that is not being met. Do you not agree that it could be so?'

'I'm sure you must be right, my lady, but does that mean that any man whose life consists of one amorous pursuit and extravagance after another is trying to fulfil a need? If so, could he ever be expected to find what he's looking for?'

'Rather than continue the chase, you mean?' Lady Inchall smiled at the pun, lighting up her wrinkled face with a network of silken strands. 'Men have different values, my dear,' she said kindly. 'What may seem like an extravagance to one may seem perfectly normal to another. Some men cannot bear the idea of pursuit while others find it essential to their enjoyment. And, indeed, he *can* be expected to find what he's looking for, and to know whether it's right for him, too. A man whose experiences are greater than most is not likely to repeat the mistakes he made as a novice, is he? Not unless he's a fool. It's true that they'll be sitting in there…' she nodded her lace-topped head towards the dining-room door

'...discussing us as if we were horses, but the pity of it is that most of them know more about horses than they do about women. I think Sir Chase is probably an exception to that, which is why women respond to him so immediately. It shows, doesn't it?'

'You, too, my lady?' said Lady Dorna, whose fan had sunk lower and lower as she listened.

'Me, too, Adorna dear,' said Lady Inchall, chuckling mischievously. 'You wait till *your* legs start to wobble and your wrinkles multiply, and I'll wager *you* dream of having a fine lusty man in your bed just as often as you do now. Eh?'

Lady Dorna fell back upon the cushions, laughing merrily behind her furiously overworked fan while others smiled, enjoying the luxury of truth.

Caterina nodded, thinking that she liked the dowager Lady Inchall and that when she herself was elderly, she would dispense similar pearls of wisdom to self-absorbed young women who thought they had all the answers.

It was already getting late, and while Lady Caroline Lamb loudly bemoaned the men's absence, the two sisters enjoyed the female company in the drawing room littered with Lady Ensdale's collection of embroideries, some of the stumpwork pieces dating back over one hundred years. On one small side-table stood an open mahogany box holding a brass-mounted glass dial that moved.

'Lord Ensdale's newest toy,' called his wife, waving a teapot at them in mid-pour. 'It's a something-meter,' she chirruped. 'Chase knows about naval machines. Ask him what it is, dear.'

Caterina thought she must be mistaken, for Sir Chase had been in an army regiment, not the navy. Browsing through some family travel diaries and chatting to friends, they were interrupted at last by a loud burst of laughter from the dining room, followed by the men's entry, bright red uniforms and deep blue naval tunics mingling with black-and-white evening dress, ostrich plumes, the flash of diamonds, the wink of gold and pearls. The ladies, yawning only moments before, suddenly sat up and smiled with expectation, their eyes plotting the progress of Sir Chase and Lord Rayne, deep in conversation.

Deprived of her chaperon, Caterina smiled at the two Ensdale brothers as they came to engage Sara and herself in conversation, and so easily did the moments pass that, when she next looked up to find Lord Rayne, he had been captured by a tall brunette whose plumes dusted the plasterwork ceiling.

But without needing to look, she knew who had come to stand at her back, and before she could move away, Sir Chase became part of the group until the Ensdales took Sara off to look at their mother's Queen Anne dolls' house. 'You are not joining the card tables?' she said to him, watching the trio depart.

'No, Miss Chester. I'm joining you instead. Shall we sit?'

'But what about Lady Dorna?'

'What about her?'

'I believe she's expecting you to keep her company.'

'And I'm expecting you to keep me company. Come, if you please.'

The large room was well stocked with tables of all sizes, sofas and chairs, folio stands and marble busts of Roman generals, but Sir Chase led her to the far end towards a deep velvet-covered couch with bowed animal-legs and gold-tasselled cushions. 'Here,' he said, 'we can hear ourselves speak.'

Not best pleased by this easy capture, Caterina placed herself well into the corner, wondering how to broach the difficult subject of her father's guile without becoming quarrelsome. 'Perhaps you should do the talking, Sir Chase, for you *do* have some explaining to do.' Arranging her silver skirt more carefully over her knees, she took a sidelong glance at his skin-tight breeches of silk stockinette, fearfully expensive and worn only by men with well-muscled legs. Her eyes travelled upwards over the white brocade waistcoat, gold chain, pearl buttons and impeccable cravat to his square chin, and she was reminded again of that exhilarating career around Richmond Park only yesterday morning. His steady eyes reflected her thoughts of his hands holding hers, her thigh against his, her shoulders leaning as they cornered at speed. She blushed and looked away. 'You might wish to explain your purpose in making such a ridiculous offer to my father without speaking of it to me first. Yes, I understand that it was a wager, intended to give my father a chance to be free of the debt at my expense, but do good manners not dictate to you that I ought to have been consulted?'

'And if you had been, would you have agreed?'

'No, of course I wouldn't!' she snapped. 'You must have known that.'

'Both your father and I knew that, which is why you were not asked. As you say, it's a wager, and it's up to me to win it, isn't it? Whether you help your father over his difficulty is entirely up to you, but we agreed to keep the good news from you until after this weekend. For reasons best known to himself, he sent me a message to say he'd changed his mind about that.'

'It was my doing, Sir Chase. It's not so difficult for me to tell when Papa has something unpleasant on his mind, though I had never thought in my worst nightmares that he could have involved me in something quite so underhand as this. You will understand that I can have nothing to do with such a scheme.'

'Ah, so you winkled it out of him, did you? Pity. I would rather you'd heard it from me first. I could probably have said it with more tact.'

'I would rather not have heard it at all, sir. I have already made you aware of my views regarding marriage, and I can assure you that when the time comes, I shall be responsible for making my own choice. I dare say my father would have you believe I'm getting desperate.'

'On the contrary, Miss Chester, he assured me of no such thing. He gave me the distinct impression that it's he and your stepmother who are desperate.'

'With a debt of twenty thousand guineas to pay off, who would not be?'

'Mrs Chester has been told of the debt, then?'

'Certainly not, Sir Chase. She must never know of it.'

'And you are not inclined to help your family out? Well, well.'

Incredulous, she stared at him. 'Help them out, sir? Would *you* marry to your father's instructions to pay off a debt that was not of your making? Would you be the object of a *wager,* Sir Chase?'

'If the lady proposed was yourself, I would jump at the chance.'

'Poppycock, sir! Don't try to bamboozle me with such flummery. I'm not such a gudgeon as you think, you know. I hope I may call myself a dutiful daughter, but only a goosecap would go along with this kind of tomfoolery. I have my pride, and I have my aspirations, and neither of these lead me towards men like you.'

'Ah, yes, I seem to recall something similar to that when we spoke yesterday. Men of my sort, wasn't it? Yet you seemed rather vague about the details. Are you any nearer explaining them today?'

She was not. Men of his sort occupied women's fantasies, safely hidden where they could do no damage. They were not easy to explain. She took a deep breath, fearful of the words even before they were spoken, feeling the heat of them and the scorn they would provoke. 'I have been brought up, Sir Chase, to avoid excess of any kind, and in the life you lead—'

'Oh, please spare me the hypocrisy!'

'I beg your pardon?'

As he winced at her intended lecture and shook his head, his craggy face registered both frown and laughter. 'You have been brought up, Miss Chester. Yes, I can see that. But don't try to sell me that nonsense about disapproving, when you know you'd do exactly the same if you were in my position. That's what's bothering you, isn't it? The fact is that you're not. No, it's no use looking daggers at me. The reason why you're so annoyed with your father is that he's taken the reins out of your hands again—'

'That's not true, sir!'

'And that's once too many, isn't it? You see, I know what it is you want, something you've never yet been offered, something deep inside you waiting to be used. It's called passion. It's what your father refers to as silly nonsense.'

'He said *that?*'

'I heard it in your voice when you sang, and I can see it in your eyes. I felt it as we drove together, wildly. You were breathless with it, and guilty with it, too. You are angry with men, your father, your brother, those pathetic creatures who offered for you, and me in particular because you're interested, for once, and you dare not say so because you're insulted by the urgency of it all. Blame your brother for that, and don't try to answer me. Go to bed and think about it. We have a few days together, and by the time we're ready for home I'll have a better answer from you.'

'You can have your answer now, Sir Chase,' she said, panting a little. 'I can earn money. I can pay you. Just give me enough time, and I can pay you back, every last penny.' Her words tumbled out, headlong.

'That isn't the answer, and I won't wait. No.'

'Please?'

'Shh…hush, m'dear. I know what it costs you to plead, so we shall say no more about that kind of solution. It's not for you, and I won't have you pleading. You'll marry me. Become used to the idea.'

'No, sir, I shall not. We live in different worlds.'

'You think so, do you? Is that what you thought when we sat side by side and sprung my team over the turf yesterday? Eh? Is it?'

'That was a mere moment or two.'

'Wrong, there were other moments, too. We both know that.'

'We have nothing else in common. It will take only a day or two for you to find that out.'

'Yes, we have,' he whispered.

His arm lay along the back of the couch, his hand drooping near her shoulder. But now, in the silence, as she acknowledged the full import of his quick uncompromising reply, one forefinger touched the bare skin of her upper arm just below the petalled sleeve, sending a shock through her body that instantly washed away the snub she would like to have delivered. The finger bent, caressed, and withdrew, leaving its memory behind to linger upon her arm, holding her motionless.

'Yes, we have. And if I can discover so much about the real Miss Chester already, just think how soon I shall find the rest of her. Different worlds, indeed.'

In some respects, Sir Chase had to agree that their worlds were different, if the hullabaloo at Paradise Road was anything to go by. No wonder the father was at his wits' end and the daughters longing for escape. 'You've been invited to sing, I believe,' he said, gently changing the subject.

She nodded. 'Tomorrow, or Sunday.'

'Is that what you were rehearsing? The Mozart aria?'

'You know it?'

'I know it well. I heard the opera in Naples last year.'

If she had not been so disturbed by him, she would have asked what he knew of Mozart's operas and Italy, particularly after listening to his conversation at dinner in which he discussed the hazards of travelling through France at this time. From his pronunciation of the place names, it sounded as though he had a good knowledge of languages, too.

Her silence may have had every appearance of a sulk, but Sir Chase appeared to understand the reason for it. 'I know,' he said, gentling her with his deep voice. 'You had hoped to be free of me for a few days, at least, and now you find me here, too. Well, perhaps that's not such a bad thing. It'll give you the chance to get used to me.'

'Your understanding is at fault, sir,' she said with as much composure as she could summon, the caress still luring her thoughts to one side. 'I have no intention of getting used to you. In a place this size, it cannot be as difficult as all that to keep out of your way and, heaven knows, there are plenty of ladies who are more interested in your whereabouts than I. Lady Dorna Elwick, for one.'

'Thank you for the warning. I'll bear it in mind.' He turned to look over his arm. 'Ah, I see the ladies are retiring already. I shall light you to the staircase.'

'Thank you, but there is no need.'

Pretending not to have heard, he rose gracefully and offered her his hand, holding it rock-firm as she eased herself out of the deep squashy corner. She felt the steel in his arm and caught a perfume of something like pine trees after rain.

'Sir Chase,' she said, in an urgent whisper, 'I hope you've not spoken to anyone about...well, you know... about this?'

He did not pretend to misunderstand her as she feared he might. 'Early days,' he replied, keeping hold of her hand. 'The other guests will probably note my interest in you, but they'll not take it too seriously, will they?'

'Won't they?'

His eyes laughed at her. 'A man of *my* sort and a filly who shies at her fences? Oh, I don't think so, Miss Chester. They might be interested to see if I can wean you from Rayne's side, but that's about all.'

'What has Lady Dorna been telling you?' she said, sharply.

'That you and he were once...er...'

'What?'

'Er...*friends,* I think she said. Good friends.'

'That's all Lord Rayne and I ever were, Sir Chase. Good friends, as we are now.' If it occurred to Caterina that she was giving away more than was strictly necessary, it was of far less importance than the preservation of an innocent friendship, and if Lady Dorna had implied otherwise, that notion must be scotched. Lord Rayne had offered her protection from unwanted advances, but the two men had been, and still were, friends of long standing, and she would not trespass on that ground for no good reason. She had no wish to inflame Sir Chase's jealousy, either. She had no wish to inflame any part of him, come to that.

'Thank you for your honesty. That's exactly what he said, too.'

'You *asked* him?'

'Naturally. I asked you, too, if you remember, but you gave me short shrift, little wildcat. So I asked Rayne himself.'

'You had no business to do that.'

'I had every business to do that. Granted, it will make no difference to any competition. I shall still win. But I like to know who the competition is, exactly. Rayne and I go back many years, and we've never had any qualms about trying to steal each other's women. I just had to make quite sure, in this case.'

'Really? And what's so different about this case? No, don't answer that. The others were not being obliged to pay someone else's crippling debt, were they? That must have made things much easier for you.'

'Yes, it probably did, but I've never been averse to challenges, and this one is worth more time and preparation than usual. This one, you see, is going to end in marriage, isn't it?'

'This one, sir, is going to end before it's begun.'

They had reached the bottom of the large white staircase where footmen waited with candelabra to light the way. Sir Chase slowed her down with the lightest pressure on her hand, holding her a little apart from the others. 'I think you will find, Miss Chester, that we have already begun. Too late to turn back. You're committed. We both are.'

'And what happens at the other end, sir? You lose all interest, do you? Then I might as well be in remote Cornwall with the Earl of Loddon's old mother.'

'Well—' he smiled at her cynicism '—I don't have an old mother in any remote corner for you to join, so I shall have to insist on you joining me instead. But we'll talk about the finer points another time, shall we?'

She could not say so, but she would rather have talked about the 'finer points' there and then, rather than later, if 'joining him' meant keeping him company at gambling parties or orgies with his rowdy rich friends. To say as much, though, would have betrayed an interest she had been striving to deny.

Perhaps he saw the doubts cloud her eyes, even in the dim corner of the Great Hall. 'You need not worry about that side of things,' he said. 'You may be in for a few surprises, but not shocks. I have never thought it good practice to shock a lady more than once in a relationship. They don't like it, do they?'

'No, sir, they don't.'

'So on that encouraging note of agreement, shall we say good-night?'

'Good night, Sir Chase.'

'Good night, Miss Chester. Sleep well.' Raising her hand to his lips, he kissed her knuckles lightly before releasing her, and she knew without looking that her every step was being watched as she exchanged a kiss with her hostess and followed the footman up the stairs.

Sara caught up with her before she had reached the top, unable to contain her excitement. 'He's laid claim to you already, Cat,' she whispered with more than a hint of drama. 'Everyone can see it.'

'That's probably what he wants them to think,' Caterina replied, a little more sharply than she intended. 'And where was Seton when I needed him?'

In the peace of their medieval bedroom, she sank with relief into a plump gilded chair that looked strangely out of place against the linenfold panelling. The bed, a delicate white-and-gold four-poster large enough for a family, was hung with cream-and-green satin, the embroidered counterpane turned down to expose welcoming layers of cool white linen and soft green blankets.

Millie set to work on Sara's fastenings, smiling at her chatter, respecting the elder sister's brooding silence. Sara turned on her stool as a pair of silver slippers came tumbling towards the claw-footed leg. 'Are you so very set against him, Cat?' she said. 'They say he's wickedly experienced, and the men all seem rather to respect his opinions, and no one speaks ill of him, and Papa would not have listened to his offer if he'd disapproved, would he? Is there no chance you could bring yourself to like him just enough to marry him?'

'Oh, Sara! For pity's sake!'

'What, dearest?'

'Surely you don't believe that liking a man is good enough reason to want to spend the rest of your life with him? I know most married couples lead separate lives once there's an heir, but that's not what I want. I thought you understood that, of all people.'

Sara slipped off the stool and came to kneel, naked, at her sister's feet. 'Forgive me...do forgive me, Cat. I'm being thoroughly selfish. Of course I understand.' She placed her blonde head upon Caterina's lap. 'And you're right, you must *not* accept him if you find him so abhorrent, as you obviously do. I could never ask you to do that. Never. It's just that...oh...I don't know. I'm *so* in love, Cat. Seeing Mr Ensdale...Constantine... again, has made me see that we mean something special to each other, more than I feel for Titus. It's like a glow, you know. Well, you probably do know, don't you? You felt it for Lord Rayne, didn't you? A lovely gentle feeling of wanting to be with him, to hold his hand, and I know he feels the same way about me, but I've told him—' She stopped, retreating from the delicate subject of Caterina's disasters.

But it was too late. 'Told him what?'

'That I'm not free to accept...well...any offers until...you know.'

'Until your elder sister is riveted.'

'Oh, Cat, that's so unladylike. Where did you learn that expression?' Sara lifted her head from the lap, fixing her sister with sorrowful eyes.

Holding a tunnel of white lawn across her arms, Millie stood behind her. 'Ready, Miss Sara?' she said.

Sara raised her arms and let the nightgown slip over her, wriggling it down to her knees. 'Take no notice of me,' she said from behind a row of pin-tucks. 'If Papa has got it into his head that you must wed first, then nothing is going to change his mind, so we may as well accept it, mayn't we? I dare say I could persuade Constantine to wait for me and I dare say you'll find a man you can love one day.' She sighed and got to her feet, pulling at the white folds.

'Don't give up,' Caterina said, as Sara returned to the stool.

Smiling back good-naturedly, Sara allowed Millie to unpin her hair and to shake it loose over her shoulders like a golden cape and, with the light of several candles shining through the white gown, outlining the lovely curves of her body, she reminded Caterina of what they were both missing with such intensity that it was all the latter could do not to cry out that she *would* accept him, if only to seal Sara's happiness.

But Sara was not entirely correct in supposing that the genteel well-mannered affection she was feeling for the Honourable Constantine Ensdale was what her sister desired from a potential marriage partner. As Millie's sweeping brushstrokes groomed the spun gold, Sara could not have known how her elder sister's thoughts had veered towards the green-and-white bed where, in her fantasies, she lay in the arms of the one whose wicked experience would teach her how to unleash the passion he had recognised.

Unlike Sara, it was not a glow but a burning heat that consumed her. Nor was it the gentle need to hold his hand but a fiercely raging desire to hold his head and to delve into his thick unruly hair, to cover his face with kisses, to breathe in his scent of pines and to roll with him in a bed of ferns, crushing white wood-anemones beneath them. It was not a well-mannered longing Caterina felt, nor could she say whether she felt love in any of its forms. Nor was it what she had wanted from Lord Rayne, despite that distant infatuation. All she could say for sure was that, until her meeting with Sir Chase Boston, some relentless pagan fire had smouldered inside her ready to be fanned into flame by his insistence that she would belong to him. Even his lightest touch on her arm had scorched her. If she could not accept that a duty to her father was a good enough basis for a marriage, then how much better would it be to base it on her physical need to surrender? Could she ever face the fact that there would be other women? Did he feel anything like the passion with which he had credited her? Would she be able to control her feelings while he continued to provoke her so? Had she any right to resist him, dashing her sister's hopes of being with the man she wanted?

Slowly, dreamily, she began to loosen the cords that bound her hair, closing her eyes as she imagined, all too easily, that the softly disturbing sensations on her scalp were being made by his fingers as a prelude to lovemaking.

Conflicts continued to bedevil her as the sound of Sara's regular breathing overtook their whispered forecast of the days ahead. There had been some talk, Sara had told her, of an excursion to the ruins of Old Sarum in the morning, which had caused Caterina immediately to wonder whether it was an outing likely to appeal to Sir Chase and, if it was, what she would propose doing instead. So essential did it become to resolve the issue, even before it had presented itself, that she slipped soundlessly out of bed and, pulling on her silk house robe, decided to go and speak to Lady Dorna about it. She was the one who would understand how important it was to have an excuse at her fingertips.

Pulling the door quietly behind her, she stepped out into the passageway dimly lit by a candle on a linen chest against the wall, but the distant creak of a floorboard made her hesitate. From the darkness at the end of the passage, a tall figure emerged, clothed in a floor-length dressing-gown, stepping warily like a man on ice.

She held her breath and pulled herself back into the thickness of the doorframe to watch as the shadowy shape bent to listen at one door before tapping it. Then, as if quite sure of his welcome, he opened it and slipped inside before the narrow sliver of light was cut off, leaving the passage as deserted as before.

Of one thing Caterina was quite certain—the door was to Lady Dorna's room. The rest, she thought, was only to have been expected for, although she'd not seen the man's face, there was little doubt in her mind who would be keeping the merry widow warm for the next few hours. The awareness that she had actually seen the despicable man taking advantage of one offer while pestering *her* with his suit was an insult she would never forgive. The rake could not, it seemed, hold himself in check even for one night and, no matter how fervently others wished it, he was not the one she could ever give herself to.

With that resolution replaced firmly in her mind, confirming all her first impressions, she returned to her bed to spend hours of unhappy sleeplessness.

Refusing to lay any blame at Lady Dorna's feet over her zealous diversion of Sir Chase's interest, Caterina nevertheless felt a bitter disappointment in the dependability Lord Rayne had been quick to defend. If he meant that the horrid man could be depended on to jump into any willing woman's bed then, yes, Sir Chase certainly fitted the description perfectly. Lady Inchall had been wary of reputations, but now Caterina had seen with her own eyes that his reputation had some substance after all, cheapening the fantasies she had concocted. Far from feeling a smugness at being proved correct, the hurt lay like a lead weight in the pit of her stomach for, until then, she had heard nothing but awe and admiration from the women, and envy from the men.

No, she could not blame Lady Dorna, for she had no

knowledge of Sir Chase's offer of marriage, and if Caterina regretted the astonishing speed of the help she had provided, she could hardly quibble at it.

She could have told Lord Rayne what she had witnessed, but chose not to since it would surely cause tensions over the next few days. On the other hand, the two men had conferred about the triangular relationship, and it was this that she brought up as the two of them lingered on the way to the breakfast parlour.

The two brindle greyhounds flopped into sphinx-like poses as Lord Rayne slowed to a standstill outside the large door where the aroma of bacon and sausages seeped through the cracks. 'He may as well know, Cat,' he said, in answer to her hesitant query. 'I've told him I'm your escort while we're here, and if he wants to get you alone he'll have to get past me first. I don't care whether he has your father's approval or not, he need not think I intend to make it easy for him.'

She could not quibble at that, either, although, if she had not known better, she might have wondered whether Seton had intentions of his own regarding the one he was protecting. While she approved of his resolution, she was reminded how difficult he had found it only last evening when he'd been detained by adoring women. She could hardly expect his entire devotion for four whole days, nor did she underrate Sir Chase's perseverance.

'Thank you,' she said, hearing distant strains of some age-old rivalry drowning out the clanking of a knight in shining armour. 'So you'll be going with us to see Old Sarum, will you?'

'Who's she? Sounds like a witch.'

'Silly. It's a hill-fort two miles away. We may call in at Salisbury, too, on the way back.'

He opened the door for her, smiling. 'Certainly I shall come, but don't allow Chase to choose your mount. Best leave that to me.'

'Why?'

'Child, he'll go for the flashy racers. He always does.'

That sounded like music to her ears, but now she was in militant mood and unlikely to accept any suggestion Sir Chase had to offer, even if she agreed with it.

She had thought they would be among the first to sit down to breakfast, but the informal meal was in full swing with the white flash of morning newspapers and a chorus of greetings, the discreet hovering of servants at the sideboard. Lady Dorna was at one end of the table sitting next to Viscount Sambrook, beckoning her. Predictably, Sir Chase sat at the other end.

But concerning the outing to Old Sarum, Lady Ensdale declined to join the party. 'There's nothing much to see, dears,' she called, describing airy circles with her crumbling muffin, 'except some big ditches and stones. And it's quite windy, too. So we shall have a game of croquet on the front lawn and take a nuncheon at three-ish out on the terrace. Go off and have a gallop, you young things.'

Lady Dorna did not include herself among the latter, but Lord Sambrook, the good-looking young viscount, quickly appointed himself as one of Caterina's personal escorts, and since that suited her purpose very well, she said nothing to discourage him, even when he offered to choose her mount.

As they left the breakfast parlour together, Sir Chase wedged himself neatly between them, obliging Lord Sambrook to abandon her at his friendly request. 'A word with the lady, if you please, Sam.'

Caterina's examination of his face searched for some small sign that might indicate a night spent in Lady Dorna's bed, but there was nothing. But nor did her scrutiny pass unnoticed. Placing a hand on the wall, he stood before her. 'Well, Miss Chester? What do you seek? Signs of repentance and a change of heart?'

'I would not be able to recognise either of those, sir. Guilt, now. I think I'd be able to recognise that.'

He blinked, and she thought he flinched a little, but could not be sure. 'Is that so? Do you have some grounds for—?'

'No,' she said, sharply, wishing she had curbed her tongue. 'If you will excuse me, I must change into my habit. You will be keeping Lady—'

'I shall be coming with you, so don't allow Sambrook to choose your mount. He doesn't know one end of a nag from the other.'

'Thank you, Sir Chase, but I believe I shall be well served by my escorts.' Pointedly, she glared at the barrier of his arm. 'Do I pay a toll here?' she said.

'If this was a more private place, Miss Chester,' he replied in a low voice, 'you would certainly pay a toll.'

She knew exactly what kind of toll he had in mind, but her safety was assured, and when he lowered his arm, she neither smiled nor thanked him as she walked away. Once more in the white and greenery of her own room, she took herself firmly in hand, telling herself severely that he would have said the same kind of thing to any half-passable female, that his arms were no more muscular, his chest no broader, his hips no narrower than any other half-passable male.

She was still wearing her white muslin day dress and gazing out over the lake when Sara returned to the room. 'Cat, what are you about, love? I thought you'd be changing.'

'I *am* changing,' Caterina whispered to herself. 'Almost hourly.'

In some respects, the excursion went according to Caterina's plan. With her two most dedicated escorts and others close at hand, Sir Chase was kept at a distance and seemed content to have it so. He certainly did not try as hard as she thought he should, or could, to engage her in any kind of conversation, which was not quite what she'd had in mind, especially as he appeared to know more about Old Sarum than the rest of the party.

Once up beyond the massive circular earthworks on the plateau high above the rest of the countryside, Sir Chase sat his big grey like a very superior architect with a group of clients, pointing out the various features belonging to an era before the birth of Salisbury when this remote place had housed both town and cathedral, and long before that, too. Watching him from a distance while being chatted to by Lord Sambrook, closely guarded by Lord Rayne and challenged to a race by Sara and the two young Ensdales, Caterina would rather have joined the group who listened with rapt attention to their guide. Pride held her back. Not even a moment of her interest would she give him.

Winning the race round the great mound by several lengths, she asked Lord Rayne whether he had chosen her mount, sensing by the shrug of his shoulders that there was some embarrassment. 'Oh, Chase had yours already side-saddled when I got to the stables,' he said. 'I suppose it would have been petty to have it changed. It's a goer, isn't it?'

So, she was riding his choice, after all. She looked across to the powerful yet graceful figure on the grey, admiring his ease in the saddle, the smooth fit of his coat and breeches, the set of the beaver hat upon his dark thatch. His stallion responded to every unseen movement of the hands on the reins, perfectly controlled and obedient, and she felt once more the soft caress of his finger on her arm, holding her passive and biddable for that short space of time.

'Let's go and listen,' she said. 'I want to know why it was left to ruin.'

'Too windy to live here, I should think,' said Lord Sambrook, as if the wind had not been blowing when it was built. 'Come on, then.'

So it was that she found herself following Sir Chase rather than the other way round, if only to stand on the outer edges of the group to listen to snatches of the discussion on landmarks, spires and distances. Putting aside personal animosities, she had to admit that there was more to him than she had thought.

It was the same in the cathedral at Salisbury. With her two escorts and Sara's group, she went off in the opposite direction from Sir Chase but found, after all her contrariness, that her ears strained to hear what he was saying to the others. Pointing out the vaulting, the arches and pillars, the bosses and capitals, he appeared to know every detail while she sat in a pew just near enough to hear, pretending to study the kneelers and the complex east window. Her plan to keep him at bay had worked too well for her own comfort, for now she was bound to admit that, in most respects, the morning had been a wasted opportunity.

They were back at Sevrington Hall in time to join the others on the terrace for a light nuncheon, discovering with a mixture of relief and apprehension that the absentee Lord Byron had arrived at last and was now the recipient of Lady Caroline's attentions, whether he willed it or not.

Caterina was in no mood for fulsome introductions, at that moment being more interested in the spread of cold meats and hominy pies, in home-grown salads, warm cakes and biscuits, nutty fruit-breads and home-brewed cider. Sir Chase made no attempt to sit next to her or to help her to the food, which she saw as one more tedious result of Lord Rayne's vigilance, and when Lord Sambrook vacated the chair at her side for an instant, it was Lady Dorna who came to occupy it, eager to hear how she had enjoyed the ride. Caterina did her best to overemphasise her enjoyment as soon as Sir Chase came to sit within hearing distance.

'And did Seton play his part?' Lady Dorna whispered, smoothing a dainty hand absently over Caterina's dove-grey velvet sleeve.

'Oh, yes,' said Caterina, bearing in mind her own self-inflicted constraints. 'I was well guarded indeed.'

'Mm…m, I saw.' Lady Dorna twinkled, impishly. 'He is rather delicious, isn't he?' Her hand continued to smooth, sensuously.

'Delicious? Who, Seton?'

'No, dear, not my brother. Your other escort, the *viscount,*' she hissed as her eyes followed the young man who leaned over the balcony to call to someone below. 'Just look at those legs, Cat.'

Caterina did not look at the legs but at the lust in Lady Dorna's eyes that not even a child could have missed. 'Viscount…Sambrook? You've taken a fancy to him, have you? I thought you—'

'More than a *fancy,* my dear,' the widow continued,

almost growling the word. 'I can scarce wait for tonight. Such a lover, Cat. And what energy he has.' Her hand flapped as she tipped her head back to soak up the sun, as if the viscount's kisses were already pressing into her barely covered bosom.

Caterina was inexperienced, but there was no mistaking what was meant by Lady Dorna's typically explicit tributes and, although she blushed to the roots of her hair, she had the presence of mind not to delve any deeper into the secrets of the widow's bed when it was now quite obvious who her lover had been last night. Not Sir Chase, but the man who had clung to *her* side all morning like a damned leech.

To compare what she had seen last night in the shadowy passageway with what she *thought* she'd seen, her eyes swung of their own accord towards Sir Chase's strong profile as he sat listening intently to one of the lively young ladies who had expressed such an interest in him last evening and who would no doubt have been with them today if they had taken carriages. The woman knew all the wiles, the sidelong looks, fingertips touching her neck and earlobes, touching him with the tip of her fan to make a point, touching her lips with the tip of her tongue, leaving her mouth agape to show him her teeth. *He will not look at me with that going on before his eyes,* Caterina thought angrily.

But he did. Slowly turning his head as if he could sense her distress, he looked directly into her eyes and held them. And although he could not have known in what way he had been misjudged, his regard of her contained more than a hint of amusement and sympathy, understanding her self-defeating attempts to distance herself at any cost, sharing with her the chagrin that simmered just below the cool surface. There was more in the look than that, bidding her to search more closely, to disturb her body-rhythms, to overwind her heartbeats and to find in his eyes the kind of passion she had not found elsewhere, to be shared with him, when she was ready.

Gentlemanly, he turned back to the young woman's one-sided conversation, leaving Caterina speechless with the ache of desire. Lady Dorna had missed none of the silent exchange, and her hand had long since withdrawn from Caterina's velvet sleeve. 'Heavens, Cat dear, but I wish he'd look at me like that,' she whispered.

But Caterina heard nothing, felt nothing but a strange fluttering sensation between her breasts and the slow pulsing of something in her deepest parts, something new that she had no name for.

Chapter Four

If the Sevrington Hall guests hoped that, with Lord Byron's arrival, his insecure lover might give them some respite from her constant outpourings of devotion, they soon discovered that her next attention-seeking device was to see the younger female guests as threats to her position. At first, Caterina and Sara thought this might be another quirky side to Lady Caroline's humour they had not seen before until her sulks and tears were followed by several turbulent exits and re-entrances, a semi-fainting fit and some irritated whispers from the guests themselves.

Lady Ensdale did all a hostess could do to suggest alternative activities, but Lord Byron, languid, boyishly good looking and affable, was not inclined to share any of the responsibility, accepting Lady Caroline's childish tantrums as one of the perks of his new fame to which he was entitled. Indeed, he appeared to be both amused and flattered by it, placing Caterina directly in the firing line by singling her out as the object of his interest, preferring her quiet company to Lady Caroline's melodrama.

Bemused, then concerned, Lady Dorna, Lord Rayne and Sir Chase all played a part in shielding Caterina from both of the immature lovers, but Lord Byron appeared to be playing his own kind of sport when he refused to join the men in a game of cricket below the terrace. Not a sportsman, he was slightly built and lame in one foot, his dress too foppish to be either masculine or practical, his liveliness more in his subjectively poetic chatter than in general conversation. Caterina thought him rather silly and extremely affected.

Fortunately, neither Lord Rayne nor Sir Chase were inclined to accept his protestations and, with a hand under each of the poet's arms, they hauled him out of his deep basket chair and almost carried him down the stone steps, to the laughter and applause of the assembly, pushing the umpire's long staff into his hand with the intention of keeping him there. Needless to say, the rules of cricket were not Lord Byron's forte, and the game became progressively more hilarious and even riotous.

But the sight of so many comely men stripped down to their shirts with rolled-up sleeves and open necks was, for the audience of women, enough to keep even Lady Caroline quiet. As the men came to join them, one by one, grinning to the applause, the glow of their exertions was prolonged by the stares that skimmed over details usually concealed by waistcoat, coat and cravat. Caterina had never seen Lord Rayne so revealed, never so handsomely tousled or accessible and, as he flopped down beside her, there was a moment when her eyes were filled with an admiration he had once kindly refused.

There was no need for words; each knew exactly what the other was thinking: if Caterina was still as interested as she once had been, he was hers for the asking. His gaze lingered and caressed, drinking in her maturing beauty and the womanly poise she had been at such pains to acquire as a fledgling swan, trying to draw from her some kind of mute agreement to begin again on a more exalted level.

But Caterina's lovely eyes swung away from his message as another laughing player approached them from the cricket field and, watching her, Lord Rayne found his answer upon her face as clearly as if she'd spoken it out loud. It vanished in an instant as she tried to hide the parted lips, the slight widening of her eyelids and the brief flare of lust that brought a blush from throat to ears, but he had seen it, as no doubt Sir Chase had, too. Such signals, Lord Rayne thought, would be difficult to conceal from a man like him. Damn him.

Sir Chase took the steps of the terrace two at a time and, swinging a chair up with one hand, placed it firmly between Caterina and Lord Rayne, seating himself with a huff of relief. He, too, was unkempt, radiating waves of heat from his bare forearms and open shirt-front where, between white ruffles, a black fuzz pointed like a spearhead towards his waistband. He saw Caterina's flicker of interest as he began to fasten his lower buttons while accepting a glass of cordial with his free hand, then her quickly averted gaze as the shirt sagged open. Yes, he could see the direction of her thoughts as well as the next man, though he had also seen the purpose in Rayne's eyes and knew that the friendship of which they had both assured him was not to be underestimated.

By now it had become apparent that Caterina had innocently won Lady Caroline's jealousy and that Lord Byron preferred not to remedy the obsession thinking, possibly, that the competition might be good for his lover. Whatever his reasoning, it caused Lord Rayne and Sir Chase to join forces in protecting Caterina from the poet's attentions on one side and from his woman's sniping on the other. It was partly this that brought about Lord Rayne's assessment of the situation and a decision to stand back and allow Sir Chase to take Caterina in to dinner. He did not, of course, ask her if she liked the idea, for she would have been bound to insist that she did not.

The other part of his decision was directly linked to the discovery of her feelings for Sir Chase, which she was doing all in her limited power to disguise as intense dislike, for reasons that Lord Rayne found rather obscure. Her inability to keep hidden those magnificent passions that had always been an essential part of her character had now shown him that his promised protection of her was not exactly what she needed or desired. He would have to make it look as if only force of circumstances prevented him from being in the right place at the right time, though he had to admit that, had he not seen her expression with his own eyes and had it been any man but Chase Boston, nothing short of a whole battalion would have broken through his guard.

Walking slowly down the white staircase in a haze of pale aquamarine and white silk, the two Chester sisters drew all eyes as they had done before, though none of the guests assembled for dinner could have known how unusually on edge Caterina was, after being the butt of such hostility that afternoon. The unsatisfactory morning had also taken its toll of her emotions, mixing and remixing them into an amalgam that refused to settle, even as Sir Chase strode forward to hand them down the last two steps.

So unlike the tumbled and perspiring sportsman she had seen earlier, he was in every way as unnervingly attractive, confusing her anger, which no one but he understood. Sauve, impeccably dressed, self-assured and coolly appreciative of her maid's handiwork upon the deep chestnut mass of ringlets, he smiled and feasted his eyes while passing Sara's hand to that of their hostess's eldest son.

'I understand,' he said to Caterina, 'that this is to be the evening for music. Are your nerves in good order, Miss Chester?'

Before she could help herself, her quick glance darted across to the beautiful lissome young creature who had been the cause of her discomfort that afternoon, who now clung to Lord Byron's arm as if daring anyone to engage his attention. 'I had almost convinced myself,' she said, 'that I should alter my programme. But then I changed my mind about that. If she takes exception to some of my more romantic songs, someone will have to stand by with the fire-buckets, won't they? I can hardly be held responsible for her reaction.'

She could hardly add that it was Sir Chase's presence that had also strained her nerves that day, nor was she looking forward to a protracted meal before singing, which was routinely the nature of these occasions. She could never eat anything, but to sit next to Sir Chase for two hours beforehand, she thought, would do little either for her appetite, her concentration, or her nerves, usually so well controlled.

'I shall make it my business to find the nearest fire-bucket and have it filled with cold water,' he said, straight-faced. 'You can rely on me. My aim is tolerably good, though I've never doused a woman before. Have you met the musicians yet?'

The beautifully arched eyebrows twitched with annoyance. 'No, sir. Last time I enquired, they had not arrived. I would usually have had a chance to speak to the leader by now. I don't even know whether they're bringing a pianist with them, so Sara doesn't know... Oh, I'm making a fuss,' she whispered. 'Lady Ensdale has been more than kind, but...tch!' She sighed.

'Where is your music?'

'We took it and the harp into the music room.'

'Then we shall go and take a look.' He offered her his arm. 'I am about as good a pianist as I am with a fire-bucket so, if all else fails, I can step into the breach.'

Naturally, she believed he was funning, and when he pretended not to know how to lift the top off the beautiful Clementi pianoforte at the far end of the music room, her heart sank at the prospect of having to refuse his help. But when he sat at the keyboard and rippled his long fingers with effortless fluency over the keys with scarcely a glance at them and a touch as light as the best accompanist, something inside her began to melt and burgeon like new growth in springtime, bringing a smile to her eyes at last. She began to sing, coming in exactly after his broken chord as confidently as if he'd been Signor Cantoni.

From the hall, the distant gong sounded for dinner, breaking discordantly into their song, and they stopped together. 'Your aim with a fire-bucket is no longer in question, Sir Chase,' she said, trying not to laugh. 'I'm sure you're an expert at that, too.'

Closing the lid, he gathered the music together. 'Well, then,' he said, 'do you feel a little easier about it now? If the musicians get stuck in a snowdrift, we two and Miss Sara will manage well enough on our own.'

'Alas, sir, in May that's unlikely, but thank you. Now I don't even care about Lady Caroline.'

'Or about Lady Dorna and Viscount Sambrook?'

They had set off towards the dining-room door, but here Caterina stopped, realising that he had somehow guessed the reason for her earlier incivility. This was no time for explanations. 'A truce?' she said, hearing the echo of her voice in the large empty room. 'Do you think that would be best? I really don't want to… well…'

'My dear Miss Chester, I have always been in favour of truces. By all means let us call one for as long as you wish.'

'For this evening, Sir Chase?'

'For this evening.' Picking up her gloved hand, he brought her fingers to his lips and bowed his head over them, showing her the thick waves of his black hair, bringing back the faint scent of pines to her nostrils. Lifting his brows, he peeped up at her with steady brown-green eyes that read her mind as easily as they had read the music. 'Shall we go and put a brave face on it?' he said, keeping her hand in his.

How many sides did this enigmatic man have? Caterina wondered, casting her thoughts back to the brilliant four-in-hand whip, the polished conversationalist, the laughing sportsman, the top-of-the-trees Corinthian and now accomplished musician. These were sides of him she had witnessed for herself: there would be yet more for her to discover, if she chose to.

By comparison, how many sides did she have? And why was Sir Chase so keen to find them? Could it be to prove to Lord Rayne that he was still able to take a woman from him? But no, not that, for he had made his offer before his impertinent questions about their relationship. Then what? Why had he forced her brother into debt when even a simple investigation could have revealed the true nature of Harry's finances? What was this precipitous offer of marriage all about, when her father must have warned him of her disinclination, as she herself had done?

Acutely aware of his exciting presence at her side throughout the next two interminable hours, she had time to observe him at close quarters and to find that she approved of so much, although she had prepared herself to do the opposite. More unsettling than his easy grace was his ability to anticipate her needs, as he had already done with the music. Then, his purpose had not been to show off his own skills but to ease her mind of its hidden anxieties. And all through the meal, aware of her lack of appetite, he placed the choicest morsels before her, making no comment when she preferred water to wine or picked sparingly at her food.

Her other neighbour was Titus Ensdale, a pleasant well-mannered young blade wearing an impossibly high cravat that appeared to support a shock of blond curls enclosing a cherubic face. His obvious elation at sitting next to Caterina and Sir Chase was almost enough to curtail his appetite, too. 'I say, Sir Chase,' he said, leaning forward stiffly, 'would you consider showing me how you do up your cravat, sir? Is that the Waterfall, or the Torrent? It looks like a bit of both. Dashed stylish, sir. Beg pardon, Miss Chester. Shouldn't be talking men's talk across you, I know, but this is the first time I've been able to get near enough.'

Smiling, Sir Chase accepted the compliment. 'You're quite correct, Titus, it's a bit of both. My man confused the two, and now he can't help himself. If you come to my room before breakfast tomorrow, you'll be able to watch how he does it.'

'Oh, sir! That would be capital…just capital!'

So the meal passed as smoothly as an egg custard and, by the end of the dessert, a message reached them that the orchestra had arrived, at last, several hours late. A house fire had blocked the road eight miles away, and the re-routing of the carriages through narrow country lanes was not the best possible preparation for an evening of music-making. Nor did it auger well for Caterina's hopes of polish from the elderly pianist whose eager acceptance of their host's offer of unlimited hot punch to warm his fingers caused them to play two notes at once and to turn over two sheets at a time, while his warmed brain failed to register the error for several bars.

An overture by half of the musicians, followed by the first movement of Mozart's *'Eine Kleine Nacht Musick'* had revealed a few wobbles among the strings, but Sara's gentle harp solo had led the audience to expect that all would be well. But not Caterina, whose sidelong glance at Sir Chase was returned with equal dismay, and when her moment arrived, it soon became all too clear that the pianist's hands and brain were not working in harmony. Some noisy flapping of music-sheets, the escape of one to the floor, its subsequent misplacement among the others, and a pause while he blew and polished his nose did little to set the scene for her first aria, and when he lost his place completely, Caterina calmly stopped and waited, sure of what would happen next.

The tall figure was already on his feet, striding towards the dais with a determination that the flustered pianist was in no mind to resist. Vaulting off the piano stool, he stumbled out of the way only seconds before

Sir Chase occupied it and, before the astonished audience had time to wonder, the first galloping, tripping, lilting notes of her song flowed out from beneath his hands, his eyes smiling at Caterina as if somehow they had both known that this would come about.

At this kind of event, Caterina had had experience and good training, and now she gave herself completely to the music, to every word and nimble note, pouring out the enchanting sounds of Mozart's *'Love is a Little Thief'* in its original Italian in a seamless joining of voice and piano that spellbound all those who listened. They marvelled at the flight of top notes as much as at Sir Chase's perfect timing that allowed her to take off and soar alone before catching her again on his wrist, so to speak, rollicking to the end where the applause almost overlapped them. Laughing with giddy relief, the two joined hands, hearing cries of, 'Again...again!'

So they obliged, after which everything else seemed like an anti-climax, so close had they come to disaster. Caterina sang with the orchestra and with Sara, but it was the song with Sir Chase that was talked about afterwards when they stood around in the drawing room, mingling with the musicians.

Lord Rayne was among the first to congratulate them, Lord Byron a close second, but his praises were not at all to the liking of Lady Caroline Lamb, who thought they were both excessive and unnecessary. She not only thought so, but said so, quite loudly enough for all to hear.

Sir Chase, however, was ready for the attack, even if Caterina was not, and before the venom could be stopped, he had taken her elbow to usher her through the open glass doors to the terrace. Behind them, the crowded room had fallen silent except for the jealous woman's tirade and two or three voices attempting to mollify her and, although Caterina was not near enough to hear the words, they acted like another twist to her already wound-up state.

'Whatever is the matter with the woman?' she said, wincing with anger. 'Is she mad?' Walking quickly to avoid the screeching and howling, almost running, her feet made little noise on the stone steps leading down to the side of the house and the high wall beyond. 'Go back!' she commanded, over her shoulder. 'Go back, if you please. I am best left alone for a while.' Her voice wavered. 'Please…leave me.'

Her steps quickened, but the determined click of his shoes told her that he was ignoring her request without an argument. When a half-open door appeared in the wall, she slipped through it, intending to push it closed, reinforcing the need for her own company. But his hand and foot resisted the attempt.

'Go back!' she yelled, hoarsely. She began to run between plots of bushy rosemary and sage that lined the gravel pathway, the tiny stones pressing through her fine satin slippers, the white-loaded apple boughs catching at her hair in the darkness. Stumbling around tall canes and cold frames, clumps of fennel and parsley, she searched for some secluded corner of the kitchen garden that would offer her solitude, a chance to unwind, alone and unaided. It was dark, unhelpful, uninviting, and her pleas for privacy were not being heeded.

The last few days had led irrevocably to this, filling a dam of unrest and anger inside her to overflowing. Usually, she would have had to wait until the social evening was done before helping the euphoria to settle after a performance, but this occasion was different in every way, for now her personal freedom was being threatened and the man set to take it from her had already begun an assault upon her emotions more than any before him, and in quite unacceptable circumstances. Always an intoxicating event that put her high in the clouds, her singing was a release, a therapy, and a massive boost to her creative urge, but tonight's performance had been unreal in other ways, too. And while her northern pragmatism frowned at any excess of fervour in her daily life, her natural sensitivity and artistry, whether she willed it or not, were being adversely affected by events before, during and after her recital. Out of control, her emotions were rushing ahead of her feet.

A solid five-barred gate to the topiary gardens obstructed her flight, camouflaged in the dim light by dark sculpted shapes below a sky of purple and apricot. The iron lever would not respond to her pulling before a large hand closed gently over her wrist, easing it away, moving his powerful bulk into the space she was seeking between strife and seclusion, between past and future. There was no room for anyone but herself there. The top of the gate pressed hard into her shoulders as she whirled to face him, pulling at her captured hand, pummelling at his chest with the other before he caught it, deftly.

He brought her hands together, and the sounds of her distress subsided to hoarse pleas to be left alone, lacking the former commanding tone, again ignored. Her head lowered, resting on their fists, and still he denied her the chance to argue by remaining silent. But her lips and cheeks were upon his knuckles as well as her own, vaguely recognising the warmth and texture of him, taking in the indistinct redolence of maleness through her breathing, his firm grip through her fingers, the intimate closeness of his thighs pressing her against the gate. Her senses swirled at the first taste of him as her lips moved softly along the back of his hand, the tip of her tongue exploring the light silky hair that lay there, delving into the crease of his thumb and its soft delta, staggering her breath at the stealthy approach of abandonment.

Dreamily, she felt the lift of their hands, taking her mouth with them, presenting her with another palette of smooth male skin to taste, a deeper experience that moved to accommodate and teach her. The hands fell apart, hers to reach up and hold, to wander freely, to search for his ears, his hair, while her body responded to her findings with an immediate blindness that slammed down the shutters of her mind and bent her like a bow into his body, consuming all the restraints of the past few days as fire consumes dry tinder. Without a single thought to hinder her, she fell headlong into the blaze where senses melted and mingled, where she was drawn deeper into oblivion, lured by the sublime pressure of his lips over hers.

Steering her with a finesse polished by years of experience, he enclosed her yielding body within his arms at the first leap of flame, his heart singing with elation at the fierce intemperance of her responses, his kisses joining hers, leaving hardly a space for breathing.

Tightly coiled after recent events, her emotions had at last found a release through fires that had smouldered, ready to ignite at his touch, and it would be up to him to control them before they could be a cause for regret. His hand gripped her shoulder, feeling the soft warmth of her skin beneath her sleeve, and it took all his efforts not to allow a search down the supple back into forbidden territory. His kisses deepened, hungering for more while staying awake to her innocence, for this was something that would require his most skilful handling if it were not to slip through his fingers like a moonbeam.

For how long they sought each other's kisses they were never able to recall, there being a mindless craving to be sated and, in Caterina's case, an overflow of pent-up anger and tension to be released into the one man who knew how to manage them, the only one, it seemed, who had come close to understanding her. But after the first fires had raged madly out of her control, she began to sense that he was directing her, showing her a change of pace, giving her the chance to regain her breath while his kisses travelled, surprising her, gently drawing her mind back into focus. When his hand moved on to her breast, the shutters of oblivion opened with a sigh, showing her both the bliss and the danger, which is what he cleverly intended.

Deep inside her, something trembled and disturbed her with thoughts of capitulation, telling her that she would accept him in spite of all her protests. On so many levels he was more than a match for her. Why not melt for him…now…here? His gentling hand moved, caressing, well practised, warning her that she was already out of her depth, that he was a man of experience and that she had everything to learn.

Her hand had been deep in his hair, but now she brought it down with a gasp like one who wakes too quickly from a dream, only half-aware of her part in it, but sure she had needed no persuading to go there. Taking his wrist, she lifted it away, pushing herself out of his embrace with her body still throbbing, her hunger still unfulfilled, still wanting, but now more sensitive to the danger than before. And the foolishness. To such a man, she told herself, this kind of encounter would be commonplace. He must not think she was like all the others, easy to take as far as he pleased, whenever he wanted them.

Trembling and thoroughly unnerved by her lapse, silent and subdued, she slid away from him, angered by her own unusual weakness. Puzzled by it, too. She would have sidled further away along the gate's length, but he caught her by the wrist, reaching her in one stride. 'No more running,' he warned her. 'You cannot be for ever bolting, Caterina.'

She felt his warm breath on the back of her neck as he stood behind her, and knew she was still only a hair's breadth away from changing her mind. 'I must go,' she said, holding a hand to her throbbing lips. 'This is not… not what I wanted to happen.'

'It's what your body wants. I think you might listen to it more. You listen to it when you sing, why not at other times?' His deep voice was soft upon her bare neck, and dark with overtones of those last few passionate moments.

'I'm surprised you of all people can say that, Sir Chase, when you and my father between you have decided to ride roughshod over what my body is telling me. I know what it's saying well enough, as most women do, but men delight in having the last word, do they not?'

'Then hear it from me.'

'No, you obviously think—'

'You cannot know what I think.'

'That I have done this kind of thing…that I am…'

'I know you have not. Do you think I cannot tell?'

Still captured by one hand, she turned to lay an arm along the top of the gate, supporting her forehead. 'I don't know what to think, except that I have gone too far. This would not have happened if…' *If Lord Rayne or Lady Dorna had been closer at hand. No, that was unfair. She was not a child to be tied to their apron-strings.*

'It happened,' Sir Chase said, 'because at that moment you needed me, Caterina. You cannot deny that. Ask yourself if you would have done the same with any other man. Would you?'

'No,' she whispered. 'I would not have done that with any other man.'

To her enormous relief, he betrayed neither by word nor expression the triumph he must have felt at her admission. Nor did Caterina herself know what had caused her to admit such a thing except natural honesty and impulse. The words echoed between them in the silence, and when she raised her head at last, she saw in the faded indigo sky that a fine sickle moon had come to hang over the dark topiary shape of a cockerel, fitting neatly inside the curve of its back.

'Just look at that,' he whispered.

Hearing the smile in his voice, she allowed him to take her hand in his and to keep it there, and for a while longer they stood without speaking of that which was too fragile and new to discuss. The beginning of acceptance.

'We must return,' she said, in a low voice. 'I would not want anyone to think—' She stopped, not wanting to say what they might think.

'We've been to take the air, Miss Chester,' he said, running his fingers through his hair. 'Would you allow me to tidy you, m'lady, before we're seen? I did it once before, if you remember? When we drove together in Richmond.'

'I remember.'

He smiled, replacing a few wayward tendrils behind the satin ribbons while she stood meekly, savouring the touch of his fingers on her hair, which only recently she had imagined. 'Sir Chase,' she said, 'what happened just now was…well…not…'

'Not enjoyable?'

'Not what I had intended.'

'There now,' he said, lifting her chin with his finger. 'That's better. Now no one will think anything. Ready?'

'Yes, thank you. Did you hear what I said?'

'I heard you. It was not what you intended. Yes, well, I knew that. Now, shall we say no more about it at present? There will be other better times for discussion.' Taking her by the hand, he led her without further comment back the way they had come and then, instead of making an entrance into the brightly lit drawing room, he opened another glass door that led directly into Lord Ensdale's great library and study. 'We shall be less noticeable this way,' he said, helping her through.

A candelabrum shed light upon surfaces of glass, brass and wood, upon clock faces, telescopes and globes on stands, and on unnamed instruments for measuring unseen things. It was where Lord Ensdale kept his collection of scientific instruments, a lofty room with shelves of leather-bound books, a room familiar to Sir Chase. Glad of the chance to compose herself, Caterina lingered on her way through, catching sight of the mahogany box she'd seen in the drawing room on the previous evening. 'Lord Ensdale's something-meter,' she said, bending to look more closely. 'Lady Ensdale said you knew about naval things. Is this a naval thing?'

Flicking back the brass catch, he lifted the lid. 'It's a naval chronometer,' he said. 'It gives the time of the day on the dial, see, and it also helps mariners to work out their position at sea by giving them a longitude reading.'

'So you *do* know,' she murmured.

'Just a bit.'

'So why does it rock backwards and forwards like that?' she said, as his finger swung it.

'So that when the ship rolls, the instrument stays level and accurate. This brass ring-mount is called a gimbal. They put ships' lanterns in them, too, so the oil doesn't tip out when the ship leans over.'

'You've been in ships?'

'Yes, Miss Chester,' he said, lifting the clock out of its mount. 'I suppose one is more or less bound to travel by boat when one goes abroad.' His mouth was on the verge of a smile, reminding Caterina of the taste and feel of him.

They stood facing each other, both remembering, hardly hearing the door open beyond them. But the candles wavered in the draught, and there was Lord Rayne in the doorway, clearly surprised to find the two of them discussing a chronometer.

'Well, my word,' he said, coming into the room. 'What's this, Chase old chap? A Royal Society lecture, is it? May I stay to listen?' His two greyhounds slipped through the door like shadows and flopped down upon the Persian rug.

Caterina frowned at him. 'Royal Society? Don't tease,' she said.

'I'm serious. Didn't he tell you?' Spinning a globe on its stand, he stopped it with his finger on England.

'That's enough, Sete,' said Sir Chase, returning the instrument to its box.

'But shouldn't Miss Chester ought to know the extent of your abilities, Chase? And anyway, what's so secret about your Royal Society membership? I'd be honoured if they invited me to join. Yes,' he continued, smiling at Caterina's astonishment, 'he and Lord Ensdale go up to town together to the meetings. Experts on scientific—'

'*Leave* it!' snapped Sir Chase. 'When Miss Chester wishes to know more about me, she'll ask me. She doesn't need to be force-fed with details of my interests.'

'Sorry. I thought she might like to know.'

'I *would* like to know,' said Caterina, softly. She strolled past them towards the door, pausing as Lord Rayne opened it for her. 'So, where were *you* when you were needed?' she said. 'No, don't tell me. It doesn't really matter now.'

The door closed behind her with a click of disapproval.

Leaning against the book-lined wall, Lord Rayne folded his arms, watching his friend's long fingers roam over the polished surface of the mahogany box. The fingers drummed, then stopped.

'So, where *were* you?' said Sir Chase.

'Keeping out of the way. Timed it well, did I?'

'Perfectly, thank you.'

'Was I needed?'

'Not at all.'

'I may not always be so obliging. I care for her, too,' he warned.

'So you said. I believe you. And I also believe she'll do her damnedest to hang on to her freedom till the last possible moment. I wouldn't be surprised if she were to make a bolt for it and find herself in some kind of Queer Street. Is that likely, do you think?'

'You read her well,' Lord Rayne murmured.

'She's done it before, you mean? Apart from the two weddings?'

'Bolted? Yes, once. Nick and I found her. Don't ask me any more than that. It's all water under the mill.'

'I see. So where is she likely to head for, if she does?'

'Any number of places, my friend. However…' Lord Rayne unfolded his arms and went to sit in Lord Ensdale's swivel chair.

'However?'

'Well, I shall be going down to Brighton on Wednesday to take a look at the Prince's stables. Nick wants a report. If I were to make it known in the right quarters, Miss Chester might ask to be taken down there, too. In fact, I guarantee it.'

'Excellent. Where would she stay? Not *with* you, surely?'

Lord Rayne smiled at the tone of concern. 'No, Chase,' he said, gently. 'Not with me. She can have the house on the Steyne and I'll put up at the Pavilion. There's always room there. Or there's the Castle.'

'I wouldn't like it to look like an elopement, Sete.'

Stretching out his long legs, Lord Rayne lay back, regarding the shadowy ceiling with a quick frown. 'Wrong direction, old chap. Anyway, it will not have the slightest resemblance to…that kind of thing, so don't get your breeks in a twist about it. She hasn't even said she wants to come yet, and it's not me she wants, but you.' He sighed. 'But I'd rather it was you than any other fool.'

'Thank you, I appreciate that. I wish I could be so certain.'

'Then you should take my word for it. I've known her longer than you. What's that you're holding?'

On the palm of his hand, Sir Chase held out a small

medallion rimmed with gold. Small enough to be either a button or a brooch, it was made of white jasper with the image of a negro in black relief kneeling in an attitude of supplication, his wrists and ankles shackled with heavy chains. 'Seen one before?' he asked, holding it up to the pool of light.

'No. What's this round the edge? *Am I not a man and a brother?* Ah, so this is the Wedgwood medallion, is it? I wondered when I might see one.'

'It's Lord Ensdale's. I have one, too.'

'So I don't suppose our lovely Caterina knows you're a member of the Slave Emancipation Society?'

'The lady is making a point of not asking any questions that might conceivably betray a shred of interest. She finds it more profitable to dwell on my reputation for fast living. It adds fuel to her argument,' he added, stifling a yawn, 'and I don't want to disarm her completely. Not yet.'

'Then you must allow me to drop a few pearls before her every now and again, as I did just now. It can do nothing but good. You can protest, mildly, and I'll ignore you, and she'll be even more impressed by your natural modesty.'

'Pitching it too strong, lad. My natural modesty shines through without that kind of fudge. Go and blow your own trumpet.' Replacing the medallion at the back of the desk, he took a small silver and mother-of-pearl snuffbox from his pocket and, flicking it open with his thumb, offered it to Lord Rayne. 'It's my own sort,' he said. 'I think you might like it.'

'I'm honoured.'

Observing the ritual of snuff-taking, Sir Chase felt that there was still more to be said. 'Why are you suddenly being so damned cooperative, Sete? If I didn't know you so well, I'd think you had a trick up your sleeve.'

Lord Rayne sniffed and cleared his throat, blinking a little. 'Very interesting,' he said. 'Thank you. Because, I suppose, if I put my mind to it, I could get seriously under your hooves. But that would salve only my pride and would probably upset Caterina into the bargain. And where would be the sense in that? I've told you I care for her. I want her happiness. I'm sticking around her because she wants me to, which is why she'll want to go down to Brighton with me. Besides, once *you're* leg-shackled, I shall be allowed to find my own woman without you barging in and taking her off me, just for the hell of it.'

Throwing back his head, Sir Chase roared with laughter. 'Codswallop, man. You could have any woman you choose, and you know it.'

Lord Rayne yawned, running a hand through his dark hair and gently tousling it. 'Oh, yes, they're queuing up for me out there,' he grinned. 'Such a bore. By the way, the price of my cooperation is to know how you do that natty cravat. It's not a Waterfall, is it?'

Sir Chase treated his friend to an exaggerated sigh. 'You drive a hard bargain, Sete. Come to my dressing-room before breakfast and my man will demonstrate. You're right, it's not exactly a Waterfall. Now…ready for the crush?'

Lord Rayne gave the impression that he was debating the prospect when in fact he was thinking of Caterina's last remark and her rather flushed appearance. He would like to have known what caused it.

On the other hand, Sir Chase's thoughts had returned to a certain painting of a ship sailing out of Liverpool harbour which he'd seen only a few days ago on the wall of Stephen Chester's study. It had four square ventilation holes in the hull.

The truce had been a useful tool in allowing some dialogue that might otherwise have gone unsaid for days, if not weeks. Nevertheless, Caterina was able to delude herself that Sir Chase had taken advantage of it to propel her into making a decision that could, if she'd been left to her own devices, have been delayed for months. In retrospect, it had been a tool of more benefit to him than to her, and the next days were spent in thinking of the very deep water she had wallowed into which would now be almost impossible to wallow out of, even more so than the two near-miss marriages. This time, she had allowed intimacies from which one could hardly walk away without considerable personal embarrassment.

There was another side to this, too, concerning the emotional part of her that had responded to his touch like a caged bird waiting for a chance to fly. It was a part that refused to settle after such an experience, so vivid and alive was the memory of his mastery to which none of her dreams had come close. She could regret having allowed it to happen; she could regret responding to it as she knew she had, but she could not forget it, nor could she look back on it without a certain melting sensation creeping through her body that had as much to do with the man himself as with the experience of being made love to.

The remaining two days at Sevrington Hall passed without incident, partly due to the early departure of Lord Byron and Lady Caroline Lamb, who had decided not to test the good nature of their hostess any further. It was a decision with which everyone agreed. Caterina decided that to stay closer to Lord Rayne would be best if she were to retain some semblance of control over the delicate situation, and this is what she did, with his willing help. It was, she thought, as if he knew how much she was relying on his guardianship.

Sunday was a relaxing day of walking in the extensive grounds, boating on the lake, fishing, partaking of a hearty picnic, and a tour of Lord Ensdale's large art collection followed by games of billiards and skittles. Monday was a ride over to Wilton House where, true to his intentions, Lord Rayne persuaded Sir Chase to join him in an exhibition of superb riding skills in the indoor riding school, emulating some of the intricate movements depicted in the set of horse-and-rider paintings hanging in the Large Smoking Room. Apart from a very select few, Lord Pembroke told them, no one had ever come as near to perfecting the *haute école* exercises as well as Lord Rayne and Sir Chase Boston did that day. For Caterina, this was yet another revelation of Sir Chase's abilities of which she had been unaware, giving her yet more insight into his multi-talented nature.

She failed to make the connection, however, that it was her temporary guardian himself who had initiated this exhibition, *and* the conversation at the dinner table when the subject of warfare underlined Sir Chase's personal responsibilities to the Prince Regent, and the high regard in which he was held. As before, Sir Chase played it down with some witty irreverence, by which time Caterina was making more revisions to her former prejudices regarding his shallowness. He was, she had begun to realise, anything but shallow. Nor had he, since that very intimate episode, insisted on being in her company.

In reply, she was coolly polite, rather distant, preoccupied with her thoughts, neither ignoring nor rebuffing him. Yet she knew at all times where he was, who he spoke to and especially to whom he paid attention. She could not fault him on that, only on the nagging offence of holding her father to a monstrous debt and using her as a means of discharging it. In short, holding her responsible for her entire family's happiness. That, and his impressive record as a womaniser. How could she possibly accept such a man as her husband?

Taking her aside after dinner on Monday, Lady Ensdale asked Caterina if she believed her father would allow Sara to stay a while longer at Sevrington Hall, and indeed whether she herself would like it, too, as her sister's chaperon. Constantine and Sara had become such good friends. What a pity it would be, the hostess said, if they could not have a few more days to get to know each other better.

Caterina's heart sank. What *would* her father say? That there was little point to young Ensdale's interest in Sara until her sister could bring herself to oblige them all? Declining the personal invitation, she said what Sara had begged her to say, that she was sure Mr Chester would see nothing improper in the arrangement while at the back of her mind loomed the prospect of a showdown from which neither she nor her father would emerge unscathed.

Sir Chase was waiting for her as she and Lady Ensdale concluded their chat. Offering her his arm, he escorted her outside onto the terrace where several couples stood talking, and she knew by the way he looked at her several times that he suspected her plans might be changing.

'If I thought there was a chance you would accept,' he said, 'I would ask you to travel with me in my coach tomorrow. But there isn't, is there?'

'No, Sir Chase,' she replied, quietly. 'Not a chance.'

'So you're set on keeping me at arm's length for a while longer?'

She had learnt so much more about him in the last few days, especially that he was well liked by everyone, that he was not the lightweight she believed him to be, that he was intelligent and cultured, talented and physically skilled, a good listener and, if the incident on Saturday evening was any indication, he would be an exciting lover, too. Heaven knows, he'd had enough practice at that. Most of all, he appeared to understand that she was more than capable of knowing what she wanted, even while he was bent on securing her capitulation, humiliating or not. Inevitably, the sacrifice would be hers, not his.

They had moved apart from the others, coming to a halt where no ears could overhear them, where she could just see in the last of the light how the strong planes of his face shifted slightly to await her reply, how his skin stretched smoothly over high cheekbones, over the straight nose and broad noble forehead. There had been times when her body had craved his closeness again, to feel the pressure of his mouth just once more. She could not find an answer to his question.

'Well,' he said, smiling, 'at least that's not a yes, is it? Did I go too fast for you?'

She looked away at the streaks of purple on the horizon. 'I think you may already have made assumptions about me…us. It may be best if you—'

'Caterina, listen to me. I do not make assumptions about you. What I know of you I've discovered for myself, and what I don't know I will find out. What you should understand is that you will accept me.'

'I think you should not leap to that conclusion, Sir Chase.'

Quietly, he continued as if she had not interrupted him. 'You *will* accept me, and we shall be married by special licence with no frills or fuss. Then we shall leave Richmond and go where we can be alone. You and I have that in common, Caterina. We perform better in our own space. Your home has become a cage, and you need to be freed from it.'

She could not deny it, but what brand of freedom did such men offer when their world resembled a giant playground? Could a man like him be taken seriously as the father of her children? 'Special licence?' she said, not quite believing him.

'Relatives in the church,' he said. 'My bishop-uncle will procure one for me, for sure. What is it? You've not accepted Lady Ensdale's invitation, have you?'

'Not for myself.' She sighed, gustily, venting a sudden anger like a breeze before a storm. 'I was *supposed* to have had some choice in the matter,' she snapped. 'Now it's a special licence. What next will it be, I wonder? A bottle of laudanum and a straitjacket?'

He laughed. 'Steady. Don't take it hard. I understand your preference to be wooed more slowly, but that will come later without your family offering advice from the sidelines. Would you not prefer that?'

'I have singing engagements. I cannot ignore them.'

'You don't have to. We shall go together. I shall be your chaperon-manager-husband and whenever the pianist imbibes too freely I shall take over. Think of it,' he whispered. 'We made music together. We can do it again whenever you wish it. I want you, Miss Caterina

Chester, and I mean to have you.' His fierce words held her to the spot, though she ought to have walked away rather than listen to such brazen verbal lovemaking. 'You want to know why the haste?' he went on. 'Well, I'll tell you. When a passionate and beautiful woman jilts not one, but two titled hopefuls and declares that there is no man good enough for her, what red-blooded male with a string of successes under his belt would not rise to that kind of bait, I ask you? If you'd been seriously gap-toothed, a miss-prissy without any spunk, I might not be so keen. But you're not, are you, Miss Chester? You're a high-flyer. A cracker. A top-notch with—'

'Thank you, Sir Chase. I think you've made your point.'

'With a voice like a choir of angels and a passion that needs a man, a *real* man. I know how to take you in hand—'

'Please…you'll be heard.' She looked around in alarm.

'And make you responsive to me.'

'Are you talking about me or a horse?' she whispered.

'About you. You know I am. You're trembling.'

She gulped, unable to look up at him. 'I'm…I'm cold. We must go in.'

Neither of them moved. Above them, bats swooped and squeaked through dancing clouds of midges. Voices murmured. Something rippled the lake, making rings of silver. He touched her fingertips with his, sending shocks through her body.

'Well?' he said, very softly.

'You place me in an impossible position, sir.'

'You were in an impossible position when we first met, with nowhere to practise except in someone else's house. I'm offering you a way out of that with as much space as you could wish for and a future as Lady Boston. Take your courage in your hands. Take me on, Caterina.'

'And your assurances? Have you none to offer me?'

'I want yours first.'

'When we get back to Richmond.'

'You'll give me an answer then? Wednesday morning?'

'I'll give you my answer on Wednesday. Or Father will.'

Raising her hand to his lips, he came close enough for her to see how he looked at her over the knuckles, making her wish his kiss had been elsewhere. 'Then I wish you a safe journey home. I shall be following you to make sure of it, so you'll have my company at the posting inns, whether you wish it or not.'

She made no reply to that and, because it was dark, she knew that her smile would not be seen as they strolled back to the house.

Lady Dorna greeted her with some relief and, Caterina thought, the slightest suggestion of guilt as she handed her a glass of wine. Casting an eye over Sir Chase's wide retreating back, shc lifted an eyebrow. 'D'ye need some help?' she whispered.

Thoughtfully, Caterina studied the candour in the bright blue eyes. Lady Dorna might have her unpredictable moments but her intentions were good, her moralising rarely in evidence, and her womanly foibles still pristine after much use. 'Yes,' she whispered back. 'I do. Shall we talk later?'

Lady Dorna's eyes widened with mischief. 'Oh, yes!' she breathed. 'Come over here. You look as if you need some food. Where did you get to?'

'Just talking,' she said.

* * *

Leaving Sara behind the next morning was for the two of them an unusually emotional event, for the young heart had been truly netted by the eligible Constantine and, although nothing direct was said about Caterina's role in their future, Sara's face was bright with hope that their path would soon be cleared for marriage. The long return journey to Richmond gave Caterina plenty of time to dwell on the prospect of making her sister happy, and her parents also, though the same could not be said about her attitude to her brother, Harry. He had come out of it better than any of them.

After mulling over the pressures being brought to bear on her, Caterina's thoughts moved up a notch to how she might soothe her resentments by making her inevitable acceptance of Sir Chase as fraught with discomfort, *his* discomfort, as *she* was feeling over the shabby conduct of the three males, two of them her own family. It was unlikely that she would be able to aggravate her father more than she had done already, nor would he ever know how her respect for him had diminished as a result of this latest edict. He was obviously drinking too much.

But Sir Chase was the one for whom she could, if she really tried, make the winning of his wager less straightforward than either of the men expected it to be, and the rest of the journey was spent in short-listing several ideas intended to level the score. If only she had not begun to find him so heart-stoppingly attractive, the proposed discomforts would be more satisfyingly one-sided.

Their overnight stay at the White Hart in Winchester gave the travellers something quite unusual to occupy their conversation, however, for it was there that the news reached them of Prime Minister Spencer Perceval's brutal assassination in the lobby of the House of Commons, and that Lord Liverpool had taken over at short notice as the head of the Tory government.

Lord Rayne, who had purposely withheld his announcement regarding his proposed visit to Brighton until nearer the end of the journey, now allowed that event to disappear from his itinerary altogether at the prospect of being needed in the House of Lords with his father and brother. To give all the early support that lords were expected to give a new Prime Minister and to attend the funeral of the previous one, they would have to be in London. The change to Lord Rayne's plans was accepted as a matter of course not only by him but also by Sir Chase, and no more was said to anyone about Brighton.

By sheer coincidence, the possibility of a hasty and impromptu flight to her retired governess at Brighton happened to be at the very top of Caterina's new 'list of obstacles' compiled during the journey. She and Sara had visited dear Miss Vincent every year so far and another visit was due, even though she would receive no warning of it. Miss Vincent had never in the least minded being made use of, and Brighton would be the most perfect place in which to escape for a week or so, while Sir Chase scoured the vicinity for his bride-to-be.

Chapter Five

With this intention fixed in her mind and very little time to set the wheels in motion, she took the chance to speak to Lady Dorna in more detail as they shared a cosy room at the White Hart. Lifting the linen bedsheet to her nose, Caterina sniffed delicately. 'Do you suppose this has been washed since it was last used?'

'Look for the creases,' Lady Dorna advised, flinging the sheet back with a flourish. 'That's the best way to tell.'

Satisfied that the linen smelled of nothing more personal than woodsmoke and that all creases were at right-angles, the conversation reverted to Caterina's plan to abscond. 'To my old governess in Brighton,' she said. 'I have a sudden urge to visit her.'

'Of course you do, my dear,' the lady gurgled, needing no explanation. She tied a frilly nightcap over her blonde curls. 'When?'

'Tomorrow. Very early. Dawn, if possible. The problem is that I cannot take Father's coach without him knowing where I'm to be found, and I don't wish to be found until I'm ready to be.'

'Quite right, too. You cannot take that old coach of your father's anyway because it's not nearly stylish enough, and if you're going to make a dash for it, you need to do it in style, dearest. I cannot think why Hannah agrees to ride in it, except that it's all right for infants to be sick in, I suppose. What you need, dear Cat, is my new post-chaise and team of greys. Brighton is only a half-day's drive away. If you set off early enough you could be there by midday and nobody but me the wiser.'

'How well you understand,' Caterina said, hugging her. 'I really ought to tell Aunt Amelie where I'm going, but I fear she'd be bound to tell Father.'

'No need to tell anyone. I know how important it is to keep a man on the run before you accept him.' Laughing merrily, she threw herself into the feather mattress, beckoning to her maid for her cup of chocolate. 'I'll send it round to Paradise Road at six in the morning the day after tomorrow. How will that do?'

'You are so kind. Thank you.' Climbing into bed beside her, Caterina kissed Lady Dorna's pretty cheek while wondering how long she was used to keeping a man on the run before he was allowed to climb in where she herself was climbing. 'Our secret,' she said.

'Our secret,' agreed the conspirator. 'Hannah has changed,' she added, between sips. 'She used to be such a dear little goose.'

'Mm…m,' said Caterina. 'Father has changed, too.'

The reception awaiting her at Richmond on the following evening was not what she had been dreading, for Mr and Mrs Chester were genuinely pleased to welcome her home after the less than cordial departure. While they were a little taken aback that Sara had been left behind with the Ensdales, they kept their concerns to themselves, at least for the time being. To Caterina, they were bent on sweetening the bitter pill which all three of them knew she would be obliged to swallow, helped down with her favourite roast duck in orange sauce and juicy tips of asparagus.

By the time the sweet baked apples and cream had arrived, the first hesitant steps had been taken towards the main subject, which left her in no doubt that they knew Sir Chase had been one of the Sevrington Hall house party. Had they got on well together? Was she any nearer to liking him? Had he made a good impression? The questions were carefully probed, rather like a surgeon looking for a single lead shot in an open wound.

It was all so absurd, she thought. What did it matter to them what she felt about the man? They had already decided what she must do, and so had she, yet it was with a strange stab of satisfaction that she noted their astonishment, to put it mildly, at her unexpected request. Would her father kindly inform Sir Chase that she had decided to accept his offer of marriage? He would be calling some time tomorrow for his answer but, in case they believed she had done this out of any sense of duty, they were mistaken; she had done it for Sara's sake. Fascinated, she watched their spoons halt in mid-air, then lower, perfectly synchronised, mouths agape like fishes.

It was less than the complete truth, but she felt no shame. Of what use would it be to tell them how, having welcomed his lovemaking in a moment of weakness, she dare not forfeit the chance of sampling it again in the future? Nor did she want them to know that Sir Chase's uniqueness was a factor in her decision. She even refrained from mentioning the unethical tactics her father was using to get himself out of a sticky mess, for Hannah knew nothing of the debt, and Mr Chester's scruples seemed to be disappearing along with his fatherly responsibilities. It was too late now to get back at them with more verbal protests.

Suddenly, she could hardly wait to get away again.

'It's all for the best, dear Cat,' Hannah said, after the meal.

She had never been a beauty, but her quiet manner and delicate features, her prematurely greying mid-brown hair and worried expression made her look more than her twenty-nine years, though the rapid production of children had taken its toll of both looks and energy. Hannah and her stepdaughter could hardly have been less alike, and now the friendship they had once enjoyed was strained by circumstances which, had Mr Chester managed his assets more wisely for his wife's sake rather than his irresponsible son's, could have been improved considerably. It was not Caterina's place to tell him how to manage his affairs, but nor did she wish to make him feel any better about his treachery. For this reason as much as any other, her plans for the following day were divulged to no one except Millie, who had already begun packing clothes for a week.

'It's certainly best for Sara,' said Caterina. 'Is that what you meant?' The candle's flame grew steady as she placed a hand on the polished banister rail and felt a child-produced stickiness under her fingers.

'Best for us all, I think,' said Hannah, casting a furtive glance along the deserted hallway. The distant clink of glass from the dining-room caused the ghost of a frown to pass over her eyes, then the press of a finger to her lips as she leaned forward to whisper. 'We shall be needing the room, you see, when you and Sara go.

I don't mean it's good that you'll be going, dear. Not that. No. Room for more cots.'

'More…cots? You mean, you're…expecting…a happy event?'

Hannah nodded, lips compressed and no accompanying gladness in her eyes. 'Yes. Again.' Her worried pale eyes searched Caterina's face for signs of comfort before she was drawn into one tender womanly arm and held close. There was no need for Caterina to ask how she felt about it. 'A bit too soon, really,' Hannah whispered over the comforting shoulder. 'I'd have liked a bit longer to get over the last one, but I wanted babies and that's what I'm getting. Can't grumble.'

'Will it be twins again?' said Caterina, holding the skinny shoulders.

'I hope not. I didn't find it easy.'

'Is Father pleased?'

The eyes opened, smiling at last. 'Oh, I think so. He says it'll be all right. We'll manage somehow.'

'You'd manage better with some extra help, Hannah.'

The smile faded. 'Yes, I know.'

'When is it due?'

'October some time. Will you be…er?'

'Married by then? Oh, yes, and Sara, too, I expect.'

Satisfied, Hannah nodded. 'Tomorrow, I shall meet Sir Chase again after all these years, then we'll sit down together and talk about the details, shall we?'

'Yes. That would be nice. Good night, Hannah. Get some rest.' Once more, she took the fragile figure into a one-armed hug and placed a kiss upon her cheek while picturing the three of them sitting down to talk about it, asking each other what could possibly be the cause of her flying off like that without telling anyone.

* * *

For her, the night was not restful, her mind being in a state of constant conflict, wanting him, not wanting him, recalling over and over the pressure of his arms, his mouth luring her into the unknown. She was relieved to see the first light of dawn, though it came streakily through stormy clouds and bursts of rain against the windows.

The problem of manhandling a trunk and two suitcases down the stairs without waking the rest of the household was solved by the two kitchen lads whose adoration of Caterina came in useful at such times. Her dismay at the timely appearance of Lady Dorna's new post-chaise, however, made her wonder whether the dear lady had quite understood her need for circumspection or whether she was playing a different kind of game, for the equipage was not meant to be missed in any crowd.

For sheer display, the post-chaise would not have looked out of place in the Lord Mayor's Show; the bright tulip-pink chassis was picked out with leaf-green details, with black wheels and cyphers on the doors, silver-plated lamps and door handles, furnished inside with lace and quilting. The postilions, one on the nearside horse and one behind on the platform, wore deep pink and silver livery with white breeches and black velvet caps, and the horses...ah...the horses! Correctly, Lady Dorna had called them greys, but this pair were snow white and perfectly matched, their manes plaited and threaded with pink and silver ribbons. Never had Caterina wished to draw such attention to herself when she was travelling, and even less so at a time like this.

If one could ignore the stares, the waves and grins, the whoops of derision from the young men in phaetons and such, the stares and shouts from the loaded London-to-Brighton stagecoach, then it could be said that Caterina and her maid travelled in style as well as luxury. At Reigate they were shown immediately into a private parlour for breakfast while the horses were rested, and at Cuckfield the same courtesy prevailed except for the extra attentions of two persistent young blades who took the lack of chaperon as an invitation to friendship. She was glad to leave Cuckfield, glad, too, that Lady Dorna had sent two postilions for her safety instead of the usual one. The squalls of rain were passing over and, by the time they were past Scare Hill, the sun was playing hide-and-seek with thunder-clouds, lighting up the sea like a sheet of silver.

The house belonging to Miss Vincent was in Montpelier Place and not for one moment had Caterina anticipated anything but the ecstatic welcome she would receive after her journey. But her repeated use of the brass knocker in the form of a Lincoln Imp produced no more than a raised window from the house next door through which a maid called to say that Miss Vincent had gone over to Hove to tend her elder sister and no one knew when she might return. The window remained open as two more faces came to stare at the pink ensemble before it moved off down the hill towards the sea.

'Now what?' said Caterina. 'Is it to be the Old Ship or the Castle Inn?'

'You stayed at the Castle once before, Miss Caterina,' said Millie, 'and the proprietor knows you well enough. And the stage will have reached the Old Ship by now. It'll be bursting at the seams.'

'So it will. We'll try the Castle, then. Open the little window behind you and tell William, will you?'

Between the Steyne and the Prince Regent's Pavilion, the Castle Inn occupied a position where the arrival of the gaudy post-chaise was at once the centre of attention from every quarter, causing a rush of speculation about the identity of the travellers. If this was in direct opposition to Caterina's intentions, there was now very little she could do about it, her stylish gown of soft brown velvet and matching bonnet adding to the impression of wealth and breeding. For another thing, she now lacked the companion she had expected to have beside her on her excursions, and although Brighton rules were lax compared to London, Miss Vincent's company would have helped to keep both gossip and unwanted overtures at bay. It was a severe setback to her plan. It also jolted her into realising that she ought not to have taken her old governess's hospitality for granted.

Determined to make the best of things, she set about hiring a room, after charging William with a message for Lady Dorna asking for the chaise to be sent for her in four days rather than seven, by which time her funds would have run out, even if she were careful. Though she might have spent time searching for a more modest lodging in which to stay, she felt more secure at the Castle with all its facilities and a proprietor who knew her.

From her corner window, she watched the pebbly beach washed by waves of angry white surf before another heavy spatter of rain hit the glass and ran gurgling to the gutter. As she turned away, a high curricle drawn by four startling chestnuts bowled smartly down the Steyne, round the corner into North Street, disappearing from view in the time it took for Caterina to take her cup of tea from Millie and turn back to the window. Had she seen it, it is doubtful whether she would have felt so serene, as Millie began to unpack her clothes, or whether she would have responded so positively to a knock on the door asking if all was well.

The squall passed over and bright sunshine dazzled the wet cobblestones as Caterina, wrapped against the stiff breeze, walked down the Steyne towards the wide expanse of shining blue-grey. Along the cliff's top, she bent her head into the wind that saucily flattened the fine layers of cambric against her body and snatched at the veil wound round the brim of her high-feathered poke-bonnet. The peach-coloured velvet spencer afforded her little protection from the chill, but she had always welcomed the elements in whatever form, and to feel the salt air buffeting her face brought laughter to her lips, urging her to whirl and skip in its blustering male embrace. She would have brought Millie with her, but the maid's lungs had never quite recovered from her neglectful years of apprenticeship to a Richmond dressmaker, and her cough had returned with a vengeance.

It was a pity, in a way, yet Caterina was content to be in her own company, to watch the tattered lacy ribbons of surf overlap and rattle upon the shore. People passed unnoticed, for the certainty of being unrecognised in Brighton relaxed the tensions she had brought with her, and she was now free to dismiss the last pangs of regret at the concern her parents might be feeling at her sudden disappearance. Perhaps they would feel that she had insulted Sir Chase by her behaviour, but her father could not be unaware of her own sense of outrage at the method they had both used to coerce her.

Glimpses of red and white, gold and black caught her eye as she walked, uniforms of the militia stationed here at Brighton on duty at the Regent's grand home, always much in evidence and always on the lookout for pretty women, available or not. Turning her face towards the sea, she waited for one noisily chattering group to pass by, feeling their examination through her gown and wishing, for once, that she had not been quite so unprotected.

Keeping an eye on the darkening sky, she walked as far as the Royal Crescent before turning back, intending to call in at both subscription libraries, Fisher's and Donaldson's, on her return to the Castle Inn. The rain had stopped again as she emerged with her books, and it was no more than curiosity about the stabling of Lady Dorna's precious greys that led her along North Street to New Road where the Castle's new stables had recently been extended.

There, under the carriage shelter, was the showy pink post-chaise with a group of admirers pointing out its crane-neck springs, its blinds and sword-case, its polished brass chains and leather straps. Keeping out of the way of busy grooms, she sidled into the stable as another burst of rain sent everyone running for cover. The glossy white rumps of Lady Dorna's pair were easily seen in the long row of stalls.

Waiting for the hard roar of rain to abate, she looked along the line of silky tails, noticing a quartet of pale blonde belonging to chestnut hindquarters, her heart skipping a beat at the shock of recognition. Sir Chase's team and curricle? Already? No, how *could* they be? Had Lady Dorna told him, after all?

'Whose are the four chestnuts?' she asked an elderly ostler.

His grin was leathery. 'You 'oping to buy 'em, miss?' he said. 'They'll cost you. Sir Chase Boston's they are. He knows 'is 'orse-flesh, does that one. As fine a whip as ever I've seen, and I've seen some. Used to be down 'ere a lot when he was in the Prince's regiment. Takes 'im just over four hours to get 'ere from London. Mind you, pulling a curricle behind a four-in-hand must be like pulling a salt-pot.' He laughed at her expression, mistaking it for astonishment. 'He's somewhere hereabouts,' he said, weaving his head from side to side. 'But perhaps he's…oh…well, then.' Turning back to his young audience, he was just in time to see her dash through the rain out of the yard, one hand clamped firmly over her bonnet, the other clinging to her packet of library books.

Mercifully, she was able to reach her room at the inn, squeezing past the latest influx of damp guests and managing to avoid any sight of Sir Chase, but thoroughly shaken by the discovery that he was not inclined to allow her any of the space he must have known she had come here to find. Undoubtedly, the tulip-pink post-chaise would have helped in his enquiries. He may already have quizzed the two postilions who would be taking it back tomorrow, and they would see no reason not to tell him which day they would be coming to collect her.

Angrily, she pulled off her wet shoes, prepared to tell Millie that they must either find alternative lodgings or return to Richmond the very next morning. But Millie's flushed face and racking cough had every resemblance to her old bronchial problems, and while the poor maid struggled to keep up the pretence of being well, helping her mistress to change and assuring her that nothing was amiss, Caterina had not the heart to send her out to find another place to stay. Nor did she wish to search for the postilions who might be anywhere in Brighton by now, for the result of her return to Richmond would mean premature recriminations of a sort she didn't wish to think about. It would be better for her to stick to her original plan as far as possible, keeping Millie in the warm and pleasant bedroom and herself well out of sight.

This was not as easy as it sounded, the inn being like a well-stocked beehive with comings and goings along every passageway and entrance. The inn boasted a ballroom, two dining-rooms and several private parlours, one of which Caterina would like to have reserved, if she had brought funds to match.

After an hour or so of tangled reflection about how best to handle this unexpected complication, she began to suspect that, if Sir Chase had wanted to confront her immediately, whether to insist on taking her back to Richmond or to stay with her here at Brighton, he would surely have marched upstairs to tell her so by now. He must know which room she was occupying; he must have discovered on his arrival exactly who was with her and that she had intended to stay with her governess, since that is what, in passing, she had told the obliging proprietor. Perhaps then, as at Sevrington Hall, he was allowing her to dictate the pace and, if she desired his company, he would be on hand to oblige. Otherwise, he would stay near enough to be there if needed, quite a comforting notion in view of the bevy of young officers who had followed her from the library hoping to find out where she was staying.

Nevertheless, she was not so blind to the reason for Sir Chase's prompt appearance at Brighton, which was to prevent her escape. For a man whose offer of marriage had just been accepted, he appeared to be taking her unorthodox behaviour with more equanimity than many others would have done. Mischievously, she wondered how far she could push him before his unusual tolerance wore out.

Dinner that first evening was taken in her room with several copies of *Ackermann's Repository* magazine to keep her company, and a small book on Old Sarum and Salisbury, about which she had learned so little on her recent visit.

Sleeping in a small bed in the alcove, Millie had passed a restless night but, even so, would have gone with her mistress to the shore early next morning if Caterina had allowed it. The two Chester sisters had always made a point of bathing in the sea during their summer visits to Miss Vincent, the one favourite activity where Caterina knew she would be quite undisturbed.

Her short walk from the Steyne down the cliff path to the bathing-machine, even at that deserted hour, was straightforward enough, though the cramped wooden cabin was dark and uncomfortably damp. The ladder was taken up, the horse led across the beach to the water, turned round and backed-up, the steps replaced and the doors opened to reveal Caterina wearing her linen bathing-gown, in no mood to be either assisted or dunked by the two titanic 'dippers' who stood waist-high in the water. 'Tide's coming in, miss,' one of them said, 'and the pebbles slope down very steeply here, you know. You sure you can manage alone? It gets deep.'

Caterina had done it before, and now there was almost a sense of desperation in her need for independence. This might, for all she knew, be her last chance to strike off on her own with not even Sara to caution her. Impulsively, she spurned their advice. 'Thank you, but I can swim. I've been here before.'

The ice-cold waves leapt relentlessly up her thighs and front, instantly soaking the gown and making her gasp with shock as it stuck coldly to her skin. Shifting stones underfoot caused her to stumble before she plunged headlong into the incoming tide and struck out into the open sea, feeling the lift under her body and the exhilaration of freedom, the salty taste on her lips and the clean sharp sting of coldness engulfing her. There were very few others bathing, their bathing-machines well away from hers and no one to observe except two people walking their dogs and throwing sticks for them to chase after.

Strongly, she took a delight in pitting herself against the tide, using all her energy to make some headway, taking little notice of time or tiredness, thinking of the man whose energy would match hers on every level, and revelling in the exertions that emptied her mind of recent cares.

Panting, she turned on to her back and saw to her horror that the bathing-machine was now no more than a dot on the distant shore. It was only then that her tiredness became apparent: her arms ached, her lungs felt tight with effort and a sickening wave of panic surged through the utter weariness, preventing her limbs from responding to her orders, thrashing them madly through the heavy water. For a few wild and terrifying moments, her energy fell apart at the possibility that she would not have strength enough to reach safety, but the tide was still in her favour and she must not give in to such fears, she told herself. She must...she *must* get back.

Through the deepening waves, she kept her attention fixed on the tiny bathing-machine, but the swell knocked her sideways and the encumbrance of the linen gown dragged and ballooned with each laborious stroke, holding her back. How she wished she had swum naked. She would have shed the offending garment, but she needed both arms to stay afloat, and the pain and cold were numbing her, becoming unbearable. The bathing-machine had now disappeared from view, her feet and legs losing all feeling, her cries gobbled up by the threatening waves. Then she knew what it was to be truly alone, and that to survive was something she must do with nothing more than her good lungs, courage, and solid determination to help her.

Racing and tumbling crazily through her mind were thoughts of what she would miss by losing her hold on life now, of all times, just when the promise of a future with that amazing and exciting man was hers for the taking. So near. So close. Within her grasp. No, she could not let it go when she had only just tasted its sweetness, his arms, his kisses. *Keep going,* she told herself, sobbing with the pain. Another stroke…then another…and another.

Through a haze of agony, gasping with burning lungs at every breath, she caught sight of the black sleek head of a man at her side, but dismissed it as a dream of him, no more than a fantasy to keep her going. Shining with sea water, he yelled at her not to give up, that he would stay with her, to keep on, that it was not far…not far… nearly there…come on…come on, girl. Confused, too tired to think, she responded, pushing herself beyond the limit, vaguely feeling some release where the waterlogged gown had been, making her more efficient in the water. Once or twice she felt the touch of him upon her arm as they collided, saw his wet face close to hers, shouting at her that she could do it, that she *must* do it. Then at last the waves became rollers, lifting her, washing her in a final surge towards the steps of the bathing-machine, and she scarcely felt the grab of a hand on the back of her linen shift, lifting her like a netted fish, supporting her until she was sprawling face-down upon the cabin floor.

Gasping, moaning with exhaustion, she lay there as the door slammed shut, while outside the sounds of the man with the horse and his impatient commands echoed eerily through her head. The cabin was not where she had left it but had been moved further back as the tide moved in, and she had been obliged to swim further to reach it. Now it lurched crazily through the pebbles with a roar, swilling the water across the floor on to her face, floating her shoes upon it.

To dry herself and change into her clothes, weakened and trembling, took far longer than usual, and the two 'dippers' had knocked several times upon the door before she could assure them that she was managing, after a fashion.

'Good thing you had a bit of help, young lady,' said one of the beefy-armed women, eyeing Caterina's bedraggled state. 'If that gen'leman hadn't come to your aid, I reckon you'd 'a been a goner out there. Here, let me fasten you up. You were much too far out, you know.'

Caterina stared, still dazed and dizzy. 'Gentleman?' she wheezed. 'There was a man?' Her chest burned with the effort of speaking.

'Aye. Did ye not see him? He raced across from over there,' the woman said, pointing towards the Steyne, 'throwing 'is clothes off as 'e went. What a runner, too. Great big strapping chap with black hair, ran straight in and fair sped through the water, he did. Brought you back, holding you up by your shift. Don't know 'ow he managed it, mind, but 'e did. Deserves a medal, 'e does.'

'Where is he? Has he gone?'

'Aye. Just picked up 'is clothes and walked off, putting 'em on as 'e went. Now that's a gen'leman for you.'

Caterina paid the man with the horse, and the two

women, making her way on legs made of jelly slowly across to the shallow cliff, dragging herself painfully to the top before resting. There was no sign of her rescuer, and only a few early strollers out to raise an eyebrow at her unkempt appearance.

The dramatic life-threatening events of that morning were too significant to be dismissed as simply a lucky escape or an act of bravado by Sir Chase, for she was in no doubt about the identity of the man who had leapt into the sea for her safety and for no other reason. Now she was forced to appreciate that his presence here could not be ignored when she owed her life to him and, at the very least, her thanks and cooperation. She would rather not have been beholden to him while the terms of her acceptance were still so offensive to her, but she was a grown woman and the time for childish petulance was over. She could no longer use incivility or ungraciousness as a weapon against him.

Clucking like a hen over her chick at the state of her mistress, Millie scolded at her extreme fatigue and shaking legs, telling her that the water must still be like ice at this time of the day, no matter what the physicians recommended. Her hair, she said, rubbing at the sticky strands, was going to be impossible to comb out.

'Then cut if off,' Caterina sighed, clutching at the blanket around her shoulders. 'Just cut it, Millie. I don't mind.'

'Like Lady Caroline Lamb's, you mean?'

'Yes, I think it will suit. Short hair is fashionable now, and so much easier to manage.' She screwed up her face at the burning sensation in her windpipe. 'Use my embroidery scissors.'

Curl by curl, the chestnut locks fell under Millie's

skilful fingers and the neat shape of Caterina's head was revealed looking, at first, like a spiny sea urchin. Washed in warm water and rubbed dry, however, she was transformed by short curls that coiled like springs to make a tumbling mop just long enough to soften her high forehead and nestle into the back of her neck, enhancing the graceful tilt of her head.

Warmed, rested and reclothed, she rehearsed what must be said to Sir Chase. Then she promptly changed her mind. 'Go down,' she told Millie, 'and request that a message be given to Sir Chase Boston immediately. Would he please meet Miss Caterina Chester in the main parlour as soon as he is able? And I would like you to wait for a reply, if you please.'

If Millie was surprised by this development, she concealed it well.

Studying herself in the mirror over the mantelshelf, she wondered how one tackled the unique experience of thanking someone for saving one's life. He had walked away afterwards as if to show that the two of them were quite unconnected until she chose of her own volition to make that connection willingly and in person. Either he was very sure of her, and himself, or he minded little which way she decided—in which case, she reminded herself, he would hardly have taken the trouble to follow her to Brighton or to watch what she did that morning. Would he? Well, whatever his shortcomings, he could never be accused of not trying hard enough to win his wager, though it was hard for her to understand why he should be feeling any sympathy for her father's predicament.

Millie returned, smiling. 'I met Sir Chase downstairs,' she said, 'just about to enter his private parlour. So I gave him your message. He's waiting for you.'

'But I cannot be seen knocking on the door of his private...'

'Outside *here,*' said Millie, pointing to the door, 'in the passage.'

Caterina's hand flew to her breast to quell the sudden pounding. He had seen her as good as naked in a clinging wet linen shift. He had held it bundled around her middle, using it as a handle to lift her like a rag doll into the cabin. She owed him an explanation.

The hand moved to her cheek, touching a tiny pearl earring. 'Am I...?'

Millie prinked at the fine frill of blue muslin around her mistress's neck. 'You look amazing, Miss Caterina,' she whispered, lifting the paisley shawl a little higher. 'He was glad to get your message, I could tell.' She opened the door.

The narrow passageway had windows along one side and three steps down to his level, and when she laid her hands in his, she could feel again the rock hardness of his support and the shakiness in her legs as she descended. His hair was still damp, roughly raked back, but already springing onto his forehead, his skin fresh and healthily glowing, his changeable gemstone eyes filled with concern and relief. As always, his attire was immaculate, as if he'd spent hours with his valet choosing, fitting, arranging and polishing.

She hesitated on the bottom step while she was still above herself yet not above him. 'Sir Chase,' she whispered, 'I owe you an explanation.' Fascinated, she saw his eyes wander in admiration over her new fashionable hairstyle and return to her face. She was paler than usual, her voice pitched to a more husky tone, and they were on the brink of presenting quite a different picture to each other, a new side to their characters and a new phase to their relationship.

His hands pulled, gently, his eyes unable to hide his triumph. Their lips met, comforting each other briefly for the hazard they had shared. She could not begrudge him that. 'You do indeed, Miss Chester,' he said. 'Shall we go down? Will you take my arm? We'll go slowly.'

He might, she thought, have been referring to their future dealings together. 'Yes. Thank you.' Not a word of censure from him. No frowns of disapproval at her latest mutinous expression of independence.

'Shall I send for some tea…chocolate?' he said, closing the door of the parlour. 'Have you taken food since…?'

'Since my swim? Yes, some soup. But I didn't taste it.' She sank gratefully into the chair to which he led her, smiling inwardly as he placed a soft chenille rug over her knees. 'A cup of chocolate would be good.'

He rang the bell. 'A day of rest, I think. Don't you agree? Perhaps a gentle stroll later on to keep the legs moving, then a good night's rest.' Requesting a pot of chocolate and some cakes, he placed himself opposite her in a high-winged armchair, looking for all the world as if a fast sprint, an exhausting swim and the rescue of a maiden in distress were his daily diet.

'Sir Chase,' she said, finding that the words flowed quite easily, after all, 'I owe you my thanks as well as an explanation. I would never have made it back to the shore without you. I feel very foolish. I was not trying to…well…I was simply enjoying myself, you see, not thinking of anything…much.' It was not strictly true. She had been thinking of him. She had thought of him ever since. 'If you had not been there, I'm sure I would not have been able to manage alone.'

'My dear Miss Chester,' he replied, 'I think you need say no more about it. Had I not been there, you *would* have done it alone. Your love of life is stronger than you think at such times. You might have been a few minutes slower—' he smiled '—but then, I have a tendency to hurry where you're concerned, don't I? Now, shall we put it to the back of our minds for good? We have more interesting developments to discuss, I believe.'

'Well,' she said, hoarsely, 'you may be able to banish it to the back of your mind, Sir Chase, but I shall find it harder to do so. I have not had my life saved before. It's a novelty to me.'

'Of course. I quite understand. I hope it remains a novelty. But I am in a similar position regarding marriage proposals, which are a novelty to me but not to you. May we discuss that, if only to put me out of my misery? Come in!' he called to the tap on the door.

The door opened, and soon the table was covered with cups and pots, plates of cakes and biscuits as big as cartwheels, the distribution of which gave Caterina time to take in what Sir Chase had just admitted to her. Replacing her cup on the side-table, she said, 'You've never offered for anyone before?'

'Never. Believe me, I'm an utter novice.'

'Then you may be wishing you had not. There's still time to change your mind.'

'Ah,' he said, looking at her over the rim of his cup, 'that sounds rather like a hope that I might. Or even that you regret what you said to your father on Tuesday evening. So, my dear lady, I have to tell you that it *is* too late. I am not so charitable. I shall not allow you to change your mind.'

'That was not my intention,' she whispered. 'You misunderstand me, sir.'

Leaning forward, he reached out to take her hands in his, making her look at him. 'Do I?' he said, softly.

'I understand that you are still angry with me, and with your father. Am I correct?'

'Yes.'

He nodded. 'But you will become my wife, for his sake?'

'Is that what he told you?'

'Yes, that you are a dutiful daughter, if somewhat headstrong.'

'Then he has misled you. I am not dutiful. I am doing this for my sister's sake. I left him in no doubt of that.'

'Well, you know,' he said, 'I was never one for filial duty in all things either, especially in affairs of the heart, and I'd much rather you married me for love of your sister than out of any sense of duty. Perhaps one day you'll discover an even better reason, but meanwhile I'll accept that. Were there angry words? Is that why you left so suddenly?'

'No angry words. I had already decided before…'

'At Sevrington Hall?'

'Yes.' It was too late to take the admission back. Now he would know what had persuaded her, apart from Sara.

'Then you still have a choice, and I shall not insist on spoiling it.'

'A choice, sir?'

'Your father seemed quite convinced that you would want to seek the advice of your governess, and now we've met again in the most *unusual* circumstances and you're probably fearing that I shall not let you out of my sight.'

'Yes, I suppose I had thought that.'

'No. You must choose whether to keep your own company while we're here, or whether to share your time with me. Do you have a preference?'

Her croaky reply came with a convincing readiness. 'Oh, yes, I would prefer to share it with you, Sir Chase, if I may. So far, I have not been too much at ease here on my own. My plans have gone rather askew, and now Millie is far from well, so I cannot take her out with me.'

'Reasons I shall have to be satisfied with, but better than I feared.'

'Oh, I'm sorry. I didn't mean it to sound quite like that. Yes, to be perfectly honest, when I first discovered you were here I was about to return at once in that horrendous pink post-chaise.'

'But you resisted the temptation. Very courageous.'

'Then I realised that you were perhaps allowing me…er…giving me…'

'Giving you your head, lass?' he said, tenderly. 'I was warned you might make a dash for it, but one doesn't cure a filly of bolting by keeping her in the stable, you know. You're free to run until we're married, and even then you'll not be confined. You have nothing to fear there.'

'Then you'll be leaving me to my own devices while you go away?'

'I didn't say that. You'll certainly *not* be left to your own devices.'

'Oh.' Her hands remained in his as unspoken queries advanced and retreated in both their minds, too delicate, too contentious to be spoken. 'There is one thing,' she said, 'which concerns my stay here at the Castle. I would not mention it except that it's been a source of concern to me.'

'I can help. What is it?'

'I expected to stay with Miss Vincent, you see, and I brought only small funds with me. So I may have to return sooner than I intended.'

'I have a confession to make,' Sir Chase said, keeping a very straight face. 'I intercepted your message to Lady Dorna. You will not be travelling home in four days' time in that appalling conveyance again. No—' he held up a hand '—I'm sorry, but no future wife of mine is going to be seen in that vulgar monstrosity with its tassels and twiddly bits everywhere. You will be returning with me, and I shall be settling all bills for accommodation, so there's no need to concern yourself on that score.'

'Sir Chase, I cannot possibly allow you to do that. I have no objection to travelling back to Richmond with you, but all I need is a loan to be sure that I can—'

'Miss Chester, have you formally accepted me, or not?'

She blinked. 'Er…yes, I think so.'

'That's what I thought.' Stretching an arm across the tray of cups, he collected a small package wrapped in brown paper and tied with string. Placing it on her lap, he continued, 'Then perhaps you would oblige me by wearing that, just to remind yourself in case of further misunderstandings about who pays for what. I do like to have these matters clarified so that we all know what we're about. You'll not be leaving *me* at the altar, my girl.' When she sat gazing at it, he nudged it with one finger. 'Come on, open it. It won't bite.'

Knowing what it would be, she pulled open the bow and peeled back the paper to reveal a small polished wooden box with a mother-of-pearl rose set into the lid. Inside, resting on a white satin cushion, was a gold ring set with a large emerald surrounded by diamonds flashing with rainbow fires. It was almost too precious to touch.

Seeing her reluctance, Sir Chase removed it from its

bed and, taking hold of her left hand, slid it on to her finger. 'There,' he whispered, 'I think that makes it official. Did the other two get this far?'

'No, sir, they didn't.' He had already gone further than they had in other directions. Even so, she sensed that there might be an element of competition in his needing to know, in his references to her previous engagements.

'Good. This is yours, whatever happens. Will you wear it, to please me?'

'If it will please you, sir, I will wear it. Thank you.'

'But?' he said, lifting her chin with his knuckle.

'It's very precious and beautiful.' It was not what she had wanted to say.

'So you can see now why I encouraged you to stay afloat this morning. It would have been such a pity to have missed the chance to wear it, don't you think? Was it worth swimming for?'

She had to smile at his banter. 'I didn't realise it really *was* you by my side. I heard you somewhere inside my head, but I thought it was a...oh, dear...what am I saying?' A rosy pink blushed over her cheeks at the memory of what had happened, her reference to his exact whereabouts in her mind giving away more than she had intended.

It appeared to please him, however. 'That's as good a place as any, for the time being. But now we shall hear no more about the funds and loans, because that is my department, and yours is to grace my side, as you do so perfectly.'

She sat very still, gazing at the magnificent jewels against her skin, suddenly subdued and, for once, unsure of how to proceed. She had been betrothed twice before, on neither occasion with rings or mentions of escape. This time was quite different, and irrevocable for all the wrong reasons. 'I have nothing to give you, Sir Chase,' she said, 'but you need not fear I shall change my mind at the last moment as I have done before. Things have gone too far for that.'

'Caterina, listen to me. I know what's gnawing at you. This was not the way you wanted it. You feel helpless, and thwarted, and deceived, too. But despite the circumstances, I feel we should be able to get on tolerably well together once things have settled down. Domestic things, I mean. As soon as we've tied the knot we can be away from Richmond within days. Leave it to me.'

'Marriage, so soon?'

'Oh, yes. I want you out of that place.'

Not, then, I want you in my arms, Caterina. I cannot wait another moment for you. Nothing to do with the emotions. Businesslike. Efficient. So that we all know what we're about.

Shivering, she reached for her cup and saucer, taking a sip of cool chocolate before answering him. 'That is soon, sir, but Hannah will be relieved to hear it. She needs my room rather urgently.'

'That was tactful of her, and no mistake.'

'Not really. She and my father expect an addition.'

There was the slightest pause before he let out a slow breath. 'Then I'd say our timing was near perfect. Now, is there any other matter you need reassurance about? We can talk over the details when you're feeling more yourself, perhaps?'

Near the front of her mind had lurked the secret hope that he might seal their betrothal with a kiss. A man like Sir Chase could not be expected to miss an opportunity like that without a very good reason. But he did not, and she could only assume that it was because she was not quite herself. Or because he did not care to.

'Of course,' she said, replacing the cup. 'May I take one of these cakes up to Millie? Then I must visit the apothecary. Her cough needs attending to.'

'Write a note telling him what you need, and I'll send my man with it.'

She tilted her left hand to catch the light, feeling the strangeness of the ring's pressure and excited by its exquisite presence, its relevance to her future.

'Like it?' he whispered.

When she looked up, half-smiling, there were pearls of moisture along her lower eyelashes. She nodded. 'I like it very much, sir. Thank you.'

In many respects, the events of that morning brought together the loose ends of a tangle, holding them securely and leaving Caterina with the impression that she had, after all, exercised some choice in the matter of her betrothal, whether this was imagined or factual. Whatever notions she had sifted through her mind about making things difficult for him now began to look futile and childlike against his obvious determination to pursue her, even to the extent of keeping a watch on her safety. His reputation as an habitual victor was not without foundation.

She did not, of course, intend to cry off at the last moment any more than she had intended to on the last two occasions. Not at the start, anyway. But the giving of a ring did not automatically level the playing field, nor did it banish her resentment, nor make her into the responsive woman he apparently wanted. Recognising her anger and the reason for it, he could not be faulted for his careful and gentlemanly manner, and if there was a tendency to be masterly at this early stage, it had been for her comfort rather than his own. Only in his unseemly haste to 'tie the knot,' as he put it, did Caterina still feel entitled to procrastinate.

There was, however, a problem there, too, for while she was being reluctant to oblige him in this, the strong emotional side to her artistic nature had begun to respond to him despite all her attempts to ignore it. Worse, she had already been foolish enough to reveal what she should have kept hidden from him. He was not supposed even to guess at her growing partiality.

Once they were man and wife, it would prove very difficult for her to pretend indifference to his lovemaking, her ultimate weapon destroyed completely. On the other hand, was his restraint that morning an indication of how things would be in the future? Was he expecting her to dictate the pace, or would his masterly side take over, sweeping away all her false reserve in seconds, as it had before? Whatever the answers, some progress had been made which was not altogether abhorrent to her, even if the circumstances fell far short of her need for romance. In place of that, she had acquired a resolute man and a ring, and it remained to be seen how soon he returned to his other life of gambling and fast living. How long would it be, she wondered, before he looked elsewhere for a woman to chase? And how long would she be able to hold him off?

With Millie receiving proper medication and Caterina's fatigue responding to rest, the invitation to take a gentle stroll after lunch was accepted without the added irritant of being ogled by the local militia who had nothing better to do. The Season had not yet begun, and the closure of the Castle's great ballroom was no real disappointment when the inevitable questions about her newest betrothal would have been an effort to answer. A walk with Sir Chase, Millie told her, would do her good.

As it was, time spent in Sir Chase's company was anything but dreary, as she had discovered on her first ride through Richmond with him, and once her defences began to lower, she found that their time together flew, that he became less of a challenge and more of an enigma about whom there was much more to discover than she had thought. Away from the nagging obligations of home, that first afternoon as his betrothed was memorable for a new kind of freedom he had promised her, better even than the freedom she had hoped for on the day of her arrival, for now there was security, too.

Predictably, the young officers kept a respectful distance as Sir Chase and Caterina walked arm in arm around the huge fountain on the Steyne, or delved into the book and perfume shops crowding into Castle Square, or strolled around the perimeter of the Royal Pavilion, safe from invitations while the Prince Regent was in London. Usually, Sir Chase told her, he would be obliged to inform the resident Prince that he had arrived, then wait for an invitation to attend a dinner to which the host would arrive late, and drunk, and which would not finish until the early hours of the morning, when breakfast would be served. To decline was never an option.

Though sorry for the Prime Minister's demise, Caterina was glad that something important had kept the Prince at his duties. 'Did you ever wish to decline?' she asked.

'Not at first. When I was in Brighton on duty, it was

a good way to pass the evenings. Now I've discovered other ways to spend my time.'

Believing she knew the other ways, she did not ask him.

Only a stone's throw from the Pavilion was the entrance to the Royal Stables, an impressively large domed building erected only a few years ago. They lingered, gazing at its exotic ornament. 'Would you like to take a look inside?' Sir Chase said. 'It's where Prinny keeps his horses.'

A team of magnificent carriage-horses was being led through the entrance as he spoke, greeted by neighs and the distant clank of buckets. Through the carved gates, light flooded through a massive glass dome on to a sawdust-covered arena in the centre of which a fountain jetted water into an octagonal trough. All around them, Indian-style doorways and sparkling glass made a riot of pattern as the sunlight and shadows moved across, taking Caterina's breath away with its sumptuous eastern beauty. Archways led to multiple stalls, to carriage halls, to tack rooms and workshops and, on the balconied upper floor, to the stable-hands' quarters.

'It's…it's incredible!' Caterina said. 'It's like an Indian palace.'

'Stabling for over forty horses,' Sir Chase told her. 'Cost over thirty thousand to build, and heaven only knows what it costs in running expenses. Some critics say that the horses are better housed than the Prince himself.'

Overawed by the grandeur and scale of the building, she went with him through a decorated arch into a room where stalls housed six handsome mares, their fine dark eyes rolling with curiosity at the intrusion. At the far end, two mares were being rugged-up and led out for their daily exercise.

'They'll be going up on to the Downs,' he said, reaching up to caress the nearest mare's head, pulling gently at her ears. 'Shall we ride up there tomorrow and watch? We can drive the curricle, or borrow two of these, whichever you prefer.' His hand swept down the silky forelock to the pink trembling muzzle, fondling the velvety skin, his eyes resting on Caterina, waiting for her answer, but telling her also that he would rather be fondling her than the mare.

All at once, they were in another realm that had nothing to do with horses or future plans. In here, it was shadowy, private and peaceful, away from the grooms and their chores, sounds muffled by sawdust and straw, intimate and strangely erotic with overtones of seduction in a Moorish harem glimpsed through ogee grilles and fretwork. The setting and the ambience affected her as much as his exciting presence by her side, sending a surge of weakness from thigh to stomach that she could not control, wanting him, his arms, his mouth, and more. Unable to think of a reply, her lips parted with the ache of yearning as she watched him leave the soft muzzle and take her gloved fingertips in his, keeping her eyes locked in a message as readable as words, telling her that he would comply if only she would speak the words of command. So far, in this matter, she had acted under duress. He would not give her cause to blame him further.

The mare tossed her head, whinnying softly for attention.

'Well, my girl?' he whispered. 'What is it to be?'

She knew what he was asking, but preferred to take the safer route. To give in to him so soon was not the way to keep his interest. 'The Downs?' she said. 'What if we were to do both, drive round Brighton in the morning and ride up to the Downs after lunch? Do you think I might be allowed to borrow this one? She's such a beauty.'

The spell was broken. His smile was understanding. 'Why not?' he said. 'Come and help me choose a mount, then.'

Having almost given up hope of finding in this relationship the kind of romance she was looking for, Caterina was all the more delighted to find that Sir Chase's methods were far removed from those of her two former betrothed. Roses appeared in her room and a late hellebore had been placed on their table at dinner, signifying protection. Other trinkets appeared, too: a pair of embroidered gloves, a lace handkerchief, a small book of William Blake's poems, more flowers, and two tickets for the theatre on Saturday evening.

'I have nothing to give you, sir,' she said again, accepting from him a small paper box tied with ribbon with 'John Atkins, High Quality Confectioner and Sweetmeat Maker' printed on the lid.

'Yes, you do,' he said. 'But I can wait.'

She was a virgin, he reminded himself, and he was reluctant to persuade her or to take a hasty advantage of the impetuosity that several times in the last few days had almost spilled her into his arms. He had witnessed her struggle against it, had seen desire darken her eyes, had felt her fear, and with probably only the vaguest notion of what she was holding on to, he knew she was impatient to discover how it would feel to release it. Curious and aroused, she was ready to be taught, just as ready to be freed from the constraints of Paradise Road and just as angry at the manner of it as she had been at first. Once she had given herself, however, there would be no turning back. She would have to go with him, willing or unwilling. And they both knew it.

Purposely, he did not make the decision too easy for her and, in her innocence of men of his sort, she interpreted his attempts to make these few days memorable for her as a desire to show her his good side, as opposed to the one about which she had found so much to criticise. In a sense, she was right, but there was more to it than that for, in the short time left to them, he took her into other situations where it would have been possible for her to drop her guard and allow him some access to her, as she had done at Sevrington Hall. After the Royal Stables, he had come close on several occasions, but the theatre was to be their last outing before their return home on Sunday.

Like other Brighton entertainments before the season had begun, the Theatre Royal on New Street had not yet swung into action with the same gusto of high summer when it would be packed to the roof and noisily sociable. In early May, the acting talent still lacked the big names, the musicians eager but unpolished. Believing that Caterina would be ready to give the second half of the performance a miss, Sir Chase suggested they might leave.

But she resisted the idea of abandonment. 'Absolutely not,' she said during the interval. 'They may not be the best we've ever heard, but they don't deserve a mass walkout halfway through.'

'Two of us is hardly a mass,' he commented drily. 'Don't exaggerate.'

'I *feel* exaggerated,' she snapped.

'You certainly have an exaggerated sense of loyalty

to a group of amateurs. If I'd known they were as bad as this, I'd have taken you to the Assembly Rooms at the Castle instead.'

'I'd much rather be here. But *you* must be missing the gaming tables. These last few days must have been quite a strain for you.'

'Oh, they have, Miss Chester. You can have no idea of the strain I've been under. Gambling, drinking, debauchery, the ruining of innocent young women. How I've missed it.' He yawned behind his knuckles. 'Shall we go in for our second dose of voluntary torment?'

'*Now* who's exaggerating?'

Sir Chase was not in the least dismayed by this sudden waspishness, for it had nothing to do with whether they should go or stay. He had seen how, when the tensions built inside her, she found a release in scolding and reckless bids for solitude, picking a quarrel when she felt herself changing towards him. Soon she would be facing her father again after a second escape without a proper farewell, her time as a free woman almost at an end. The prospect was unnerving. She needed a scapegoat and he was happy to oblige. For the time being.

'You've had no singing practice,' he said as they took their seats in the box beside the stage. 'Have you missed a lesson?'

'Two,' she said, curtly, as if it were his fault.

'And when is your next performance to be?'

Slowly, she swung her head to look at him as if he'd asked her to name the King of Persia. It was the first time she had thought about it. She shrugged. 'I don't know,' she said in a rush, thinking that he must be the most exciting man she had ever known. Sitting there beside her, he exuded a virility and strength in his easy grace that took her breath away. When he moved, he had the rhythm and power of an athlete and she had known a most unusual pride to be seen with him, riding and walking, driving, sitting at meals. She had worn her best outfits to complement his elegant style, enjoyed his friendship and forgotten those uncomfortable resentments until just before sleep each night. Then, she had dragged them out for a nightly airing, in case they disappeared altogether. Gradually, it had become obvious that, unless she were to reveal her willingness to him, he was not going to kiss her as he had done at Sevrington Hall. And she was certainly not going to ask him to.

'Don't ask me where, either,' she said, turning her head away.

'Where is it to be?' he said, smoothly.

'Chiswick House. Not far from home. You need not be there.'

'I shall be there. Remember what happened last time.'

'The Duke has his own resident musicians, so there won't be a repeat of last time. Signor Cantoni will be with me, too.'

'So shall I. The Duke of Devonshire is a friend of mine.'

'I might have guessed.'

Superficially, the frostiness lasted throughout the second half during which she would have regretted her misplaced loyalty to the cast had it not been for his warm large hand that took hers within minutes, settling itself upon her lap like an old friend. Soon, she covered it with her other hand, nestling all three close to the bend of her body where, when the acting grew increasingly tedious, he spread his fingers caressingly into the soft folds of muslin over her inner thigh, moving it downwards into the dark warmth of secrecy. He heard her gasp beside him, but knew she would not look at him when she was herself in full view of the audience.

Alert, vibrating, unresisting, she allowed his hand to stay there. He had made the first move, and now she need no longer accept full responsibility for what happened next. In allowing his caress, she had divulged the open secret that her pique was more for his delay than his new ownership of her.

'Little wasp,' he whispered, during one noisy scene. 'I'm beginning to read you, girl. Beware.'

'How long does this go on?' she whispered, her eyes fixed on the stage.

He smiled at the ambiguity. 'What a question,' he replied.

The five-minute walk back to the Castle Inn was made in the kind of silence that anticipated another delicate shift in their relationship, though the age-old response of all well-bred women was bound to make an appearance, as a formality, at the door of her room.

'Where does your maid sleep?' he whispered.

'In the little room next door. Her coughing disturbed me.'

'Good. I shall come to you in half an hour.'

'Sir Chase…no, er…you cannot.'

'Why can I not?'

'I don't know.' She bit her lip, in the darkness.

'Then I shall comc. Caterina?'

'Yes,' she said. 'But…oh…yes.'

Chapter Six

Wanting him was one thing, but offering herself like a betting-token as the price of a wager was quite another. When his light tap upon her door broke the silence of the room, she was still in the cream embroidered evening gown, and Millie had been sent back to bed.

He, on the other hand, had come to her in a long dressing gown of grey-figured silk tied round the hips, his feet inside velvet mules, his neck startlingly bare without the high neckcloth, his only accessory the lingering aroma of pine trees. Apparently, he saw nothing surprising in her unreadiness. He closed the door quietly and waited, his expression thoughtful.

'I've…er, I've changed my mind,' Caterina said, her voice wavering with the effort. 'I'm sorry. You must know how I feel about…things. This would be a betrayal, wouldn't it? You can see that. I can't do it. It will have to wait…until…whenever.' She spread her hands in a helpless gesture, one of them still holding her long kid gloves. Facing him, she saw his eyes glint in the flickering candlelight and thought she recognised the glimmer of amusement or admiration rather than disappointment. Irritated, she tried again, sharpening her tone. 'Perhaps you should leave now. Good night, sir. I've had the most enjoyable...' Backing away, she warded him off as he approached, but he took the gloves from her and draped them over the chair. 'Do you not understand me, Sir Chase? I have changed...'

'Your mind. Yes, of course you have,' he said, gently. 'You reach the brink, you get cold feet, then you cry off. And this time, although you want me, you cannot bear the thought of being seen to submit, or even to consent. It goes against the grain, doesn't it? Dazzling, fiery creature. It goes by another more common name, too.'

'What does?' she whispered, still backing round the room, skirting the obstacles and feeling her way round the bedposts, hand over hand.

'Pride,' he said, following her through the shadows like a grey cat stalking its prey. 'Understandable, but I have a way round the problem that should satisfy both of us. Shall I show you?'

'No!' she cried, unnerved by his refusal to be put off. She had backed herself against a small bedside table where a candle's flame wavered in the draught, bending as she dodged to one side to evade him. But she was not fast enough to escape the arms that came round her with a speed that made her yelp, and before she could even begin to struggle against his grip, she was tossed sideways onto the bed, held down by his arms and legs, her hands caught as they flew up to beat and push at him. 'No...no!' she growled. 'You might at least *talk* about it. You don't understand, do you? This means nothing to you, does it? Let go...let *go* of me!'

'Steady, girl...steady. Stop struggling and hear me out.'

'I don't want to hear you,' she panted. He was close above her, and she was able to see how his gown gaped to expose a wide V of rugged chest and the muscled column of his throat, so close that she could smell his skin and feel his intimidating warmth. The excitement of it surged through her body towards her knees, making her heart race and her objections slow to a halt. 'I don't want to do this with you,' she whispered, trying to convince herself of its truth.

'And it will suit you better if I insist, thereby giving your body what it craves and clearing your conscience at the same time? Yes, I know. But if you believe that it means nothing to me, my beauty, you're quite mistaken. I would never waste my time with any other woman who's raised as many objections as you have. Now, let's see if we can move things on a bit with some gentle persuasion.'

Having released her hands, his own fingers were engaged in undoing the ribboned drawstring around the neckline of her dress and, when that was loosened, he eased her over on to her side so that he could reach the hooks of her bodice and draw it down past one shoulder. Casually replacing her, he eased the other side down.

Anchoring her elbows close to her sides, Caterina clung to the top of her gown while her mind, in contrast, lay helplessly adrift, her senses honed in readiness, sure that he would, despite her insincere protests, unleash something within her that had been caged and waiting too long for freedom. Only a man with his experience, tarnished or not, would know how to accept what she had to give with its odd assortment of pride, passion and surrender. Only he would understand what she wanted from him in return, not the usual diluted lovemaking reserved for virgins, but something more that would disturb her profoundly and make this particular sacrifice worth her while. What good would it do for her to opt for anything less than the real thing with a real man? Like him.

Instead of insisting, he drank deeply from her dark eyes and knew from the desire growing there that he had been right: her objections were formulaic, no more than that, her arms already relaxing against the ache to hold him. Bending his head, he began a kiss intended to lure her cooperation, tender and teasing.

Once again, she flared like an inferno at the taste of his mouth, and the words of denial upon her lips were devoured in a blazing contradiction, spurring him on beyond the initial languid phases of seduction. Exhilarated and encouraged, he gathered her into his arms, rolling her under him in a crumpled knot of silk as a cry of sheer abandonment escaped into the dark canopied enclosure of the bed.

In the briefest of intervals, he sat back to remove his gown in one impatient tug, hurling it aside before bending to her once more, watching for any sign of distress as she lay with half-closed eyes, waiting for him to disrobe her as she had dreamed more than once that he might do.

The close proximity of his nakedness vibrated through her like a drug. He was smooth, solid and magnificent under her hesitant fingers, rippling with muscle toned by exercise, broad above, sloping to a narrow waist and hips that had little resemblance to her own womanly curves. The strong nose and brow caught the mellow glow from the single candle, carving his features from polished oak like some dark woodland god, his eyes following the path of hers as she bathed him in open wonder and approval, telling him without a word being spoken that she had ceased to object.

He bent to kiss her again, intending to draw her mind away from the hand that slid the bodice down over her flawless breasts to her waist, and beyond. But the first contact of their skin brought another cry of desire from her lips, and she arched against him, pressing herself along his length, pushing her hips into him as if she had been taught, eagerly searching for every connection while foraging with her mouth, accepting everything he offered.

Pushing her thumbs into the folds of her gown, she eased it away with his help, impatient to learn more of him through her skin, moving, smoothing him with her thighs, sliding the soles of her feet down his long legs, feeling with her hands the deeply rippling valleys of sinew and muscle.

She stopped suddenly as a strange hardness pressed against her stomach, tearing her mouth away from his, her eyes wide and filled with apprehension. She had seen that part of a man on classical statues from the ancient world, but there remained some anomalies in her mind about the mechanics that not even the observation of her tiny half-brothers had been able to solve. What she felt now pressing urgently against her was something she had neither seen nor imagined.

Her reaction was what Sir Chase had anticipated. Although virgins had never received his attentions as a lover, this woman was different in so many other ways from the one-dimensional women he had known. Outwardly in control, inwardly she seethed with denials and inconsistencies. She was sensual, passionate, wild, fiercely free and independent of spirit, talented and, in many respects, conventional. She was largely innocent of men also, for though she had met plenty of them, only one had been allowed to come close. Indeed, it looked as if she had begun to lose interest altogether until he had demanded to be noticed.

'It's all right,' he whispered. 'There's no hurry, my beauty. I shall be careful. We have some ground to cover first. Let me show you...easy...my girl. Let's take it slowly, eh?' Showering her with a mist of new and erotic compliments, his hand began its quest along her shoulders and throat, leading his kisses along paths of smooth silk. Her eyes closed in rapture once more, unable to hold back her craving long enough to wait patiently upon his languid lovemaking.

The caresses moved over her breast like a breeze that scarcely touched her skin until it brushed her nipples in passing, causing a gasp of surprise at the tingle along every fibre of her being. Feeling her response, his hand cupped and encircled one breast, holding it captive for his lips to tease and torment. But without realising it, he had already lured her beyond that point, and now the instant response to the nudge of his knees between hers was a soft moan and the sharp incisive dig of her fingernails into his back, warning him of her readiness, sooner by far than he had imagined.

Spreading her legs to resolve the ache between them, she waited, trembling and tense with desire. 'I don't know what to do,' she whispered into his cheek. 'You must tell me what to do. Quickly...what is it? What am I to do?' There was an urgency as well as desire in her voice.

She was, he thought, already doing everything a man could dream of, and more. Without delay, he responded to her demand by lifting her to him with an arm under her back, passing over the intimate preliminaries that he'd intended, making his first careful entry effortlessly smooth, virtually painless, and more immediate than either of them could have predicted.

Awed, speechless with the exquisite thrill of his penetration, she became aware of a slow fire within that deep part of her that had ached for him, like a firm rippling caress over a private wound, taking her breath away with its sweetness.

'Breathe,' he whispered, waiting for her to recover.

Raggedly, she exhaled. 'It's…all right,' she gasped. 'Is this it? Is this what you do, Chase? Is this what we do? Like this?'

'Not quite, beautiful, wild woman. Not yet.'

'What more…is it? Ah…yes, go on…go on…'

With slow voluptuous movements, he began to pleasure her, raining kisses like snowflakes upon her upturned face, gradually filling her with each thrust.

Faint mewing sounds escaped from her throat, pushing every thought from her mind into a world of sensation, part pain, part bliss, in which she was sure heaven could not be far away. Stretching under him, she felt each gentle thrust, anticipating the next with greedy excitement, wanting it never to end, revelling in the knowledge that this man understood her needs better than she knew them herself, that he was the strong, handsome, arrogant man who had brought her to this sooner than she had believed possible, that he was the one, the *only* one, she wanted.

Contrary to Sir Chase's personal prediction that he would be expected to continue for quite some time before she came anywhere near a climax, if at all, it was only moments before her mewing cries took on a different tone. Sensing the approach of some life-changing experience, she writhed beneath him, overwhelmed by a tantalising force that hovered just out of reach. 'Chase...' she cried, hoarsely.

Instantly, he recognised the sound, quickening his pace, driving himself to take her with breathtaking speed to the point where the explosion awaited them, together, perfectly matched. As if they had been practising for years. Never had he thought it could happen like that.

For Caterina, the turmoil deep inside her was like an internal earthquake where every small part of her was suspended, even her breathing, until it passed, leaving her dizzy with a euphoria beyond any she had experienced before. Released and soaring like a bird, she lay in a kind of limbo between waking and sleeping while he rested inside her, and, by the rhythm of his ribcage under her hand, she could feel him breathing heavily as if he'd been running.

Turning to her, he buried his face for a moment in the mass of fiery curls. She thought he was smiling. 'What an amazing creature you are,' he said. 'Like quicksilver. Like a rainbow. Little fire-ball. Shall I ever get to know you, to tame you? Saints, woman, you're unbelievable. Just unbelievable.'

She smiled, but made no reply to that, nor did she plead for him to stay when he carefully withdrew and pulled her into his arms, drawing his grey silk gown around her shoulders and rocking her against him. His withdrawal made her feel incomplete and bereft, yet deliciously exhausted, but it occurred to her then that she might have found a perfect way to bind him to her more closely when his interest began to wane, to prevent him from straying as men often did when an heir was on the way. She must try *never* to be predictable, not with a man of so many talents. She had made a good beginning, it seemed.

He was smiling, drowsily. 'Somewhere along the line,' he said, 'we appear to have lost sight of something.'

'Oh?'

'Mm...m. I had it at the back of my mind that you'd have preferred something, well, rather more lengthy, something quite slow, in fact. I was quite prepared for a very...very...slow seduction.'

'And wasn't that slow?'

The smile broadened. 'It certainly was not. It was meteoric by anybody's standards, Miss Chester.'

'Oh, then you're disappointed.'

Raising himself up on to one elbow, he looked down into her eyes, a woman's eyes with a hint of childlike innocence behind the topaz brilliance. 'Disappointed?' he laughed, shaking his head. 'No, my beauty. Very much the opposite. I'm elated, surprised certainly, and utterly fascinated, but never disappointed. I know how your passion leads you on. That was how I first saw you, angry and impulsive and not afraid to show it. That's the kind of honesty I admire, even disliking me as you did. I wanted you then, Caterina, and now I want you more than ever, to discover all your sides, all your passions. Then, when I've found out what's hidden behind those beautiful eyes, I'll start again and rediscover it, just for the fun of it. Shall I?' His fingers played with springing curls of hair as he spoke before beginning a journey over the landscape of her throat, downwards over her shoulders, finally coming to rest upon the breast he'd hardly had time to importune.

'You'll need fortitude, sir,' she whispered. 'I'm afraid I have a habit of reacting rather too quickly to... er...things.'

Her admission amused him. 'Yes, but I'm beginning

to get your measure, impetuous woman, and I shall out-pace you. I think I've already proved that.'

She had to agree that it was so, especially in the water. Nor had she managed to shake him off on land, or evade his lovemaking. But now her body's responses refused to lie dormant and, even as he watched, her eyes were darkening with desire, her hips moving seductively under his stroking hand.

'Show me more, then,' she said. 'Show me wicked things that take a long time. Make it last fifty times longer.'

His hand moved downwards, spreading across her flat stomach before reaching the soft mound and the warm cavern of womanly secrets. Her sigh invited him to explore, her senses again on the very brink of rapture.

'How to slow you down, my beauty, is going to be very interesting,' he said, bending his handsome head to kiss her.

Caterina had come to Brighton in a state of mulish independence to put as great a distance between herself and her future as she could devise. Fate had decreed otherwise, and now her return journey was as different in every way from that taken in the florid pink post-chaise, Sir Chase's curricle being at the apex of high fashion. For various reasons, the curricle and four gathered just as many stares as the other, and by the time they had toiled up the long hill to Reigate, Caterina had fallen in with Sir Chase's suggestion that they should stay overnight at the posting inn there. To rest the horses, he told her, though she had little doubt that it was he who sought a bed more than the horses. With her, of course.

Their first night together had been a night to remember, sleep having been in short supply. For all Caterina knew, Millie was still recovering from the mild shock of seeing her mistress in bed with the man she claimed to dislike. In all other respects, Millie's recovery was assured as she, Sir Chase's valet, and the luggage followed on in a hired post-chaise.

Reigate was swathed in clouds as they set off early on Monday to reach Richmond by midday to a reception neither of them could predict with much accuracy. Caterina was particularly quiet, wrapped in her own thoughts of last night during which sleep had again played a minor role. Glancing at her several times with the secretive smile of one well pleased with himself, and with her, Sir Chase said little of any consequence to interrupt her memories, which he rightly supposed would be very much along the same lines as his.

Unlike him, Caterina had no comparisons to make, yet she believed he must be an outstandingly good lover to be able to bring her to such rapture time after time. Only a good lover, she thought, would have heaped so many praises upon one so new to the art of lovemaking. If only her father's underhandedness had not stood in her way, she might have been even happier with her lot. As it was, she could only be thankful that the outcome would mean her removal from Paradise Road within the week.

The question of which of Sir Chase's houses they should settle in first was never quite resolved, although both agreed that it would be useful to make a quick visit to his town house on Halfmoon Street, where the London shops could provide her with everything she required. Her forthcoming singing engagement at Chiswick House, one of the Duke of Devonshire's London homes, must come first, after which they were free to distance themselves from any other obligations. It was a prospect that sat easily on Caterina's mind, leaving her less time to dwell on the darker side of the affair.

It was Sir Chases's suggestion, as they bowled along leafy lanes and rolling downland, that she may like to takc hcr singing teacher with them so that she need not feel her talents were being in any way neglected. There were pianos at each of his homes, and it was not good for her nerves to have to rely on the kind of musicians the Ensdales had hired. Signor Cantoni might like the idea of a more permanent position as piano teacher, too, he suggested.

'For whom, sir?' said Caterina, knowing full well for whom.

'I shall expect all my children to be musical,' he said, smiling.

'All of them, sir?'

'All of them, Miss Chester. We shall give fortnightly concerts.'

'I see. Then I shall put the idea to him. Thank you. That was very thoughtful.'

'I aim to please,' he said, favouring her with a quick smile.

It did seem to her that he was doing all a man could do to please her, and much more than the two previous contenders combined. And what a pity it was, she continued to remind herself, that she must now return to Paradise Road and her father's gloating satisfaction.

Contrary to her expectations, Mr Chester did not demand to know why she had left home without a word, and her welcome was as warm as she could have wished from parents who knew her remaining time with them was limited. After being closeted with her father for an hour, Sir Chase emerged from the study on amicable terms, saving her the embarrassment of having to explain the whys and wherefores of their stay in Brighton, and no questions were asked of her except how they could help to arrange the next few busy days. Friday's marriage ceremony sounded alarmingly final.

Sara would be home by then.

Caterina's ring and her new hairstyle met with their approval.

The bridegroom's parents were invited to dine, and visits were made to Aunt Amelie at Sheen Court and to Lady Dorna at Mortlake, both ladies happy to welcome Sir Chase as part of the family, Lord Elyot having looked on him as his brother-in-arms for years. What could be better than a chase after a Chester and a prize like that, he wanted to know. It was what he'd had to do to get Amelie, after all. It was the kind of typically male remark that had the two laughing friends banished to the stables, while the blushing women remained to discuss the more practical aspects of being one's own mistress, at last.

The drive in the curricle, Lady Elyot remarked, had been timed to perfection, but Caterina didn't feel inclined to explain that the coffee-coloured phaeton could have told a different kind of tale, the repercussions of which would be felt for years. For her part, Lady Elyot did not mention the very unorthodox circumstances surrounding Lord Elyot's wooing of her that had given her less choice in the matter than anyone supposed. Not even Lady Dorna, his sister.

Their visit to Lady Dorna was predictably slippery, the news of Caterina's immediate marriage to Sir Chase setting off a train of thought that had a destination all its own. There would have been a time when Sir Chase might have responded in good measure to her very direct approach, her forthright questions about their time in Brighton, her queries about the proposal, the ring, their reaction to her pretty post-chaise, all the showy things that mattered most to her. But this time, Sir Chase countered her probings with some of his own, turning the subject round in no time at all, to everyone's complete satisfaction. Caterina could have hugged him.

They went to look at the church and to meet the vicar.

Sir Chase wanted to know what all the fuss was about.

There was, of course, too much to be done in three short days.

Perhaps, Hannah remarked, looking flustered, if Caterina had not flown off to Brighton…?

Caterina held back the obvious reply.

Considering what had to be done, everything fitted together remarkably well, and the dinner for Sir Reginald and Lady FitzSimmon, Sir Chase's stepfather and mother, passed off in the friendliest manner, since they had known Hannah as a young girl. When the evening was rounded off with a song from Caterina accompanied by Sir Chase, they were convinced for the first time that he had chosen a woman worthy to be their daughter-in-law. Caterina liked her future in-laws unreservedly, but supposed their adoration of their handsome son to be responsible for his notoriously unprincipled behaviour. A clear case of sparing the rod.

That same night, the one before her wedding, she could not sleep. Sara had chattered excitedly about what

Caterina's marriage would do for *her,* falling asleep in mid-sentence about her own plans for the future, little realising that her sister longed to confide in someone, or that *her* ideals were being scuppered so shamefully. The clocks had struck the hour of midnight and, after listening to the wails upstairs, the creaking floorboards, the click of doors, the town crier and his bell, Caterina left her bed, threw a shawl around her shoulders and took the candle downstairs.

The door to her father's study was ajar and, instead of closing it in passing, she went inside to take a last look at the place where she had first met Sir Chase. Neither of the men had discussed with her the terms of her dowry or settlements, if any. Maybe she ought to have asked about Harry's IOU, but there had hardly been a moment to spare.

Casting a dim light around the room, the candle's flame hid familiar daytime things and picked out others, less familiar, the whirling pattern on the walnut desk, a mahogany box with a brass catch like the one she'd been shown by Sir Chase, the gilded frame of the painting on the wall. A ship in full sail. Strangely, she had not noticed it before. She lifted the candle to read the inscription beneath, wondering if this was a new interest of her father's. *The Caterina leaving Liverpool,* it read.

The *Caterina?*

Puzzled, she placed the candle on the desk and sat in his chair, looking at the neat stacks of papers with glass paperweights on top and, at one side as if thrown there in a hurry, a stiffly folded letter addressed to Mr Stephen Chester in a handwriting she immediately recognised. It was postmarked Liverpool. From her brother Harry. Her father had not mentioned this, perhaps because it was a sore point with him still.

Gingerly, she picked it up and unfolded it, holding it near the flame, expecting to see some words of abject apology and regret for the pain he had caused.

Sir. At your request, I hasten to acquaint you with how matters here have progressed since we last met and how I have found them on my return, though my hasty departure was not what I had intended, had things been better handled by me. Which I regret. Hardly an apology, she thought. *You will be gratified to learn that the* Caterina *returned while I was away, unexpectedly early before a strong southwesterly and all ship-shape with no losses. Our Customs men examined her, but since they have never had reason to suspect the Africans of being lately stowed in the hold, a full cargo of 422 prime males and 30 young females, their search was soon done, and I have had the pleasure of entering the report in the files, no one suspecting that I am about my father's business. Your instructions were followed to the letter by Captain Bowes, a reliable man who was able to deliver the Africans to our agent waiting at St Kitts and to load up with sugar from our plantation there. The Captain picked up coffee and raw cotton also, on the return voyage to Liverpool, and brandy from Rio de Janiero, all of which should see us with good profits again of about 135% after payment of crew, supplies and cost of repairs, which I think are not substantial.*

I realise that my gambling debts this time were rather more than usual, but the truth of the matter is that, though I wished to stop, Boston would challenge me further, plying me with drink until I had lost far more than I ever intended. The man seems never to lose, yet I believed I could break his luck. Fortunate for us, with the Caterina*'s profits and soon the safe return of the* Hannah, *then the* Welldone *in September, God willing, this should be a record year, and the recovery of my IOU will as usual be easily undertaken. I trust you will also manage to buy back the phaeton from him. I shall one day purchase a team of my own.*

Be assured that your interests are well protected here, Captain Bowes being the most discreet of men. He pays the crew too well to fear that they will disclose what cargo is carried, and since he took a full load of woven Manchester cottons on the way out, no one here is aware of the second side of the triangle. Long may it be so, though I sometimes wonder if we can continue to evade the British West Africa Squadron who prowl the coast. But they must, as you know, find slaves on board to have evidence enough to prosecute, and they have only four ships to do it.

I will inform you again as soon as the funds are safe in Chester's Bank in Manchester; meanwhile I pray that you will relay my regards to Mrs Chester and to my sisters. And I remain, Sir, your humble and Most Obedient Son, Harry Chester.

Post Script. A parcel of ginger, vanilla, tobacco and snuff is on its way addressed to our agent in London, Mr Snell.

Lowering the letter to the desk, Caterina stared at the wavering candle flame to steady her thoughts, then turned to the letter again, trying to reconcile what she knew of her father with the other side of him revealed in this sheet of closely written evidence. It would damn him as a felon if it were seen, and Harry had not even the sense to write it in code. Without doubt, this was the most serious state of affairs she could have imagined, worse by far than being too poor to pay Harry's IOUs.

Her father was, in fact, more than able to pay off Harry's debts every year, even this last one, which was greater than usual. There was no reason for her to have been involved; that was the greatest deceit for which she would never forgive him.

But the counterpart of this letter from Harry uncovered a gluttony for wealth she had never suspected, a willingness to trade in human lives that was truly repellent, and to break the law in doing so. The 1807 Act of Parliament made it illegal for any ship to sail from an English port for the purposes of slave-trading, but time and again this had been ignored by merchants and ship owners who knew how unlikely it was that any of them would be caught in the act, there being so many ways of concealing such lawlessness. Last year, the penalties for slave-trading had been made more severe, and now anyone found in breach of the law could be transported to Australia for as long as fourteen years. Enough time for a man's life to be wrecked as he had wrecked others' lives, with the ensuing loss of family and the confiscation of property. The gamble was immense. How could her father truly believe that it was worth risking everything he held dear for wealth he was too miserly to share, even with his own loved ones?

Caterina was stunned. Appalled. The room was still, holding its breath. The whole house was asleep. Her mind, however, began to clear as the sediment floated to the bottom. She became logical and as cool as a lawyer holding together the pieces of a legal puzzle with many questions yet to be answered, beyond which was a festering anger and a hurt as great as any she'd ever suffered, for this was a betrayal of trust that affected them all, not only her. She owed it especially to Hannah to find out the full extent of it.

Dispassionately, she viewed the immediate options open to her.

First, she could confront her father with the letter and ask for an explanation, an idea that was dismissed even before it had formed. He would tell her it was none of her business and that the day of her wedding was no time for such matters. He would offer to tell her after the event. This was not the day for a showdown.

Then perhaps she should cancel the wedding, or postpone it until the matter was cleared up? No, she had promised not to do that. They would all want to know the reason, and that would mean exposure and ruin for them all.

Were those the only reasons not to cancel? she asked herself. Again, no. Marriage to Sir Chase was beginning to look like the only relatively secure element in her life, and she knew that she wanted him above anything, whether he was right for her or not. She could not cancel this wedding, as she had done the others.

Should she confide in her future husband, then? No, it was too risky. He might already know about her father's ships. They may have done a deal, for all she knew, a wager in which, if he should win her, he would take a share of the profits. Blackmail, in other words. Her father would bet that she could not be won. Sir Chase was experienced in winning both women and money, and her father would do anything, apparently, to keep his money out of anyone's reach. At the same time, it made sense for Sir Chase to make her father pay dearly for taking his choosy daughter off his hands. Is that what was happening? Did Sir Chase know of the slaving? Had he threatened to expose him via some complicated game using money and daughters, IOUs, wagers and time-limits? Is that why he'd forced Harry to keep on losing?

No, she would keep this disgraceful affair to herself until she could discover whether he had colluded with her father. The thought of it almost broke her heart, but she had a vow to keep about not weeping for a man's love. And she needed a clear head to solve this gargantuan problem.

Ought she to tell Hannah, though? No, her stepmother was in a delicate enough condition already, and such news would do nothing but harm.

What about Lord Rayne? No, he'd been away for so long, and was not likely to know anything she didn't know herself. She could not involve him in this business.

Aunt Amelie, then?

No, tell no one, she said to herself, firmly. Make your own enquiries, then confront Father privately when you have more facts. The whole family was at risk.

All the facts? What about his lead mines in Derbyshire? Could she lure Sir Chase up there to find out more about *exactly* what father owned? After all that deception and play-acting about his lack of funds to meet a dowry, the hardship of having a new family to support, the cramped conditions—why, he could have bought the largest house on Paradise Road for the price of Harry's gambling. *Her* price.

But from the thought of slave-trading Caterina recoiled with utter disgust. To think that her father was making himself a secret fortune at the cost of human suffering was far, far worse than the position into which he had forced her. She would come out of it alive and with a future. Slaves would not.

And what of Harry's notorious IOU? Who had it now?

Coldly, and with determination, she folded the letter and laid it upon her lap, beginning methodically to work her way through piles of bills and letters to find any piece of paper that looked like a promise to pay. With no clear idea of what an IOU looked like, it took some time before she found a scruffy note folded into four, placed at an angle in one of the pigeon-holes of the desk, obviously scribbled with the aid of some very potent alcohol. Even so, it was legible enough to be frighteningly genuine.

'Mine, I think,' Caterina whispered. 'I have a right to it, Father. If you want to know where this and Harry's letter have gone, you'll have to come looking for them, won't you?' Taking the candle, she left the room and tiptoed upstairs to bury her treasure in the secret drawer of her travelling writing-desk, which Aunt Amelie had given her only the day before yesterday. Then, lying sleepless beside Sara, she told herself repeatedly that she had made the right decisions for, with a father transported to Australia on a convict ship, Sara's chances of connecting with the Ensdales would come to nothing. It went without saying that Caterina's own sacrifice would have been useless, in that event.

On the cupboard door before her, the pretty white gown with embroidered lilies-of-the-valley hung waiting for tomorrow's marriage to the man who had stolen her heart in exchange for twenty thousand guineas. It was a very great amount for anyone to forfeit, and the details of it were yet to be discovered.

In many respects, the day that ought to have been the happiest of her life had become the most difficult, fraught with ugly questions, with assumptions, and with a revival of the anger that had recently been diverted through days and nights of fierce delight. Now this anger had returned with an added vengeance, and there were few at the wedding ceremony who failed to notice how strained were the bride's efforts at sociability.

The only time she had been able to divert those negative emotions was when they stood side by side at the altar, given away, literally, by her father, pledging to obey this wonderful man in all things. Feeling his protectiveness and his boundless vitality, she asked herself what more she could want from a man but his boldness in knowing exactly what he wanted and how to get it? Like herself. What other man would have chased down to Brighton after her, or thrown himself into the sea to bring her back, or given her the space to work out her anger and direct it towards their loving? What man could love as he did, teach her, guide her, take her every whim and mood through the most difficult days of their relationship?

She took his hand and felt the strong comforting grasp of his fingers close over hers. It was not the done thing, but he cared no more for that than she did and, as soon as the vows and rings had been exchanged, he took her hand back into his with a smile that held the most blatant look of triumph she'd ever seen.

'I have you, my lass,' he whispered.

His smile was for her alone, drawing from her a similar one that he understood the meaning of better than anyone watching. It was one of the rarest and most poignant moments of the ceremony and lasted until the vicar gave a discreet cough behind his hand.

Her father, however, was one rendered oblivious by his favourite tipple to everything except his astounding success and, when his hands were not holding a glass or plucking at his high neckcloth, they were smoothing his hair from back to front. With one eye on the expense and another on the advanced timing of it, it pleased him to host a wedding he described to his guests as select rather than small.

Since the discovery of her father's terrible secret, it was more than Caterina could do to look him in the eye with anything like the love she had held for him only last week. She still found it hard to believe what he was doing, which could ruin them all, for he'd been a kindly father, though never overindulgent. But such outrageous exploitation of others' lives sat very ill beside his demands for her to be dutiful and obedient to others' needs. Apparently, her absent brother's duties lay in a different direction.

With her usual motherly directness, Aunt Amelie took Caterina aside after the ceremony. 'Are you avoiding me?' She smiled lovingly. 'You are, aren't you? What is it, dearest? Is this so very painful for you? You seemed to be quite reconciled the other day. Has anything happened?'

Radiantly lovely in the white embroidered morning gown with ribbons fluttering from each shoulder, Caterina had not intended her anxieties to be so obvious. 'I am reconciled, Aunt Amelie. And, no, nothing has happened between us. Sir Chase will be a considerate husband, I believe.'

The colour that flooded her long neck was observed by Lady Elyot's concerned eye. 'Well, I'm glad to hear it, love. So that's not going to be a problem. Good.' She laid one gloved finger against her niece's rosy cheek. 'I'm glad. I would have been surprised to hear otherwise. You and he have a lot in common, you know.' Lady Elyot knew her niece better than anyone, and she was astute enough to see that most of her questions had been sidestepped. So she took the angry young woman into her arms and held her like the mother she had been during their years together in Richmond, thinking that if Chase Boston didn't know how to please a woman, then no one did. 'Promise me,' she whispered, 'that you'll come to me, and write, if you need help. Or advice. I'll listen to you, you know that. Promise me?'

'I promise. You've always been my confidante. I shall tell you what we're doing, and I *shall* need your advice. I shall miss you more than anyone else. My lovely writing-desk will go everywhere with me.'

'That's good. Look, here's Seton. He wants a word with you.'

Lord Rayne took the bride's hand and, with eyes that told their own private story, drank in her beauty with envy written so clearly in them that Caterina's blush hardly had time to fade.

Smiling to herself, Lady Elyot moved away to her husband.

Lord Rayne sidled Caterina away from the crowd. 'Well, my lovely Cat?' he said. 'How many hearts will you have broken today?'

'Rubbish,' she whispered.

'Badly bruised, then. I would have had you, Cat. Did you know that?'

'Hush.'

'I cannot hush. I want you to know that I *could* have offered for you, and now it's too late and I shall probably go into a slow decline. Shall I do that, just to prove how sincere I am? Shall I make you feel guilty, Lady Boston?'

'Seton, hush! You may not talk like this. Not now. You think you and I could have made a partnership, but it's not so, dearest. We could not. It has nothing to do with being too late. I've changed and so have you. But

I want you as my best friend. Say you'll be that to me, Seton, that you'll be there when I need you. Please?'

One eyebrow flicked upwards. *'When?'* he said. 'Not if?'

'Whenever I need you.'

'I shall be there. Just send for me.'

'Thank you. And find someone wonderful to marry.'

Lifting her hand, he bent his head to kiss her fingers, and the look they exchanged said all that could be said in the crowded drawing room on Paradise Road where so many eyes were upon them. 'I did,' he whispered, 'but I was too slow off the mark.'

'Wish me happiness, then?'

'Apart from myself, there is no one better for you than Chase Boston. You're two of a kind, and I wish you every happiness together.'

'That's what Aunt Amelie said, too. Thank you.'

This, she thought, from the man who had come close to breaking her heart, for whom she had wept bitter tears and vowed never to weep so again. But she *had* changed, and now she understood that those tears were for the first stirrings of a woman's love which were nothing compared to the melting fires she suffered when Chase Boston looked at her, his winnings of one evening. Seton would find a woman, or a woman would find him. He would take another mistress, perhaps. What a pity to waste time. He would make a wonderful husband and father.

There could be no further exchange as Sir Chase came to take his bride's arm. 'Lady Boston…my lord?' he said. 'Am I interrupting? I do hope so.'

'Yes,' said Lord Rayne, winking at Caterina. 'You've taken my woman again. Thank heaven you'll be out of my damned way at last. I might get a clear run now. Keep him from getting under my feet, will you, Cat?'

Laughing, Sir Chase placed an arm around his wife's waist, drawing her to him in a bold display of possessiveness. 'No need for that, whelp. As far as I'm concerned, no other woman exists. You're safe. Just get on with it.'

'Oh, I'm not a speed merchant like some I know,' Lord Rayne said, walking away. 'Positively indecent, I call it.'

His innocent but apt remark did not bring the expected smile to Caterina's face and, as Sir Chase looked down at her, he was moved to sympathise. 'We shall be away soon,' he said. 'Tell me when you're ready to leave.'

'Any time now. We must go and take our leave of Father and Hannah. Do you need to speak to him in private?'

'No, my sweet. What about?'

'Anything.'

'No, I doubt it would do much good if I did.'

She understood the reference to her father's noticeable heartiness and her shame deepened as she noticed Hannah's concern at his dependence on the brandy. 'Then let's get away from here,' she said, quietly.

'Are you all right? Did Rayne say something to upset you?'

'No. Nothing at all. I'm fine.'

'Then we'll take our leave, sweetheart. Have you said your farewells to Miss Chester?'

Caterina nodded. It had hardly been a farewell, Sara having been so immersed in her own good fortune that all the things she might have remembered to say had been somehow left aside. Her thanks had been implied, rather than spoken, her good wishes for her sister's happiness wrapped neatly into her own subjective parcel of expectations.

Attuned to his new wife's sensibilities, it had not taken Sir Chase very long to see that she was suppressing a new wave of resentment that he believed had begun to fade during their days together in Brighton. When he asked about it, she denied any cause for concern, though he did not believe the denial. When she asked him, on their drive from Richmond to London, what he knew about something called 'the triangle' that ships sailed on their return to Liverpool, he began to suspect that he knew the cause of her latest tensions, though his reply purposely betrayed no alarm, no curiosity about her reason for knowing.

'A three-sided voyage,' he told her. 'Before the Act, ships would sail from English ports down to Africa's west coast loaded with goods, and barter these goods for slaves. The second side of the triangle was to take the slaves across to the Caribbean Islands or the east coast of America, sell the slaves to owners of sugar and cotton plantations, then buy coffee, raw cotton, molasses…'

'Molasses?'

'Raw sugar. It's made into blocks of sugar, and into brandy.'

'Oh, I see.'

'Then, with a load of goods that we want in England, the ship would complete the last side of the triangle to home.'

'So now we cannot buy raw cotton and sugar any more.'

'Yes, we can. It's put the prices up, certainly, but English merchants are not allowed to use slaves as currency, as they used to do.'

'Then I wonder if the Carrs' mills in Manchester have suffered. They used to belong to Aunt Amelie's late parents, you know. The factory still prints cottons.'

'More than likely.' His interest appeared to lapse, and he did not ask where she had heard of the triangle.

Caterina's silence was as eloquent as words, and the journey to Halfmoon Street in the flashy curricle continued in a state of thoughtfulness. As a concession to the occasion, the team of chestnuts had been decorated with white ribbons that fluttered from their brow bands and cruppers, drawing waves and smiles from those they passed on the road. When Sir Chase asked her if she would like to drive, she politely excused herself. When he asked her what she was thinking about, she sighed and could not bring herself to tell him. Moments later, she asked him the same question.

'About tonight,' he said, without hesitation.

'Don't,' she whispered.

'How can I not?'

'I think…I would prefer…tonight…to be on my own, if you please.'

'All right. I understand. It's been a hectic day and there'll be plenty more nights.' He waited, but she did not respond. 'You're free now, sweetheart. Free at last. You can learn to fly. We'll do whatever you please.'

Caterina had doubts about the plural 'we' and decided to put it to the test. 'I wonder if we might go up to Buxton soon? To take a look at the house and see old friends.'

'Why not? Want to show me off, do you?' He smiled at her, then gave his attention to an oncoming stage-coach in a hurry.

'Yes,' she said. 'I do.'

'Then we'll go. Derbyshire is beautiful in May.'

'You know Derbyshire?'

'Very well indeed. We'll get this weekend out of the way, then we'll make your purchases, then we'll pack and go. We have no need to return to Richmond unless you wish it, now we have Signor Cantoni with us. Is there anything you need to pick up?'

Her hesitation was only slight, but he noticed it. 'No,' she said. 'I have all I need, thank you.'

'Then we shall waste no more time there.'

If her father wanted to ask if she knew anything about the missing papers, she thought, he would have to wait. If only she could discover more about Sir Chase's part in all this. The questions gave her no respite, for it seemed that just as she had begun to learn acceptance of one problem, another even greater one had come to take its place.

Just off Picadilly, Sir Chase's well-proportioned house on Halfmoon Street was tall, white, terraced and as elegant as Caterina had imagined, in style very like the one on Paradise Road, with servants' quarters below and a further four floors of spacious living rooms above. Iron railings painted black and gold, a bright red door with a fanlight above, a brass knocker in the shape of a stirrup, an iron shoe-scraper and three newly scrubbed steps led them past the bowing bald-headed butler into a high white hallway lined with the dusky autumnal pink of Persian rugs. On one wall hung a barometer, opposite which a tallcase clock stood quietly ticking, showing the phases of the moon above its dial to anyone who cared to know.

'Your new London home,' he said, leading her by the hand into the pale green panelled salon at the front. 'I've had no time to change anything, but if it's not to your taste we'll find one that is.'

'It's charming,' she said. 'I've been thinking.'

'Yes?'

'That now I have a husband—' like it or not, she almost added '—I ought to know something about him. If anyone were to ask me, I shall not have much to tell them. I don't even know for certain how old you are. Oh…*what* a handsome piano.'

He had led her through double doors into a large adjoining room where long sash windows looked out onto a long narrow plot of apple trees in full bloom. A grand piano of polished rosewood was reflected in the oak floor, and a tidy pile of music lay at one side as if waiting for the owner's return.

'A fairly recent purchase,' he said. 'Will it do to practise on?'

Speechless with sudden emotion, she nodded into the back of her hand. 'Yes, indeed it will. Signor Cantoni and the others will be arriving soon. Will he have his own bedroom?'

'Certainly. I have plenty of rooms, and he'll be treated as one of the family. I'll show them to you, but first…' Taking her into his arms, he nudged her face upwards so that he could see into her eyes, obliging her to yield up all the fears and hidden accusations for him to see, if not hear. 'First,' he said, 'we must come to an understanding. Yes, I know what you think, my beauty, that now I've won my wager I shall go my own way and leave you to make shift for yourself. Well, that's *not* what will happen. There are things on your mind that only you can resolve in your own time, and I shall do what I can to help. It's in my best interests, isn't it?'

'I don't know. Is it?'

'Of course it is, my girl. I want all of you, Caterina, not only your companionship, but your respect and love, too. You thought not to hear that word from me so soon? Eh? Well, I was never one for half-measures.'

That much was obvious. She was bound to smile.

'There. A smile at last. But if you're not willing to take me back into your bed, that's a price I have to pay for the unseemly haste, and I shall wait until you are. There's a lot to find out about each other, my beauty. Such a lot has happened to us, very quickly. Perhaps too quickly. But now we can take one day at a time and enjoy each other as we did at Brighton. You did, didn't you?'

'Yes, I did.'

'And the nights?'

'Yes, and the nights.'

'And now you're continuing the protest, even though it hurts? Is that it?'

'It's all I can think of.'

'Then you have only to say when your angers have gone, and we can carry on where we left off. Is that agreed?'

She knew it was a dangerous game she was playing. Take too long to discover how deeply he was implicated in her father's illegal affairs and he might grow tired of waiting. He was understanding, but what man could be expected to be so obliging when his rights were at stake?

'You are not supposed to be so cooperative,' she said. 'How am I to thwart you when you're so tolerant?'

His reply to that was spontaneous and suitably masculine, the hard pull of his arms bending her to him, his expression anything but long-suffering. 'Because, my fierce one, I've just spent a fortune to get you here, protesting all the way, and I'm not about to lose you through impatience. If there's one thing gambling has taught me, it's how to play a patient waiting game and not to give up.' The deep voice was husky with desire, and if Caterina had thought he cared little about her protest, she now realised how wrong she was. He cared very much indeed.

His head bent to hers, taking the kiss she'd intended to deny him, a kiss of three days' waiting that told her explicitly about his need of her, a kiss that left her dizzy and weak. Breathless, instantly aroused, she had to cling to him to keep her balance.

It was all she could do then not to give in, to forget the hurt of deception, the anger of being used. But the memory of her father's smug expression as he shook Sir Chase's hand earlier, wishing them both a speedy journey to wherever they were going, hardened her heart and strengthened her resolve to discover the extent of his treachery. As Sir Chase had said, the two of them had much to find out, but meanwhile she could not help but assume that this business was more complicated than a wager.

Having earlier decided on a strategy of unpredictability in her lovemaking, it had never been her intention until now to take it to the limit, denying him her bed altogether. Even now, her wish to spend that first night alone collapsed after the first hour of lying sleepless in her large comfortable bed, and she had eventually gone to the door of his room, tapped lightly upon it and walked in, standing outside the circle of light from the oil-lamp beside his bed. He was reading.

The book was lowered and he was on his feet in one bound, coming to meet her without a trace of complacency, holding out his hands, leading her towards the bed, lifting the covers and arranging them round her as she lay her head on the pillow, appalled by her own temerity.

Without explanation, he seemed to know both what she wanted and what she didn't want, and the night spent in his arms was chaste in every respect, comforting them both after their nights apart, as well as being a test of his personal discipline, which was extraordinary for a man with a desirable bride.

They had talked all this evening through dinner and beyond, and because Signor Cantoni had been invited to join them, the conversation made it easy for Caterina to discover more about her remarkable husband by means of small prompts rather than by questions that revealed her ignorance. They talked of mutual acquaintances, of music, of travel on the continent and the wonders of Italy, of the Peninsular War, politics, the Prince Regent's problems, life in the army, of architecture and the latest crop of landscape gardeners. And if Signor Cantoni thought it unusual for a singing teacher to be invited to a newly-weds' private dinner, his natural sensitivity and perfect manners forbade him to mention it.

Caterina was very fond of him. His own voice was a remarkable instrument, ranging from falsetto when he was amused down to a gravelly bass when seriously rambling, his features equally supple and expressive, his hands the same, describing words in the air. Thick dark hair made him look like a younger version of Beethoven without the scowl, and his willing acceptance of Sir Chase's offer meant that, for the first time since leaving Italy, he had a permanent home and a generous fixed salary. Though he favoured himself, he had not quite decided which of them was the most fortunate.

The conversation that evening also revealed that Sir

Chase was one of the exclusive Society of Dilettanti, men whose main qualification, apart from wealth, was a patronage of the arts. According to some sceptics, the other qualifications were having been to Italy and getting drunk. None of this surprised Caterina greatly, having observed the paintings on her husband's walls by the popular Mr Turner, by Sir Joshua Reynolds and Richard Wilson, by an up-and-coming watercolourist named John Sell Cotman, by Stubbs (horses, of course) and an oil by Thomas Lawrence, who had painted Aunt Amelie's portrait.

Sir Chase's membership of the Royal Society was now much in evidence from the number of scientific instruments displayed all over the house on walls and tables, all of which he knew how to use. The scholarly side of her husband, Caterina decided, was less gossip worthy than his extrovert side, which was why news of his public affairs travelled faster than that of private ones. But as for any suggestion of slave-trading, merchanting or ship-owning, there was as little indication as for any other money-making venture, including the famed gambling, for which she needed no more evidence than she already had.

After last night's forgivable lapse of purpose, she half-expected some comment from him about her lack of determination but, apart from lifting the curls from the back of her neck in one large fist, which held her very securely to the spot, and planting a soft kiss below them, he said nothing as he held the door for her to return to her own room. She felt the exciting sting of his grasp for quite some time afterwards.

One who saw nothing unusual in two newly-weds sharing the first days of their marriage with others was the sixth Duke of Devonshire who greeted them at Chiswick House that same day as if they'd been married for years. Since he was himself a mere twenty-two years old and as far from matrimony as he would ever be, this was perhaps to be expected, being sophisticated in so many areas, but naïve in matters of romance. A well-known London courtesan had only recently complained that he had given her two old wedding rings as a gift which she had passed on to her butler. His charm and perfect manners, however, were reason enough for him to be a favourite with everyone. An added reason was his generous hospitality at his many large establishments.

Known as Hart to friends and family from his previous title of Marquess of Hartington, the Duke had inherited his late father's wealth only one year ago and had just begun to take stock of his legacy, including some crippling debts that appeared to have had no noticeable effect upon his lavish spending. Parties and entertaining were his love, Chiswick being especially well placed on the outskirts of London for smaller select gatherings of a more artistic nature, which is why he had invited Caterina to sing for him at one of them.

With obvious delight that two of his friends had arrived together, he welcomed them even before their town coach had come to a halt below the impressive steps of his 'villa', as he liked to call it. Introduced to the Duke for the first time, Signor Cantoni was treated to a welcome in his own language where, also for the first time, Caterina heard her husband join in with perfect fluency. Every day, she thought, brought a new revelation.

They went with the tall young man with the affable countenance into the grand house built in the style of an Italian villa and set in acres of perfectly laid gardens. His personal musicians, he told Caterina, were at her entire disposal. Taking them across marble floors past statues and busts, stone friezes filched from ancient Greece and plaster walls removed from Pompeii, they entered the airy music room beneath the dome where the great Frederick Handel himself had performed more than once.

But as so often happened, no sooner were the rich mellow tones of Caterina's voice picked up from every polished surface than a slow trickle of listeners flowed on tiptoe towards the source, their ears straining to catch every luscious sound, and when the two artistes turned to look, the crowd applauded the rehearsal as if it had been a performance.

Laughing, Caterina took a bow. 'Well, now, there's no more to look forward to,' she said. 'What a pity.'

There were several faces she recognised who came forward with smiles of welcome and congratulations for a marriage none of them had anticipated, though they knew Sir Chase Boston well. Who did not?

One of them was their mutual friend George Brummell who, with typical understatement, good-humouredly took Sir Chase to task. 'Dashed if I can tolerate this habit of yours any longer, Chase, of snatching the goods before the rest of us can get a look in. I was about to saunter over to Richmond to claim the heavenly Miss Caterina Chester for myself and, but for a pressing engagement with my coat-tailor, I'd have done so. When did you marry him, Miss Chester?'

'Yesterday, Mr Brummell.'

'There you are, then. It was yesterday I was all set to claim you. Too bad of you, Chase. Too bad.' Moving his quizzing glass up and down Sir Chase's large frame, he halted its progress at the cravat. 'Tch!' he remarked. 'A drink, somebody, before I call this coxcomb out.'

A liveried servant appeared bearing a silver tray of cut-glass beakers and a bowl of fruit punch, placing it at a small table by Sir Chase's side. His skin was the colour of polished ebony, his solemn face exceedingly handsome, his hair like astrakhan. Sir Chase thanked him; the man bowed and left. Others were chatting and laughing too loudly to notice, but Caterina did, and when she and Brummell sauntered to a bench with their drinks, it was she who remarked that she'd not expected the Duke to employ black servants, on principle.

'On what principle, my dear Lady Boston?' said Brummell. 'The man's not a slave, he's on the same footing as any other servant. Everyone employs them nowadays, even if only to show their liberal-mindedness.'

'Do you, Mr Brummell?'

'Lord, no. I can't afford any more servants. But Chase does.'

'I beg your pardon?'

Laconically, he turned to her wide eyes to search for more behind the amazement. 'Ah, I see. You've hardly had time to find out these details yet, I take it. Why is the man always in such a blinding hurry, I wonder?' His eyes turned towards the assembly, resting upon the finely proportioned figure before he continued. 'Somewhere, my dear, your lusty husband employs a negro woman; if not in London, she's safely tucked away in one of his other places. Oh, dear, don't look like that, child. She's a servant, that's all. He'll tell you, if you ask him. He's coming over.'

'No, don't mention it, *please*. I'll ask him in my own time.'

'Very well. Ah... Chase, just asking your bride what your plans are. Will you be at Prinny's "do" next weekend?'

'No,' said Sir Chase, noting Caterina's frown. 'If fortune favours us, we shall be several hundred miles away.'

The conversation flowed gently without Brummell caring too deeply about the seeds of mistrust he had just scattered over the new Lady Boston's fertile imagination, which already had begun to nurture all kinds of reasons why her husband would employ a negress in his service unless he had bought her or, worse, unless she was his mistress. That there could be a dozen other reasons for the woman's existence in his household did not occur to her, primarily because she was looking for some evidence that would fit her vague theory about his duplicity. Why else would he keep a beautiful young negress hidden away unless he wanted to avoid questions being asked? Was he, like her father, involved in the slaving racket? Or was he an abolitionist out to take revenge on her father, to ruin him with blackmail or exposure? Was she being made to play some bizarre part in this power game?

With a supreme effort of will, she pushed the information to the back of her mind during her performance that evening so well that none of the guests had the slightest inkling about her newest fears growing like hothouse plants, feeding off what remained of her resentments. Her contribution to the musical evening was so well received that she and Signor Cantoni were asked for several encores until Sir Chase drew her away for some refreshments.

Still nursing serious doubts about him, Caterina nevertheless found it impossible to conceal the delight she felt at being by his side, as his wife, the one he'd chosen and paid a fortune for, as he'd reminded her only recently. Conveniently, she chose not to recall his use of the word 'love'.

Sir Chase's past mistresses concerned her very little. What concerned her now was the possibility of an existing mistress, even if she were a servant, which would be quite unacceptable, and heartbreaking. It was a subject she had never spoken of, nor was any wife expected to pay any attention to her husband's *affaires,* let alone discuss them with him. She was not supposed to care enough for that.

To balance Brummell's cynical information, Caterina discovered yet more about her husband's abilities, for their host was eager to involve his guests in dancing the quadrille, which Sir Chase had already mastered, as Caterina had. Between the envious looks of the assembly, they executed the complicated moves like a dancing master and his best pupil—a caper merchant, he laughingly called himself after the compliments. Then there was the waltz, for which the Duke held morning classes at his Burlington House, shockingly improper to dance with anyone except one's nearest and dearest, or under the strictest supervision.

But to waltz in the arms of Sir Chase Boston was a fantasy that women took to their dreams, for here was no sharing of partners but bodies pressed close, the woman arching against the man's supporting arm, her own arms held wide and raised in surrender. That night, in their adjoining rooms at Chiswick House, they lay alone and thinking of the waltz and how they needed each other, but aware that the chasm between them was widening instead of narrowing. She did not go to his room, and he did not visit hers.

* * *

Had he not promised her a few days' shopping in London before heading northwards to Derbyshire, Sir Chase would have taken her away immediately from the claustrophobic public scrutiny where his own and Caterina's experiences of the marriage-mart were well documented and regarded with some healthy scepticism.

George Brummell and he had known each other since their Eton days, had been in the same regiment and shared many an escapade and, although he liked much about the man, there was a prickly side of which to beware when George envied something he could, with more effort and commitment, have got for himself. His remarks concerning Caterina had not been quite as innocent as they appeared, and Chase had little doubt that the ensuing coolness she had shown when no one else observed was a direct result of something Brummell had said to her. He would have liked to know what it was.

The more positive result of their stay at Chiswick House was an invitation to stay with the Duke at another of his homes, Chatsworth House, for as long as they wished while they were in Derbyshire. It was a prospect that pleased Caterina well, giving Chase an extra incentive to set a day for the first stage of their journey. The sooner he could be alone with her, the better it would be for both of them.

She and Sir Chase were emerging together from Jackson's Habit Warehouse in Covent Garden, about to climb aboard the high-perch phaeton, when Caterina felt Sir Chase's attention being drawn to a group of gawping young dandies on the opposite side of Tavistock Street. He would normally have ignored them but, from his delay, she saw that one of them had been recognised. Without cutting the fellow, it was too late for them to escape.

'Oh no,' Sir Chase muttered. 'Look who it is. Can you believe it?'

Caterina could. Even without the five-storey neckcloth, the bee-striped waistcoat, the brilliant blue long-tailed coat with the exaggerated lapels like wings and the tight pantaloons, his mincing walk alone would have been enough to proclaim him a peep-o'-day boy. With winks and waves he was making it clear to his cronies that he knew the owner of the raffish phaeton and his stylish lady, and that he would remind them of it. The lady was, after all, a relation.

Neither of them had bargained for the untimely interference of yet another face from the past in the unwelcome dazzling form of Mr Tam Elwick, younger brother of Hannah, née Elwick. Caterina had heard news of his return after years of travel, but she had hoped it would be some time before they met again, for Tam's irresponsible behaviour had once caused her some problems.

The foppish young man tripped daintily, flashing unnecessary spurs at each step, swinging a silver-topped cane and lifting a colossal bucket-shaped hat off his head, swinging it in a wide arc to reveal a mass of nut-brown curls. The years, Caterina thought, had not dealt too kindly with him since their last meeting, for now Tam had learned to smirk instead of sporting that memorable mischievous smile when he had been twenty-one and she an impressionable seventeen.

'Tamworth Elwick at your service,' he reminded them, bowing stiffly as if he might be wearing a corset. 'How d'ye do, Cat? Your servant, Boston old chap. Well met, eh?' The bucket was replaced at exactly the correct angle.

'Sir Chase and Lady Boston are very well, thank you, Elwick,' said the deep voice in a singular display of rank. He had not wanted even the remotest relationship with this upstart, for though their parents were near-neighbours at Mortlake, the sons had nothing else in common worthy of first-name familiarity.

'Ah...er...oh, yes. The *wedding.*' Tam giggled. 'Of course. Well, congratulations to both of you. Yes, indeed, *what* an achievement, eh? Married, after all that, my lady. Must try to keep up with events, now I'm back, mustn't I?'

'Are you back at Mortlake, then? Or staying in London? I'm glad to see you're no worse for your Grand Tour,' said Caterina, smoothly.

With typical drama, he rolled bloodshot eyes. 'Oh, not the Grand Tour exactly,' he said. 'What a bore! I was dragged round the whole island of Great Britain rather like Defoe, but even further. Father thought it was too dangerous to traipse across the water. He didn't want me *killed,* you see, only out of the way. I don't suppose your elite regiment caught a boat either, did it, *Sir* Chase?' Neither of them were intended to miss the tone of bitterness at his father's harsh treatment when he had longed to join the army, to prove himself as a dashing daredevil of a man like Boston.

'Oh, I did some traipsing through Europe a few times. As you see, I'm still alive to tell the tale,' Sir Chase replied with a noticeable lack of sympathy.

Tam would have given much to adopt the same deeply cultured bored tone of one who'd seen the world, but didn't care who knew about it. 'So what are you two up to? Living in London, are you? Bit different from those heady days in Bath, eh, Cat? Er...Lady Boston?' There was now a malicious glint in his eye after the snub, and the questions he fired like shots were not intended to be answered. 'Remember? Had 'em all on the run, didn't we? What? You and Seton, or must I use *his* title now? What a fiasco that was, and your father chasing all over the countryside after you, and then your so-broken heart to mend. Oh, what a to-do, eh?'

'I believe your friends are waiting for you,' said Sir Chase. 'It's been a pleasure meeting you again. Please give our regards to your parents when you return to Mortlake.'

'Oh, but Lady Boston and I have so many pleasant memories to share,' the persistent man said, stepping between the two of them with almost suicidal imprudence, 'of the times when she and I would…'

But here his determination was no match for Sir Chase's. Finding an iron fist tightly bunching the high neckcloth beneath his chin, Tam Elwick was propelled forcibly backwards in an ungainly stagger until, pressed hard against the wall, his eyes began to protrude rather unpleasantly. Held there for a count of five, not a word was wasted on him until, with an attempt to nod his head, he gained his release. He gasped, fumbled at his very disturbed throat and walked away to rejoin his friends with rather less affectation than before.

Caterina could have used the ugly situation to explain what Tam Elwick had been referring to, or to challenge Sir Chase about his jealous response when there was no need. Which may have been what a more incautious woman would have done. But she said nothing as they drove home through London's streets, nor did Sir Chase demand to know more about the pointed reference to Lord Rayne and the broken heart in Bath, and she could only guess whether that was due to a lack of interest or to his anger. Unfortunately, she did not know him well enough to risk finding out.

Chapter Seven

The visitor to Halfmoon Street arrived as Sir Chase was just about to retire for the night. Crossing the hall, he placed the silver candlestick on the table and waited to see who was being shown in. 'Sete?' he said. 'What brings you here?'

He had known Lord Rayne for many years, and still the only way he could tell when his friend had been drinking heavily was by the slow and very precise way of speaking, as if he was delivering a lecture.

Lord Rayne was, in fact, intending to deliver a lecture. 'A word or two…if I may…in private,' he said, ponderously. 'Miss Chester gone up, has she?'

Sir Chase didn't bother to correct him. 'Yes. Did you want to…?'

'No…er…no! Indeed, I do not. I have not come here to upset *her.*' As usual, his appearance was faultless, but his host detected more than a whiff of tobacco smoke and spirits on his clothes as the door closed.

'Thank you for the warning. In here, if you will.' Taking up the candlestick, he led Lord Rayne into the salon and waited for the butler to disappear. 'Will you take a brandy? A glass of wine? *Do* sit down, Sete. It can't be all that bad, can it?' Crossing over to a sideboard, he poured two glasses of brandy, puzzled by Seton's unusual displeasure.

'Well, you may not think so,' snapped Lord Rayne, 'but I think it is as bad a thing as ever I have heard, and I have heard a few in my life. How you have the gall to enter into an arrangement like that with Stephen Chester's son, of all people, when you must know he is unable to stump up the bronze, is more than I can—'

'Sete, for pity's sake, man! What the devil are you talking about? Look, drink this and *sit down* before you forget where your backside is. Where've you been, White's?'

'No, of course not. They would not allow Tam Elwick's sort in there.'

'What does he have to do with it?'

'Do with what?'

'What you've come here to tell me.'

Lord Rayne sat down rather heavily upon a long settee, took the glass from his friend and gulped down the amber contents in one go. 'I have…argh!…I have come here, Boston, old chap, to tell you exactly what I think of you. That's what.'

'Right. But before you do, tell me where you've been, and with whom.'

'Timson's Club. Met Tam Elwick there. Wished I had not gone.'

'I'll bet you did. Lost a lot of pennies, did you?'

'I did not lose. I won, from that pinheaded little sapskull. So then he was peevish. So he told me he was there when you fleeced Stephen Chester's ninnyhammer of a son for twenty grand, and by my reckoning that was a short time before you made an offer for the hand of Stephen Chester's eldest daughter, Miss Cat—'

'Yes. And so? Is there a law against it?'

'Against what?'

'Offering for a woman.'

'For *that* woman, yes, I should think there ought to be, if there is not one already. Is there?'

'No, Sete. So what's the problem, exactly?'

Lord Rayne frowned, staring morosely into his empty glass. 'The problem?' he said. 'Oh, yes. Well, you must have known Chester's son could not honour his debt. *Did* you know?'

'I suspected it. In fact, Sete, I didn't much care whether *he* could or not. I knew he'd go to his father with it.'

'So then you made a beeline for the father, knowing that he couldn't meet it either? So then you offered to take his daughter instead? Now I know why Cat was so angry with you at the Ensdales' house party. She did not care for your scheme, did she? She did not wish to become Lady Boston because you and her brandy-soaked papa between you have forced her into a marriage she did not want. Have you not?'

'Another drink?'

Lord Rayne lifted his glass, shakily. 'Small one. You think I'm bosky, but I ain't. Jober as a sudge. Thankee.' He took the drink. 'And I have come here to rescue her. You cannot take a woman in such stance…cum…scances, Chase. Not even you can do that.'

Impassively, Sir Chase seated himself upon the chair by the wall, his eyes giving away nothing in the shadowy room, but watching his friend like a hawk. 'And what were you to each other?' he asked, quietly. 'You had an *affaire* of the heart, I believe?'

'I thought I had told you all that, once.'

'Tell me again. About Bath. What happened in Bath, Sete?'

'Did I not tell you?'

'Only that Caterina once made a run for it. Was that from you?'

'To me, not *from* me. All a mistake.'

'I see. She was in love with you, then.'

'Mm...m. Should not be talking about this. Not done, old man.'

'I'm her husband. I need to know.'

'Perhaps, but I am not so foxed that I rattle like an empty can, Chase. I would like to be able to tell you that we were lovers, but that would not be true. However, I do not intend to stand by and see her hurt. I have told Miss Chester that she must send for me whenever she needs help.'

'And has she sent for you?'

'Eh? No, I have sent for myself. She needs rescuing.'

'From me.' It was more of a statement than a question.

'Yes, from you. You cannot take a woman in this way. I have told you.'

'So you have. But am I to understand that she would have accepted you if I'd not insisted she accept me instead?'

'I doubt it. Doubt it very much. Told me so.'

'Told you what, exactly?'

'That we would not suit. Friends, she said. To come when I need her. Besides, I have seen how she looks at you. You know how women look.'

'So you've come to rescue her even though you think she may not be so very averse to the idea of being my wife?'

Lord Rayne was truly nonplussed. 'Eh?' he said.

His friend stifled a yawn. 'Would you like me to find you a bed, Sete? Or I can take you home, if you prefer?'

'What I want,' said Lord Rayne, catching the yawn with one of his own, 'is Miss Caterina Chester. I cannot *think* why I did not realise it sooner.'

'You were away, Sete.'

'So were you, but that didn't hold you back, did it? This time, I think I shall plant you a facer, Chase. You deserve it.'

Sir Chase smiled, recalling Caterina's resistance, then her amazing capitulation. 'If you remember, you once said that all you wanted was Caterina's happiness.'

'Then I must have been too sober to express myself properly. What I meant was that I want *my* happiness. She is everything I want, Chase.'

'She's everything I want, too, old man, so if you're thinking I've done a straight deal with her father, think again. There's more to it than that. Much more.' He would have continued, but now Seton's head had begun to droop towards his glass, his eyelids already closing. 'And I shall take Lady Boston,' Sir Chase whispered, 'well away from you, my besotted friend, and well away from Brummell and Elwick and the wagging tongues of helpful relatives, pregnant stepmothers and especially from inebriated fathers who are trying to prove something to the world. Come on, my lad. Sleep it off. It's not like you to get all maudlin over a woman.'

Removing the glass from Lord Rayne's loose fingers, he eased the broad shoulders back against the scrolled end of the settee, swinging his booted legs up on to the other end. Then he reached over to the wall and tugged upon the bell-pull. When his valet arrived, he issued compassionate instructions for Lord Rayne's comfort, including the use of a coach at dawn to convey him to his parents' grand house in Berkeley Square.

On the second landing, he paused outside the door of Caterina's bedroom, opened it and went quietly inside so as not to wake her. Within the curtained bed she was sound asleep, sprawled across the sheets with one arm outstretched, reaching into his space. For a few moments he stood watching her, feasting his eyes upon the undulations of hip, waist and breast, on her long slender limbs, the mop of tousled curls, the fringe of dark lashes upon her cheek. Then, taking the edge of the sheet, he pulled it upwards to cover her shoulders and, removing the candle, tiptoed away to his own room. 'Not yours, Seton my friend. Go and do your Saint George act somewhere else. It's me she needs, not you. And you *are* beginning to get under my hooves, as you predicted,' he said to no one in particular. 'What did you intend to take place down at Brighton, I wonder?'

Inebriated or not, it took Stephen Chester only an hour or two to discover the loss of two very important documents from his new and expensive walnut desk. For the next two days he turned his study inside out, thinking that, in the excitement of Caterina's wedding, he might have placed them somewhere so safe as to be lost for ever. As he was unable to ask his wife, his temper grew more and more frayed until it was with guilty relief that Hannah accepted his announcement that he would be going into town that day. Being overcome by morning sickness, she did not bother to question why he had taken his valet and a portmanteau of clothes so, when he failed to return that evening, she assumed he would be staying overnight at his club.

In fact, he had gone directly to Halfmoon Street, intending to accuse Sir Chase of the theft of documents of massive significance which he was by now certain would be used to set him up for something much worse than a mere debt. The incriminating evidence that his stupid hare-brained son had spelled out in that letter was alone enough to give a man nightmares, and now all the conversations he'd had with Boston pointed to the distinct possibility that he had it in his power to ruin him.

Looking back through a mind fuddled with alcohol, he could see how his own story of shortage of funds and daughterly stubbornness, which he believed had been swallowed, had been his own undoing. The man had been laughing at him, plotting his downfall, taking his daughter *and* the IOU, which he would now insist on being honoured if he wanted his letter back. Now the man would know that Harry was abusing a position of trust in the Liverpool Customs House, placing a noose firmly around his neck, too.

As it turned out, Chester's arrival at Halfmoon Street was half a day too late, the master and mistress having that very morning departed for the north. And, no, the butler did not expect their return for some weeks.

'Where've they gone?' said Chester, irritably pulling at his cravat.

'I believe Sir Chase and Lady Boston intend to stay in Derbyshire, sir.'

'They can't get there in one day, surely?'

'No, sir. They'll be stopping.'

'Where?'

The dignified butler scarcely blinked at the brusqueness. Whatever the father-in-law intended, he was sure Sir Chase would be able to deal with it. 'I heard him mention Ampthill, sir.'

'Ampthill?' Chester echoed. 'Where's that?'

'In Bedfordshire, sir. A delightful little—'

'Yes…thank you!' Chester was already halfway through the red door, down the steps and rocking the shabby town coach as he leapt on to the worn leather seat. 'Great North Road!' he snapped. 'And look sharp about it.'

In contrast to her father's desperate haste, Caterina's comfortable journey was a more leisurely affair in the crane-neck travelling coach large enough to carry leather trunks besides. In a smaller coach that followed them with more luggage, Millie, Signor Cantoni and Pearson, Sir Chase's valet, were getting to know each other rather well.

Caterina had made no objection to her husband's suggestion that they should leave London promptly, and it had taken her and Millie no time at all to pack and be ready by midday, time enough to reach Ampthill before dinner. Sir Chase's mother, Lady FitzSimmon, owned a cottage there, a gift built in her birthplace by Sir Reginald as a reward for marrying him. To Caterina's amusement, the so-called cottage was a mock-Tudor mansion set in beautiful parkland on the outskirts of an attractive village within sight of St Catherine's Cross, a memorial to Queen Catherine of Aragon, who had waited in the nearby castle while her husband, King Henry VIII, divorced her.

The house, fully staffed, was hung with ancient tapestries and Lady FitzSimmons's ancestral portraits, heavily beamed above, windows twinkling with leaded glass, walls shiny with oak panelling, brass and pewter everywhere, stone floored and filled with hefty tables and Jacobean chairs no more out of date than double garden-windows that opened like doors or kitchens that held every modern device.

The two grand pianos in the long gallery were more than Caterina could have dreamed of and, if she had been more than usually preoccupied with her own private concerns until then, this seemed devised to lift her spirits as nothing else could have done. That evening, after a meal of young vegetables from the garden and local lamb with mint, she and Sir Chase and Signor Cantoni played duets and trios, singing them, too, laughing like children at mistakes, losing themselves as the light dwindled and the servants tiptoed in with candles to prolong the music to which they had all secretly been listening.

At the door of her mock-medieval bedroom, Caterina's mood had risen to such pleasurable heights that it seemed quite natural for her to cling to Sir Chase just a little longer than the night before, to accept his kisses with her own fervour and to convey the message, without realising it, that her need of him was as strong as ever. Sir Chase was in no way disappointed.

But neither of them could have known that, at about the same time, her troubled father was stumbling from his battered coach that had just pulled into the courtyard of the White Hart at Ampthill. After miles of being shaken like a string puppet, Stephen Chester's bad temper was shaken even more by his enquiries about Sir Chase and Lady Boston. There was no one of that name staying at the coaching inn, nor did anyone by the name of Boston own any property in the village.

Immediately after an early breakfast they were off again, heading north-westwards to reach Northampton by mid-morning where they ate and refreshed themselves at the Chequers, close by Allhallowes Church. Then on for the longest stretch through Rothwell and Market Harborough to the village of Wigston Magna, just south of Leicester.

'We never came this way when we travelled down from Buxton,' said Caterina. She did not mind the change of route, for Sir Chase usually had very sound reasons for whatever he did and, losing her penchant for confrontations, she found it quite pleasant to accept whatever surprises he had in store for her. It was getting late and the horses were tiring. She, on the other hand, lounged inelegantly in the crook of her husband's arm with his hand spread across her midriff over the peach-coloured spencer. Her hat had been abandoned long since, and her feet were wedged into a corner of the velvet seat.

'You wouldn't,' he said. 'This place is barely on the map. I don't think we've been through a toll-gate for miles.'

'Another of your mama's houses?'

'Not this time. We'll pay a visit to some old friends of mine, Thomas and Alice Tolby. He's a Leicester merchant. A hosier.'

'Ah, stockings. He'll be successful, I suppose.'

'Take a look for yourself, my lady.'

They had been travelling through wooded slopes and pasture land where cows stood in the shade or wallowed knee-deep in streams but, as the horses slowed to a walk, thatched cottages appeared on the fringe of the village, a mill and a pond with ducks, a small church and, through wrought-iron gates, a drive leading to an imposing early Georgian house, the home of one of Leicester's wealthiest merchants dealing in the town's main product. Northampton made shoes, Leicester made hosiery.

As a personal friend of Sir Chase, Thomas Tolby was delighted by the unexpected visit and by the chance to meet the new bride. A lively, eloquent man, he was tall and sandy-haired with every outward sign of prosperity in his well-cut sober dress, and if he was amazed by his friend's plunge into wedlock after all the active bachelor years, he was too polite to let it show. His wife, a lady of generous nature and proportions, could not contain her excitement at the prospect of entertaining them, even though their stay was to be brief.

Theirs was a stylish three-storey house built of mellow brick topped with slates of a deeper lichen-covered orange, and it was only to be expected that, inside, the merchant and his jolly wife should have no inhibitions about displaying what they had earned. Restraint was not a concept they entertained, the high ceilings providing them with more space in which to cram their paintings, ormulu mirrors, urns and showcases, tables of every shape and size and dressers loaded with silverware and Sèvres china.

Naturally, for one so prosperous, there was no aspect of commerce about which Mr Tolby was unfamiliar. It was his duty, he told his guests, to know what was going on, even if it was not going on in his neck of the woods. 'Dissent,' he told them at dinner.

Caterina would rather have settled for a less controversial topic over a meal as sumptuous as the one prepared by Alice Tolby, but she was not in a position to object.

'Yes, dissenters,' he emphasised, shovelling into his mouth a forkful of slithery sweetbreads. 'Luddites, they're calling themselves. Terrible damage they're doing. Fires, break-ins, wrecking machinery and riots. That's what the Prime Minister's assassination was all about, you know, Chase. Protests against the high price of food and low wages. Oh, yes—' he gulped down another forkful '—the murderer may well have been insane, as they say, but perhaps the poor devil had had enough of such things, huge losses, factories and men's livelihoods going down the pan.'

'Thomas…please!'

'Beg pardon, m'dear.' He laid his fork down, glaring with menace at the last reprieved sweetbread. 'It's not happening to my business, I need hardly say. I pay the best prices and I don't sell short, Chase. You know me.'

Sir Chase nodded.

'But it's happening all over the country. Ten years of bad harvests and food doubling in price, machines taking over from handworkers. What does the government expect when someone takes a shot at the man at the top? Up here in Leicestershire, the men are calling the murderer a martyr, and they've been rioting for years to get some help, as they have everywhere up north. Manchester alone has lost some of its biggest mills due to fires and riots in the past few months, not to mention all-out strikes. There are few mill owners who can survive that kind of punishment.'

'Cotton mills, Mr Tolby?'

'That's right, Lady Boston. Somebody's losing a lot of money up there.' He looked round the table. 'Signor Cantoni, sir. Will you try a little roast salmon from our own stretch of the river?'

Signor Cantoni dabbed gently at his lips with his napkin, smiling his refusal. He had known Caterina long enough to know that her aunt, Lady Elyot, was a daughter of the Manchester Carr dynasty, owners of one of the two largest cotton-printing mills. He knew what the next question would be.

'The spinning mills, Mr Tolby? Or the printing mills?'

From the head of the table, Thomas Tolby leaned towards Caterina as if he were about to address a meeting of traders. 'Well, you know, it makes very little difference whether they spin it, weave it or print it. If *one* goes out of action, they *all* do, you see? Raw cotton imported through Liverpool can't be processed until the machines are repaired and the men get back to work. Ship owners can't sell the stuff. It'll sit in the warehouses until they can get rid of it, and let's hope they're insured.'

'And if they're not?'

He pulled a wry face. 'If they're not, Lady Boston, they're fools that deserve all they get. Now, Alice, my love, is it time this cover was removed?'

If Stephen Chester had heard this damning opinion as he bumped and jolted wearily into the town of Leicester at about the same time as his daughter was eating her delicious pineapple flummery, he would probably have wondered why, after such apparent good fortune, things had begun to turn against him. He had, after all, just shipped the first of three valuable cargoes of raw cotton into Liverpool expecting to sell it to the highest bidder.

Having failed to hear any mention of Sir Chase Boston's equipage at any of the coaching inns, he had given up all hope of finding them in that area. He would have to chase up to Buxton behind or ahead of them if he wanted to catch the man before he could do any harm with the stolen papers. He prayed that Sir Chase would not tell Caterina about what he'd discovered, for that would set her even more against him, her father.

* * *

Caterina's feelings towards her father, however, were vacillating rather strangely between extreme disaffection and concern, for she had not needed to ask any more questions about cotton to understand that he was about to lose several cargoes of the stuff in a very short time unless he had a steady market unaffected by the troubles. Which did not seem likely when he was down in Surrey instead of up in Lancashire. He would have an agent and Harry, of course, up in Liverpool, but news travelled only at the speed of a mail coach.

Her first reaction to the impending catastrophe was to think that it served him right and that, whatever his losses, they could never be as severe as those of the poor wretches whose lives he had traded without a shred of conscience. Underlying this was a streak of sympathy for him, for he was still her father and she had once given and received his love as unconditionally as a child, with no questions asked.

That night, she and Chase were accommodated in the same bedroom, and it was he, when they were left alone, who asked if she wanted him to sleep on the chaise longue. Weary and abstracted, she shook her head, which he found difficult to interpret. 'What is it, my beauty?' he said. 'Is it about the Manchester mills? You're concerned for your aunt?'

'She doesn't own the cotton-printing mills,' she replied, staring at herself in the dressing-table mirror. 'They were inherited by her cousin. Her parents received a good income from them at one time, I believe.'

'So what's bothering you, sweetheart?'

She could not explain it to him. She was free now; free from her father and all the remaining responsibilities for Sara's happiness, free of restrictions, free to enjoy herself with a man who filled her dreams, but who still had much to answer for. She was too tired to explain, too afraid to ask, or to receive the answers. Instead, she turned to hold out her arms, knowing that he would immediately come to kneel by her side, to place his great head against her breast, clasp his arms around her hips and remain there as she caressed his hair. He might even have known what was tumbling through her mind.

'Trust me,' he whispered.

She smiled at that, having been warned years ago never to trust a man who said *trust me.* This time was different, and cynicism was not appropriate, and when he picked her up and carried her to the bed, she lay with her doubts and with him, unable to give herself, yet just as unable to deny him the comfort of her presence by his side.

But in the small hours of the night, she awoke from a disturbing part-remembered dream to find that tears were coursing down her cheeks, if not for herself then surely for the wonderful man whose loving she craved, whose arms she had only to touch to feel them wrapping her, whose body she was chastising for personal hurts that seemed daily to matter less and less.

She could not deny that she was already gaining everything she had ever wanted except the trust she had been asked for, which she could not find. She had once vowed never to shed another tear for a man, but now her dreaming had done it without her permission. Sleepily, she tried to excuse herself.

Even half-asleep, Chase was alert to her distress and, easing her into the warm haven of his arms, he smoothed her forehead and wiped her face with the sheet, telling her that she was his wonderful tender-hearted woman, that he had paid a high price for her, half as much as the Prince Regent's Royal Stables but then, she came without the domes and the fancy fretwork. Tomorrow, he told her, they would go on to the Duke of Devonshire's place at Chatsworth instead of directly to Buxton, and they would ride on horseback over the moors. Could Buxton wait a few more days, he wanted to know?

Buxton could wait, she agreed, snuggling into his embrace.

Borrowing two strong hunters from his friend and with Caterina in possession of two pairs of white silk embroidered stockings, they left Wigston Magna rather later than intended with the two coaches. They would travel together as far as Derby before separating, the coaches to go directly to Chatsworth House by the easier route, the two riders to take a detour via Ashbourne over the hills and moors. It was time, Sir Chase remarked very quietly, that she filled her lungs with good Derbyshire air again, though his private smile made her blush.

The three occupants of the coach, however, were chattering too much to notice the dusty old carriage that was being repaired in the smithy at Belper, just beyond Derby. It had had a brief but disastrous encounter with an ox-team, and now its very disgruntled owner was sinking his problems in the taproom of the local inn.

Along the other route taken by the riders, the pleasant village of Ashbourne led them over the hills into the valley of the River Dove, passing some attractive Georgian houses and the Black's Head Inn, which reminded Caterina yet again of her father's disgraceful trade. She wished he, too, could have been a hosier. But the lure of the rugged landscape, the magnificent views in every direction, brooding rocks, distant blue-greys changing to hazy mauve, the cry of curlews and the rattle of grasshoppers, clouds like soft veils dragged carelessly across hills to tear holes and let in shafts of brilliant sunlight, all this filtered through Caterina's eyes and heart. Softening, and coming dangerously close to the kind of happiness she could ill afford with so many recent grievances to cling to, she nevertheless broke into a gentle humming, then to singing, then to rest the horses beside a stream to listen to its song through limestone rocks.

Pulling off his coat and cravat, Chase folded them into a bundle behind his saddle while Caterina watched admiringly as he rolled up his sleeves, baring his forearms to the buffeting wind and the sun's warmth. His thick hair lifted and settled, transforming the suave drawing-room beau into a windswept local farmer viewing his stock from the hilltops, in harmony with the elements. A nibbling sheep cropped its way close to where they sat, and when Chase called to it, it replied with an identical baa-aa and a curious stare of amber slit with black. Laughing, they held hands and fell backwards into the wiry turf, covered by a canopy of scudding clouds.

Veering north-east towards the Duke of Devonshire's villages, they reached a plateau well above the surrounding countryside that erupted into a large broken ring of high mounds, a ditch, and an inner raised circle where slabs of fallen stone lay on their sides, multicoloured with lichens and moss. It was a place Caterina knew well.

'It's known locally as Arbor Low,' she said, dismounting. 'I used to come here for picnics, and to play hide and seek. Sometimes I came out here on my own to sing and…' Unsure of how she was sounding, she walked away through one of the gaps in the bank, passing between the rocks to stand in the centre, overcome by memories of her childhood.

'And what?' Chase called, dismounting and tying the reins together.

She remained with her back to him. 'To dance,' she said, diffidently. 'But I was a child then. I had little else on my mind except how to be happy.'

The outer bank was higher than most men, but Chase loped up to the top to stand on its rim and view the rolling countryside below. 'They certainly chose their places well, those people,' he called to her.

'What people?'

'The people of the Bronze Age. This place is even earlier than Old Sarum. Remember?' He went to meet her, smiling at the memory of that day. 'Remember how you tried to appear not-interested while you tied yourself in knots to hear what I was saying at the same time? Remember reading it up with a guidebook from Donaldson's Library in Brighton?'

'You were not supposed to know that,' she scolded, recalling so clearly the anger that would not allow even a hint of his magic to affect her. She was still trying to resist it, though they both knew he was winning, day by day, moment by moment. She felt his arm steal around her waist and pull her back against him, his hands spreading to hold her secure, the scent of his cool skin caressing her cheek.

'So,' he whispered, 'now you can redeem yourself, proud woman. Dance for me the way you used to when you had so little else on your mind but happiness.'

'No, I cannot.'

'What shall it be, a minuet? The Dashing White Sergeant? A hornpipe?'

'No,' she scoffed. 'Not that kind of dance.'

'What kind? A wild pagan dance, was it? Come, I can do that, too. Come on…come!' Taking her by the hand, he sat her on the nearest stone. 'You must remove your shoes to feel the earth under your feet. Off with them.' So saying, he pulled off his own boots and stockings and took her hand to lead her to the outer edge of the stones to begin a slowly swaying seductive measure, weaving like a ribbon through them, in and out, circling and moving on. 'Did you sing, too?' he said, drawing her on, waving his arms in a stately flow.

'Yes, vaguely. No one heard me.'

'Then sing vaguely with me, and only the wild things will hear us.'

It seemed to be the most natural thing to do with him, to sing no particular song that arose from the occasion and to hear the echo of his deep harmonising hum, to feel the magical sounds caught up by the hilltop breeze, to follow the flight of sunbathing butterflies into the sky. In and out of the stones they wreathed in a graceful pattern, hidden behind the great outer mound that had once witnessed other dancers long ago. She had not known such freedom for years, had almost forgotten how it felt to curl her toes into the short grass, to sing to nature, timeless and unselfconscious. Never had she thought to do it with a man like this by her side who not only encouraged her, but understood it, too, joining in, undaunted by anything.

Leading her up to leap upon one of the fallen stones, he then lifted her down in a soaring waist-held flight with arms like wings, whirling her, laughing and singing to the ground. Breathless and exhilarated, Caterina sank down between two of the larger stones to lay spread-eagled, drunk with the recaptured carefree silliness of youth.

Chase fell down beside her, taking her tousled head in his hands, taking her kisses, too, pausing for breath only to extend their primitive ritual into the natural urge to make love. Caterina had not thought about it, but knew immediately that this was what her body required to bond with the one who was so much a part of her. What other man but Chase Boston would so easily have ignored the conventions?

It had been days since their last loving, and neither of them could delay by a single moment what was already brimming over into every thought, every deed, every touch of the hand. Without a word between them to speak of reasons, their bodies entwined like dancers while Caterina, as usual, urged him past the leisured preliminaries with the urgency of a wild creature eager for consummation. Chase was not inclined to hold her back while his own need was as great and, at her first signal of surrender, he took her with the tender force that she so clearly wanted, towering over her with the domination that was one of the hallmarks of his love-making, powerful, yet aware of her smallest response.

There, on that almost ancient place on the lone moors, no one was near to hear their cries, nor did Caterina feel any shame at her impulsive change of mind, for this was as much a part of her as her previous reservations. There was no need for words: it had happened, and the release shattered them both with a power that reached them through the earth, sating them with its life-force.

Sensitive to her unstable emotions, Chase did not

tease her about her sudden change of heart, loving her for her immediate response to both their needs. Full of contradictions and impulses, courageous, talented, sometimes volatile, yet as fragile as a moth, she was the kind of woman he admired above all others. So the short ride across the Duke's land was more contemplative than usual, and they rode holding hands, containing their thoughts for the time being.

With typical understatement, the English are used to describing large estates as 'a little pile in the country'. Their first full view of the Duke's 'little pile' was from the village of Edensor that straggled down to the bridge over the Derwent, set in a gloriously wide landscape softened by trees against a dramatic backcloth of hills, the glowing honey-coloured stone settled like a solid golden box. Further up the hillside to the left was another large stone building with a clock tower on the roof.

'The stables,' Sir Chase told her.

'I've seen the house often,' said Caterina, 'but never as close as this. It's huge, isn't it?'

'Not quite huge enough for Hart. He's already planning on extensions to make it about twice the size. The gardens, too.'

'There…over there…' she pointed '…that's the long cascade. Do you think he'll allow us to paddle in it?' Higher up the hill to the other side of the house was a long flight of steps that sparkled with water.

'We'll be allowed to do whatever we wish. Come on. The coaches should be there by now.' He laughed, recognising the change in her with each mile of their journey, wondering if Signor Cantoni and Millie would notice it, too.

They had been seen from the house riding through

herds of deer in the parkland and, by the time they had arrived at the foot of the terrace in the West Garden, the lanky young sixth Duke was striding out to meet them, his long boyish face beaming with pleasure, his arms ready to lift Caterina down from the saddle, greeting her with a brotherly kiss to both cheeks. Animated and eager, he took his friend's hand in both his own, asking questions, but not waiting for an answer before telling them how their coaches had arrived and how sensible they were to come cross-country.

He had given Caterina the red-velvet bedroom, which had a wash-basin and a commode of polished mahogany. Sir Chase was in the room next door but, in a house the size of Chatsworth, a guide might have been useful when it was necessary to walk through so many other rooms to reach his Grace, and it was soon obvious why he was planning so many changes. Their journey took them through vast rooms with painted ceilings, gilded cornices and dowdy wallpapers, over marble floors and shabby carpets, past monstrous bookcases, old slabs of alabaster and furniture chipped with the countless knocks of generations, up staircases and along passageways lined with columns, plaster casts of feet and heads, malachite pedestals and clocks, urns made of the local Blue John stone and tapestries from the now-dismantled Mortlake factory showing faded biblical scenes.

'But things are in the wrong place,' said the Duke, airily. 'And there's too much gilding everywhere. Some of it will have to go.'

With a resident orchestra and the Duke's Hungarian pianist friend, Edouard Schulz, with Sir Chase, Signor Cantoni and Caterina, it was not surprising when, after dinner, they resorted to the music room where the guests willingly 'sang for their supper' to the delight of the Duke who, although slightly deaf, loved music. When it grew late, they abandoned the piano, the harpsicord and harp for a supper in the Sitting Room, all white, grey and gold, which Caterina found restful, but which the Duke wanted for his library. 'After I've enlarged the stables,' he told her. 'I can only get eighty in there at the moment, and there's nowhere for the carriages.'

Caterina's red-velvet room was connected to Sir Chase's by a small door cut into the wall that disappeared from view when it was closed. While they prepared for bed, they propped it open so they could talk and, when Millie and Mr Pearson had been dismissed, they came together only because they could no longer keep away from each other for the space of a night.

The events of the day had assembled in her mind, helping to relieve her of the cares that had dogged her for so long, replacing them with companionship, music-making and loving, peace and freedom. A heady mixture that was sure to affect her.

He had waited at the door in the wall with his head almost touching the frame, his arms folded as he took note of the last fussing delaying tactics that he knew were signs of her uncertainty. There were still doubts in her mind and now her resolutions wavered, too, but her body's messages were strident, insistent.

She turned, as if surprised to see him standing there, and he could see the conflict raging within her, reminding her of the passionate encounter on the moors and the ecstasy they had shared there, literally, on her home ground.

'Chase,' she whispered.

He neither spoke nor moved, but his look told her that she must come to him, not the other way round.

'Chase…I think…I think I want you.' Her eyes were wide and dark with desire, her fine lawn nightgown like a halo around the darker outline of her body, her hair glowing like burnished copper in the candlelight.

He could see that she was trembling. Moving at last, he held out one hand to her and she flew to him like a bird with a cry of joy at the sudden soft impact of their bodies, at the warm welcome of his lips, as hungry as hers. She melted into him and he lifted her, carrying her through to his own bed where the loving began even before they fell, sprawling them across it, rolling to the edge and back again.

This time, Caterina's need was for every tenderness he could offer, the slow, seductive, secretive caresses that he had rarely been given a chance to give, or to teach her how to give in return. In those rapturous hours, she learned about waiting and about giving pleasure as well as receiving it, about the sensitive parts of a man's body and about the joys of delay which, ultimately, heightened the sublime ascent that kept them both at the peak for longer than before, crying out with the suspense of it.

His head lay on the pillow with his nose almost touching hers, their eyes laughing, wondering, their lips playing together.

'I'm in bed with Chase Boston,' she said, impishly.

'So you are, my lady. Regretting it, are you?'

'Not yet. No, certainly not yet. But Chase, there's something I think I ought to tell you.'

'Shh!' he commanded, lapping at her top lip. 'Sleep now. You can tell me tomorrow.'

* * *

The chance to tell him did not present itself the next day nor indeed on any of the following days or nights, and by the end of their five-day visit to Chatsworth, the need to speak about her secret theft was fading, partly as a result of Chase's contriving to keep the topic of conversation well clear of contentious issues. The other reasons were to do with the increase of guests at Chatsworth and their days spent tirelessly visiting all the places Caterina had known when she had lived in the nearby town of Buxton. For her, these days were the beginning of a new life in which everything she enjoyed most was hers to do without restriction. The hours spent with her personal singing tutor and all the other music-makers were like the fulfilment of a dream that seemed unlikely to end.

Using the Duke's horses, they galloped freely over his acres, taught Signor Cantoni how to ride, splashed like children in the cascade fountain on the hillside, played games of croquet and boated on the lake. On tours of the palatial house, they were shown the fifth Duke's collection of *objets d'art* and all the curiosities he'd not bothered to catalogue, for he had been no connoisseur of the arts like his son.

One of the extra guests to appear was a certain Mr Turner, an artist who disappeared each morning to sketch the local beauty spots, reappearing each evening looking just as scruffy as when he'd set out. Though no one could have called him charming, he kept them in hoots of laughter with stories of his adventures in pursuit of his art, but if any of them had assumed that his finished paintings might be easily affordable, they were soon to find out that, for all his air of shabbiness, he had been a Royal Academician since the age of twenty who knew his own worth. His charges included not only the painting but also the cost of transporting it to the buyer and even, when he felt like it, the paper and string it was parcelled in. He did not come cheap by any standards.

Politely, Caterina agreed with Mr Turner that this was only common sense, but the controversial subject of earnings and entitlements was soon pounced on by other guests, some of whom were local landowners, and the conversation swung inevitably to the price of land and the Derbyshire's valuable lead mines. Several of these were owned by the Duke himself, as well as others further north on the moors of Yorkshire.

'Mark you,' the Duke said between mouthfuls of Wensleydale cheese and apple chutney, 'I don't need to go all the way up to Yorkshire to understand what my agent is telling me. He's always on the spot, but I have the model of the mines that my father had made for him. I'll show it to you after dinner, if I can find it.'

He found it behind a bronze bust of Admiral Lord Nelson that stood on top of a large lump of lead known, he told them, as a pig, probably because no one could lift it. The model was beautifully constructed of wood showing how the seams containing lead-ore ran vertically down into the ground connected by man-made sloping tunnels where tiny figures of men crawled on all fours to pick away at the rock, inch by inch. Caterina knew that lead mining was a highly dangerous occupation and that the miners' families lived only on what their menfolk could find and bring to the surface. They were always desperately poor and, as usual, the largest share went to the owners. But until then, she had given little thought to the appalling conditions in which the men worked, rain or shine, winter and summer. Most of the workers would have to walk miles across the open moor in all weathers just to reach the mine, with no change of clothes either before or afterwards.

With only the Duke and her husband to hear her questions about the Chester mines inherited by her father, she was surprised to see the sudden frown followed by a fleeting expression of concern cross the Duke's face. Clearly, he was perturbed. 'Good heavens!' he whispered, looking to Sir Chase for support. 'Heavens above. Of course, you're *related,* are you not? How could I have forgotten it?'

'Is there a problem, Hart?' said Sir Chase.

'Well, er…yes, there is indeed, but…' his eyes wavered uncertainly between Caterina and Sir Chase '…but perhaps this is not the time.'

'Please tell me,' Caterina said. 'Has something happened?'

'Oh, dear. Chester's mine is on neighbouring land, as I'm sure you must know. That's how I heard the news so soon, only this morning, but it didn't occur to me to mention it. Your father won't have heard yet, down in Richmond. I suppose that's one of the problems of not keeping a close eye on the place. Your father visits so rarely, I believe.'

'Never at all, your Grace. But please tell me what's wrong.'

'The worst. I'm sorry to say that his one remaining mine collapsed last night and killed seven men. He's supposed to keep them supplied with good timbers, you see, so that they're shored up as safely as possible. Your father's mine reached the water-table only last year,' he said, pointing to the underground lake on the model, 'down here, so they'd almost worked that seam out. Since then they'd been looking for parallel seams, and I believe they were sinking deeper shafts to search for more veins. But if the water that collects isn't pumped out properly, the shafts will flood and collapse. If your father had granted leases for them to look elsewhere on his land, they'd not have needed to go deeper, but this takes time to discover, and I believe he's always refused to do that. Folly, really. It may be an expensive undertaking, but seven men is a lot to lose in one go. He'll have to close it down completely now, with all his miners gone. A very sad business. Every owner's nightmare.'

Caterina's face was white. 'And the families?' she said.

'Oh, heaven knows what'll become of them. Perhaps your father will come up to see for himself, once the message reaches him. These families help each other out. They're a close-knit bunch up here.'

She felt the support of Chase's arm around her shoulders, easing her gently against him, sharing her shock. First the loss of profits on his cotton cargoes, now the terrible accident and the closure of his one remaining mine. Which would concern him most, she wondered, the loss of revenue or the loss of life and the destitute families?

'I'm so sorry to be the bearer of bad news,' the Duke said. 'Was the mine your father's only source of income, my lady? Forgive me for asking.'

'No, your Grace. I believe he may have others.'

She thought about the sugar plantations, the profits from raw sugar and the miserable slaves who toiled under the baking sun, about the fortune her father had squandered to bail Harry out of trouble year after year, and about patient Hannah and the sweet young woman she had once been, eager to please him. She thought about the secret she herself longed to share with her husband, the petty theft that would compound her father's distress. Perhaps she should not have done it, after all.

It was their last evening at Chatsworth as guests of the Duke, and Caterina sat on a bench next to Chase, watching two cats dart about between the bean canes and beds of young lettuce. White butterflies flirted over the spring greens as a stiff breeze lifted the ends of the long Kashmir scarf off her knees. With a shiver, she pulled it closer about her shoulders. 'There's something I must tell you,' she said. 'It's important.'

'Then you must tell me, sweetheart.' He took her hand and held it upon his thigh. 'About your father's affairs, is it?'

'And yours, too. I have his IOU. The one you returned to him.'

'Your brother's? For twenty grand?'

'Yes, I took it from his desk. I know it was wrong of me, but I felt I had the right to do it, and now he'll be worrying about that as well as hearing about the mine. I'm regretting it, Chase. Should I send it back to him?'

Deliberately, she stopped short of any mention of Harry's incriminating letter and the cargo of cotton that would probably not be sold for some time, or the slaving and the law-breaking that could be the end of him. That ground was too dangerous to tread just now. She felt his eyes upon her and turned to meet them with trepidation. 'You're angry with me?' she said.

His thumb moved over her skin. 'Hell, no, but it sounds as if *you* were, my vengeful fierce little bird. What use is the IOU to you?'

'None at all, except to give him a taste of the heartache he's caused me.'

'Well, then, it will have served its purpose by now.

If you're uncomfortable with it, you can deal with it in two ways. You can either send it back, or tell him you have it safe, just to put him at ease. Or you can tear it up and send him the pieces and tell him no one wants it. I certainly don't. I have what I want, thank you.'

'You *don't* want it?' she insisted.

'No, sweetheart. It's of no use to anyone now, is it? He should have destroyed it himself.'

It could be some use, she thought, in the wrong hands. So could the letter. It could ruin him utterly. Was Sir Chase involved? Was he keeping quiet about what he knew of her father's activities? She wished she could be more sure of him. 'I'll send it back to him, then,' she said.

'Yes, we shall be in Buxton by midday tomorrow. You can send it from there, then he'll know where we are. A pity he didn't offer to open up Chester Hall for us.'

'Yes,' she replied, stony-faced. 'I thought he might have offered to let us use it, but he didn't, so I didn't ask.'

'That's all right. We can stay overnight at the hotel. What's it called?'

'St Anne's. It's on The Crescent. A very good place.'

The chill wind pestered them again as dark clouds loomed up from the south-west and, prompted by the Duke's disturbing news, the matters that for a few days had given her some respite now began to reform for the next assault.

'Let's go inside,' she said. 'I think the Duke wants to beat you at billiards on our last night here. Is that likely?'

'It certainly won't cost him as much as a hand or two of whist, my sweet.'

* * *

By morning, the clouds had lowered to shroud the hilltops and to drench the Duke's extensive acres with much-needed rain. The drop in temperature brought out extra layers and many caped coats for the journey, and today Caterina's fur-edged green velvet pelisse was draped with a paisley shawl that complemented the cream-and-green-patterned day dress beneath. Green kid half-boots peeped from below the scalloped hem, and a rather mannish felt hat lay on the cushion next to her, its spotted veil dripping like water on to the toe of Sir Chase's polished boot. She had spoken only intermittently during the few miles to Buxton, for although the countryside was dear to her, the thought of spending time in the gossipy town of her birth and to make enquiries into her father's detestable affairs had completely lost its appeal.

Lady Elyot, who had once been married to her father's elder brother, had not been able to tolerate the claustrophobic society there any longer and she had taken Caterina, at her father's request, to live in far-away Surrey where, as it turned out, society was just as gossipy and insular, though perhaps with more reason. Did she *really* want to know more about her father's disastrous enterprises? Caterina asked herself. No, what she wanted most was to know about her husband's, even if that meant hearing what she dreaded.

The small town of Buxton, however, was three-quarters owned by the Duke of Devonshire, and last evening he had enjoyed discussing his plans for its development with Caterina. It could, he told her, with its warm and cold medicinal natural springs, become a northern version of Bath in Somerset. The Duke's own town house was situated right in the centre of The Crescent, built by the previous Duke, his father. He would not hear of them staying next door at St Anne's Hotel. They *must* stay in his rooms which were, like all his others, always available at a moment's notice, and they could think of no good reason to refuse his offer.

Although impressive at first glance, The Crescent had none of the classically elegant proportions of the sweeping crescents of Bath, for the architect, John Carr of York, had never been in the same league as Nash or the Adam brothers, and the arcade that underpinned the frontage was too narrow to be functional and too solid to be purely decorative. Not that this concerned the travellers in the smart coaches with the liveried footmen as the doors opened to disgorge them all before a small crowd, gathered especially to see who was to stay at Centre House, as it was called.

It was a strange homecoming for Caterina to feel that she was now a virtual stranger just like any other visitor to Buxton, unrecognised and unsure where once she had been a well-known part of a respectable family. Her father had been a local benefactor, known by everyone, but she had been away from here for longer than he and had changed beyond recognition. To have to re-introduce herself to acquaintances and then to ask them what they knew of his business interests was going to look very odd. Where did she begin? And how was she to do any of this with Sir Chase by her side?

'I may take a walk over to Chester Hall with Millie,' she said to him over a cold collation of chicken and ham pie, fruit compote and cold custard.

'It's still raining,' said Sir Chase, passing the basket of warm bread rolls across to Signor Cantoni. 'I'll take you there in the coach.' The butler and housekeeper, well known to Sir Chase, had done everything possible to make them welcome, as their master would have wished.

'Oh, we have umbrellas,' Caterina said. 'It's not far.'

'But I'd like to see where you once lived.'

She had told him, and so had Stephen Chester, of the large house in its own grounds with gardens sheltered by a hillside, and Sir Chase intended to see for himself what they had all forfeited by moving to Richmond. Chester Hall had once been Lady Elyot's home, too, inherited by Stephen Chester, but it was interesting to note that he had not sold it to raise capital to buy Number 18 Paradise Road from her. What explanation had he offered to Mrs Chester about that, he wondered, or did he keep all his cards close to his chest? Had she ever been up here for well-earned rest from the family?

From the outside, Chester Hall was everything the father and daughter had said, heavily stone-built, situated on the edge of town overlooking a beautiful wooded valley, high-walled, and approached through large wooden gates that kept out the gaze of the curious. The drive up to the front of the house took them through an avenue of dark dripping pines that gave off the distinctive aroma that Caterina loved, and it was not until they rounded the last bend of trees that they saw the old rain-battered town coach outside the porch being loaded with trunks, boxes and cases, strapped to the roof by Stephen Chester's shiny-wet valet.

'That's your father's coach, surely,' said Sir Chase, handing her down.

This was something neither of them had expected, but Caterina's astonishment was answered at once, for it was not hard to see that he had come *either* to reclaim his missing documents *or* in response to the troubles with the sale of his cargo in Liverpool. He could not yet have heard about the mining disaster, and it was obvious that he was moving on in a hurry. Whatever the reason, she could not believe he would be pleased to see them.

Chase kept hold of her hand. 'He must have been close on our heels,' he said. 'Come on, sweetheart, we're here together, so we'll soon find out what he knows. Let's go and find him.'

It was not necessary, for a grey great-coated figure with his head down against the rain strode through the solid stone portal, a large leather briefcase clamped under one arm. Catching sight of another team of horses behind his own, he whirled round with an obvious annoyance that immediately turned to amazement, then to anger. beneath the wide-brimmed hat, his face was blotched grey and crimson, his eyes bloodshot with drink, evidence of which bulged from one pocket.

The briefcase plummeted before he caught it, irritably shoving papers back inside. 'At last,' he snapped. 'I've been waiting here five days for you to show up in Buxton, Caterina. Where've you been? And *you,* sir! Especially you. You are a blackguard, sir. And a thief. And now you're here, you can explain your dishonourable behaviour to my face instead of—'

'Enough!' Sir Chase bellowed, tightening his hold on Caterina's hand. 'If you intend to talk nonsense, Chester, perhaps we may be allowed to hear it under cover. You did not invite us to come here, so you can count yourself fortunate to see us at all. We'll go inside, if you have no objections.'

'Eh? Fortunate?' Stephen Chester swivelled on the wet flagstones, taking a hard look at his daughter's pitying expression.

'Inside,' said Sir Chase. With a determination that

Caterina had grown to love, he strode past her father into the damp-smelling hall that had lost all the warmth and welcome for which it had once been famed.

Chester followed them still loudly complaining, ignoring the stares of the two old servants whose smiles and greetings for Miss Caterina and her new husband withered into deep anxiety. She touched their arms as she passed, comforting them with a smile. 'Some tea?' she whispered.

'You have taken my daughter, sir, under false pretences,' Stephen Chester raged, 'and you have reneged on our agreement in the most dastardly way imaginable. I shall call you out, sir. Name your seconds.'

Sir Chase showed not the slightest response to this tirade as he followed Caterina's steering hand into the large ground-floor salon where dust covers shrouded all the furniture, though some had been sat upon and even slept upon, too, to judge by their dishevelled appearance. The usually sunny room reeked of spirits and a sourness that wrinkled Caterina's nose.

But now she saw her chance to ask some of the questions that had burned holes in her heart for weeks. 'What agreement are you referring to, Father?' she said. 'And how has Sir Chase not fulfilled his part in it? I believe I have a right to know.'

She half-expected Sir Chase to protest, but he did not.

'You *do* know, lass!' her father snapped. 'Don't pretend you don't. He agreed to waive Harry's IOU in return for your acceptance of his offer. Well, now he's helped himself to it, hasn't he? And I'm back where I was before. I'm not only accusing him,' he said, slamming the briefcase down upon the nearest dust-sheet. 'I'm challenging him to a bloody *duel,* girl. That's what.'

'Not in your state, you're not,' said Sir Chase, sternly. 'And mind your language in front of my wife, sir. Sit down and try to get your head round a few simple facts, if you will. What's your reason for coming up to Buxton? Surely not to chase a missing IOU?'

Stunned by the severity of his son-in-law's tone which, up to this point, had always been pleasantly deferential, Stephen Chester sat down obediently. 'You admit taking it?' he whined. 'And you have the impudence to ask why I've come all this way? To find *you,* sir. And to demand the return of my documents from my desk. Either you hand them back or I'll have Caterina. Make your choice, Boston.'

'What documents do you refer to?' Sir Chase squeezed a warning upon Caterina's hand. She had been about to explain.

'Oh, come, Boston. I have no time to play guessing games. I have to be in Liverpool some time tomorrow. Don't pretend you didn't take my son's IOU and his letter, for I know the truth of it. You're the only one who would do such a thing, and I want them back. I hardly need to say why.' He shot a furtive glance at Caterina before looking away in discomfort.

'Father, I…' Caterina began her admission before she felt another silencing squeeze from Sir Chase, catching a quick frown from his eyes.

'I have them both,' he said, evenly. 'I believe Lady Boston has more right to them than anyone, Chester, since it is she who has been most inconvenienced by your son's wild behaviour. You must agree with me there.'

'No!' The word exploded in a shriek. 'I cannot agree to that. Caterina must *not* see… Have you shown her? Where is the letter?'

'In my luggage.'

His voice dropped to a horrified whisper. 'So she's seen it?'

'Yes, of course she has.'

Slowly, his head dropped forward into his hands with a groan that shook his body, shrinking it inside the heavy coat blackened by rain. His hat shielded him, but they knew he had begun to weep. 'Ruined,' he sobbed. 'Utterly ruined. Nothing left, not even credit with my family.'

Freeing her hand, Caterina went to his side, overcome by sadness that he should have been reduced to such a pitiful state, drunk, miserable, and destroyed by events. She was torn between compassion and feelings of revenge, but the ties of blood were strongest. 'Father,' she whispered. 'Why?'

'You know about it,' he wept. 'I never wanted any of you to know, and never you, of all people. It's all gone terribly wrong, Caterina.'

'I know. We've heard about the mills and the sales of cotton up in Manchester. Is that why you're going up to the Liverpool docks, to see what can be done?'

To her surprise, he shook his head, took off his hat and wiped his eyes with the back of his hand. 'Not only that. The news of the cotton cargo is nothing to what I heard only two hours ago. Nothing could be worse than *that* kind of news to a small-time shipowner.' His voice was hoarse with emotion.

'A slave-trader, Father. Why not use the proper name?'

He flinched at that. 'Not any more. It's all over. Gone,' he croaked.

'What does he mean?' she whispered to Sir Chase as he took the chair opposite, leaning his arms along his thighs. 'Is there something else?'

'It rather sounds like it,' he answered, grimly.

Chapter Eight

Instead of any relief she might have felt at the emergence of the truth, at last, Caterina was now more certain than ever that, whatever dreadful truths she was about to hear would never be enough to kill or even to diminish the love she had for Chase Boston. Yes, she had known of her love for weeks, though at what point the knowledge had first crept upon her she could not have said. Perhaps it was right at the beginning when he had marched boldly into her life: perhaps when he had saved it. Whatever the facts, she was sure there would never be another time for the pretence at coldness and rejection she had tried, and failed, to use as a weapon against perceived wrongs. Whatever emerged now would have to be accepted and suffered in the same way that most wives did, with resignation and forgiveness in return for the comfort of a husband's attentions.

She did not believe she wanted to live without him, whatever he had done to win her, whatever his payment, bargain or wager. She did not even want to try. She was his. She would accept what he offered her, would do what he asked, though she prayed he would never ask her to share him with another. That would be harder to bear than anything, yet she would, if that was the only way to hold him.

The tea-tray was brought in, giving her a chance to consider any disaster that could be worse than the one about which she had heard. After a lapse of months, that would probably resolve itself somehow, but her father was talking about something far more serious than sales.

She carried a cup of tea across to him, then to Sir Chase to whom she whispered her thanks, not needing to explain.

Owlishly, he took the tea from her, holding her eyes with a quizzical look. 'You have some explaining to do, my lady,' he whispered.

'So do you. He's broken the law, you know. He's in serious trouble.'

'I know,' he said, only mouthing the words.

'You…you know?' Yes, she thought, of course you do. Of course.

'Yes, we'll talk about it later, shall we? Right now, we need to know what else is upsetting him and what he intends to do about it.'

So, it was as she'd suspected. Sir Chase knew about the slave-ships, and now it was inconceivable that he had not planned to use the information for her father's downfall, otherwise he would surely have shown some alarm at Mr Tolby's news. And now Sir Chase would know that, because of some letter from her brother which she had stolen, she had discovered the source of her father's secret wealth.

'I'll ask him, shall I?' she said.

'Yes, he'd better hear about his lead mine, too, eventually.'

'He ought to be going there instead of to Liverpool,'

she whispered, crossly. She went to sit beside her father, taking the rattling cup and saucer from him and placing it on the small table. 'You've been in touch with Harry, Father?'

He nodded, fumbling for the spirit flask wedged in his damp pocket. 'The mail takes only a day from Liverpool. I had the latest news this morning. I have to go. Damn this thing.'

She lay a hand over his. 'No more of that. You need a clear head.'

He sighed, sending a look of extreme dislike across to Sir Chase. 'Yes, you're right. But can you persuade *him* to give me back my papers? What does he intend to do with them? Blackmail me?'

She caught the lift of one darkly eloquent eyebrow, but had no reply to give. It was, she thought, a distinct possibility in the light of all the trickery that had gone on before. She wanted to be hard, vindictive, to make him suffer, but the years of daughterly respect made it too difficult for her. 'You'll have to ask Sir Chase yourself, Father. You have far greater wealth than you allowed any of *us* to know about. Has something happened to change all that?'

'Yes, it has,' he whispered, shamefaced, 'but you would not understand any of my reasons for wanting real wealth, Caterina.'

'Certainly not, unless I'm given the chance to,' she replied, caustically.

'Well now it's caught up with me at last. I've lost all three ships. All three…gone!' The words faded to a whisper. 'Serves me right. Serves me damn well right.'

'But according to Harry's letter, the *Caterina* arrived with a full cargo at Liverpool. He saw it there himself.'

'Yes, and before they could complete the off-load-ing, some maniac set fire to it, and now there's nothing left but a charred hulk in the dock and a crowd of angry owners whose ships were damaged by the sparks, all wanting compensation. Thousands of pounds' worth of damage. Harry is certain it was sabotage.'

Sir Chase's quiet voice cut through the horrified silence. 'But you are insured, surely?'

'No.'

'What?'

Chester shook his head. 'I was uninsured.' His admission wavered on the brink of tears. 'I could never find anyone to insure me. I believe they may have suspected what I was doing, but I was always careful not to give them any evidence, and, without proof, no one could speak against me. I had to take the risk.'

'And the other ships?'

'The same. No insurance. And I've lost them, too.'

'How?' said Caterina. 'Where?'

'Storms off the Caribbean coast, typhoons, I think they're called. The *Hannah* must have gone down. She's not been seen for months.'

'With slaves on board?'

'I don't know,' Chester croaked, looking down at his feet. 'I don't know.'

'And the other one?' said Sir Chase. 'What happened to her?'

'The *Welldone* is in Kingston harbour without a crew or captain. It was the damned weather again. Apparently it's taken her six months instead of six weeks to cross from West Africa to St Kitts. She carried a live cargo of one hundred and sixty-eight, but not enough water or food for that kind of voyage. They ran out.'

'Starved, you mean?' said Caterina.

'Yes, starved. They had to be thrown overboard.

Some of the crew died, too. The captain headed for Jamaica and left the ship at Kingston, empty, infected, and in poor shape. The crew mutinied and fled, and the captain has taken everything he can lay hands on and fled, too.' His head, too heavy for him to hold, sank into his cupped palm and rested there, his eyes closed tightly against his daughter's dark accusing stare.

Shaking her head against the dreadful images, she rose and went over to the window, looking out over the untidy garden and orchard where the rain lashed furiously at the pines, feathering their tips. 'It disgusts me,' she whispered, 'how you can so disregard others' lives, using them to make your wealth, discarding them, writing them off as losses as if they were bales of something. I had not ever thought you could put your own family into so much danger, either, knowing what the penalty is. Have you no thought for Hannah? Are your tears and moans for what *you've* lost, Father? Have you ever shed a tear for those poor wretches whose lives you've used up like so much currency? What about the sugar plantation in St Kitts? Is that still a source of revenue?'

'Hardly,' he said, stung by her tone. 'There's a quick turnover of labour there, the work is so hard. The planters can never get enough of them. But the price of refined sugar has dropped now. The demand for molasses is not as it was when I bought the plantation.'

'Why not?'

'Somebody has found an alternative,' he said, wearily. 'It's called sugar beet, easy to grow and harvest over here. I shall sell my share.'

'Oh, so *you* won't starve. That must be a relief.'

'I'm not relieved, Caterina, I'm worried about Harry's position.'

She responded angrily to that. 'Oh, Harry! Of course. You must be. Clever Harry, who puts it all into a letter that he entrusts to the public mail, which anyone could pick up and read. Well—' she caught his reproving glance '—*I did,* didn't I? That's right, Father, save your concern for Harry.'

'I want my letter back,' he said, leaping to his feet in annoyance. 'It can land me in serious trouble, you must be aware of that.'

'I am aware,' Caterina said, 'that you have landed *yourself* and the rest of our family in serious trouble, Father,' she snapped back at him. 'But I imagine Sir Chase may wish to hold on to it a while longer and, if he doesn't, then I will. I shall keep the letter and the IOU until I have proof that you've finished with this abominable business altogether. I shall show it to the authorities if you don't, you can be sure of that, and you can take the responsibility for what happens to Hannah and the children and all the rest of your property. You set me up, Father, and now I'm turning the tables on you.'

'You will do as your husband tells you to, no doubt.'

'I shall,' she replied, looking at Sir Chase. 'Accepting his absurd wager was by chance the only good thing you've done for some time, except marrying Hannah, who has given you far more than you deserve. You will not think to ask me, I know, but I will tell you nevertheless, that I am *very* happy with my husband, more than ever I could have believed possible. He is all I could wish for. He is all I could *ever* wish for.'

Though the words were for her father, her eyes held her husband's and watched them change from surprise to the soft caress of love. Amusement, too, for this confession was so unlike the scalding Caterina they had encountered during their hostile marriage-broking.

Taken by surprise, Stephen Chester stared at Sir Chase as if for confirmation, but when the latter's only reply was an enigmatic smile, his bitterness surfaced in a welter of self-pity. 'Got her tamed, have you, sir? Well done. I wish you joy. I wish I had gained a wife who would say that about me with so little prompting. But there. She won't. Not now.'

If Caterina was shocked, it showed only in the slight frown that disappeared as quickly as it had come. 'Perhaps,' she whispered, 'if you had shown Hannah as much concern as you have for Harry over the years, she might have done. What has Harry done to give you happiness?'

'He's my eldest son, Caterina. My only son. He needs a good start in life, any father knows that. He'll be given everything I wasn't given. He'll be a gentleman with enough wealth and property to take him to the top. Well,' he corrected himself, 'that was always my plan.'

'To be a *real* gentleman, Chester,' said Sir Chase, 'he'll have to start behaving like one, won't he? Perhaps you could concentrate your efforts into that, rather than teaching him how to deceive his employers, abuse his father's trust and squander his money.'

'Did you not squander your father's money, Sir Chase?'

'No, I squandered my own. That was my choice and hurt no one but me. But perhaps young Chester could learn something about honesty and compassion and responsibility for his actions. And how to be discreet, too.'

'At twenty years old, sir, it's only to be expected.'

'At twenty years old, I was responsible and so, I think, were you, sir.'

'He's still quite immature.'

'All the more reason for you to keep him where you can see him, then.'

'Why, what do you know about him?'

'Enough. I took a large sum of money off him, remember?'

'Father,' said Caterina, turning the conversation away from her brother's weaknesses, 'you spoke of Hannah just now as if you had regrets. Is that so? Surely Hannah has done her best to make you a loving wife?'

There was a tiredness, a reluctance about him that made Caterina believe that her question was presumptuous. Indeed, it was a personal question that was none of her business; not the kind of enquiry she had ever made before. Then he seemed to relent, coming to stand by her side to watch the wind sway the pines, ruffling their fronds. 'She has been a comfort to me,' he said, 'in a manner of speaking, but perhaps I should not have leapt into a second marriage as fast as I did. It's always been a second-best arrangement.'

'You mean second-best to Mother? You still miss her so?'

He sighed, lifting his scrawny sandy head to watch the rain fall in hesitant runnels down the window-pane, and his voice took on a different quality, rather like a dream that would never be caught. 'Not your mother, Caterina. It was Amelie. Always Amelie.'

'Aunt Amelie? Lady Elyot? Father, what are you telling me?'

'I thought everyone would have guessed. She knows. I was the one to offer for her before Josiah, after your mother died.'

'But she married your elder brother instead of you. Why?'

'Because she was a dutiful daughter and her parents preferred Josiah's offer to mine. He had the knighthood, the wealth, and eventually the inheritance. It was only natural. I was a widower with a family of three. I had to stand back.'

'Oh, Father. I didn't realise. But then, when Uncle Josiah died?'

'I did everything I could to help her through it. It was a terrible few years and I know she was grateful, but it was never more than gratitude. She could not have stayed in Buxton with all the gossip.'

'So you still had hopes?'

'Frail hopes. She took you to Richmond with her.'

'Ah, I see. That was to make her obliged to you.'

'No, it was not, Caterina. It was entirely for your sake. But then she and Lord Elyot found each other, as you know, and there was no competing with that. I suppose my idea was that, if I'd possessed the kind of wealth that Josiah and Lord Elyot had, I'd have stood more chance of impressing her, somehow. I married again because it was obvious I wasn't going to win Amelie, and I agreed to move to Richmond ostensibly to please Hannah.'

'Although it was really to be near Aunt Amelie?'

'And to live in the house on Paradise Road where she had once lived. That's why I never wanted to move. But it was the wrong thing to do. I should have insisted on coming back here. I never felt as if I was part of the Richmond set.'

'So that's why you've never sold Chester Hall.'

'Yes, it was a place to return to, to lick my wounds. As you see. Now I shall be forced to sell it after all, though it's a far better house to bring up a growing family. You loved it here, didn't you?'

'I did, when I was younger. I think you should make Chester Hall your home, Father. Hannah would love the space, and so would the children. I shall live wherever Sir Chase lives.' Again, their smiles met, secretly.

'Sell Paradise Road, you mean?'

'Yes, sell up. Hannah won't mind as long as you're happy, and you're a Derbyshire man, Father. Stop the ship-owning and the law-breaking and begin again in Buxton where Hannah can help you to make a new life. Aunt Amelie has always been very fond of you, but she has her own family now, and I doubt she'd be impressed if she knew how you'd been making money all these years. She's as concerned about human welfare as the rest of us. How could you ever have thought that wealth would make the slightest difference to your standing with her?'

'Because I'd tried everything else I could think of, short of abduction.'

She left the hint of desperation to speak for itself, for it would not be helpful to keep open the wound when she ought to be trying to close it. She had never known of her father's strong feelings for Aunt Amelie, and although this confession could not excuse his immoral business, it did go some way towards explaining it, and his addiction to brandy.

Sir Chase's impromptu contribution made them both start. 'I'll buy the house on Paradise Road from you, Chester,' he said. 'It would be quite useful for us whenever we want to visit Richmond. How would you feel about moving up here to live instead?'

Chester looked over his shoulder in surprise, slowly turning the rest of him to re-examine the man for whom nothing ever appeared to go wrong. 'Relieved,' he whispered, still unsure of Sir Chase's motives. The caution showed in his voice. 'I would be very relieved, if I can get out of this tangle without losing everything. I cannot carry on like this.' A glistening drop of moisture gathered in the corner of one eye which he brushed away with a knuckle.

'No,' said Caterina, sternly. 'You most certainly cannot, Father.' With the skill of a pickpocket, she deftly lifted the flask of brandy out of his pocket and placed it on the tea tray. 'And the sooner you learn to do without that, the easier it will be. You'll have your work cut out in the next few weeks if you're to free yourself and Harry from the mess without it becoming an open secret, and brandy isn't going to help one bit. I don't suppose Harry will help, either.'

'But what about my letter?' he cried, glaring at Sir Chase. 'Hannah must never find out about this. Never!'

'Father, Hannah *will* be the first to know, and Aunt Amelie, too, if you don't immediately begin to wind up all your affairs in Liverpool and present Sir Chase with the evidence within three weeks. Then he'll begin to negotiate to buy Paradise Road, and you can begin to move back to your own home. Won't you?' she said, looking across at her husband.

He had crossed his long legs and was looking up at the finely detailed plaster moulding over the large bay window, his face a picture of resignation. His yawn was too prolonged to be genuine. 'Yes, my darling little termagant,' he said, smoothly. 'If you say so.'

'You're surely not serious about that, are you?' her father protested. 'A few *weeks* is hardly going to be long enough to—'

'Oh, yes, she is,' said Sir Chase. 'Devil take me, sir, she is very serious about these things, and so am I. I cannot afford to have my father-in-law mixed up in this shady business. I have been an active abolitionist too long for the mud-slinging to miss me when my wife's father is deported to join Australia's chain-gang community. That really would be too much, even for a man with my reputation. No self-respecting abolitionist could emerge from that kind of thing with his head held high.'

Father and daughter stared, overcome by amazement.

Stephen Chester had paled to the white of the plasterwork ceiling. 'So *that's* it,' he whispered. 'Where will I…er…find you? What address?'

'In Richmond. I'll contact you when we arrive.'

'Richmond?' said Caterina. 'Why are we returning to Richmond?'

'Peace, wife!' he said, severely. 'You will live wherever I live.'

'Yes, husband,' she said, blinking a little. 'Would now be a good time to tell my father about the lead mine?'

Stephen Chester's departure from Buxton would have been delayed even longer if Caterina had delved into every one of the grievances she held against him, but the mine disaster was more important and, after some heated argument, both she and Sir Chase managed to convince him that his first duty was to the miners' families, not to himself or Harry. Reluctantly, he was made to agree with them while Caterina held her anger in check at his selfishly blinkered attitude, even now.

'A leopard doesn't change its spots,' Sir Chase commented drily, after watching her silent fuming that same afternoon in Centre House. 'He'll do no more than he has to, then he'll be off up to Liverpool. But he'd better sort himself out, my sweet. He'll not find me a soft touch in this business, as he thought he had in the last.'

She said nothing to that, still irritated by the argument which, in her eyes, should not have been necessary. Whatever her father did as a result of these catastrophes would be first and foremost in his own and Harry's interests, not anyone else's. That much was certain. With that in mind, she had withheld the question concerning the way he had negotiated her marriage. It would have to wait.

There was one question, however, about which she needed more information. 'Why didn't you tell me?' she said indignantly, opening one of the sash windows with a screech. The wind was beginning to moderate, the heavy rain clouds scudding away into the distance with a watery sun spying through a small patch of blue. 'About being an abolitionist?'

He replaced a glass paperweight he had been examining. 'Because, my child, you would have added two and two together and come up with something like ninety-nine. It's a habit of yours I was made aware of quite early in our relationship.'

'Quite the contrary,' she snapped, lifting a spider carefully off the sill. 'If you had declared yourself at the beginning, I would have known where I stand all the sooner.'

'Oh? And where do you stand now that you know?'

'More on your side than I was then.'

'But I didn't want you on my side then. I enjoyed the sparring.'

'Whether I enjoyed it or not. Thank you. That was helpful.'

'You enjoyed it, too. Don't pretend you didn't.'

'There was absolutely no need to keep it a secret from me.'

'Talking about secrets, are we? Does that apply to you, too, or do you have a special dispensation to hide things from your husband?'

'I suppose you're referring to the documents I removed…'

'To the *stolen* letter and IOU. Yes. Where are they?'

'In my writing-desk. I was going to show them to you,' she said, chastened by his severity and the hard hazel eyes that followed her all the way to the door with no promise of pardon. With a last attempt at defiance, she stood half-in, half-out. 'If you're going to be…'

His eyes narrowed, and the rest of her challenge went unsaid.

Moments later, the air in the sunny drawing-room was charged with expectation as Sir Chase read the letter that supplied him with details, clenching and unclenching the muscles in his jaw. Then, laying it down on the table beside his elbow, he gave a grunt of disgust. 'Ye gods!' he said. 'What an asset to the Chester family. With a son like that, any more disasters would seem like an overdose even to Job himself.' Picking up the crumpled IOU, he scanned it briefly then calmly tore it into shreds which he laid on the open letter.

Caterina observed, loving every move he made, fascinated by his self-composure. She would have debated for weeks before doing such a thing, even with her natural impetuosity. 'You can afford to do that, can you?' she said. 'Is it really of no use to you?'

His eyes rested on her, searching her face for a meaning. 'Whatever reason you had for taking it has passed, sweetheart. Do you think I should kick him while he's down, then? Is that what you'd have me do? I don't want anything he's got now, sweet girl. I've won.'

'I just wondered what you'd do, if you had the chance.'

'Then stop wondering. It's not nearly as complex as you think.'

'What do I think? How would you know?'

'If you sit down, I'll tell you what you think.'

Obediently, she sat in the winged chair opposite him where a fresh draught from the window brought the faint scent of new-washed leaves and grass. 'It was not by chance that you won so much from my brother in London, was it?' she said, still half-hoping to catch him off guard, to uncover a new layer of meaning to events. 'You knew then of my father's slaving, didn't you, and that was your way of punishing him? Have I got it right? But instead of that, you did him a favour. That's what I can't quite understand.'

'No, I did *myself* a favour. I was never concerned about your father's feelings. They're not easy to understand, in any case. And, yes, you're right in assuming that I intended to relieve your brother of as much as he'd wager. It was not particularly difficult because, for one thing, he doesn't have a gambler's memory and, for another, he knew your father would always bail him out. What *I* find difficult to understand is why your father allows it, year after year, while he gripes about being stumped for cash. That takes some explaining that goes deeper than his need to set your brother up as a wealthy gentleman, especially when he's kept everyone else on a very fine line.'

'Security,' Caterina said. 'Taking matters into his own hands. But what did you intend to do with twenty-thousand guineas, if my father had not agreed to your offer?'

'If I'd not won the wager, you mean? Ah, but I never make a wager with something as important as that if I'm not quite sure I can win it. I'd have won you, however long it took. Your father would have extended the deadline, I'm sure.'

'Oh, you *conceited* oaf!' she yelped, springing to her feet. 'I've heard enough. You were supposed to be telling me what I think and you've done nothing of the kind, sir. I think you're conceited, cocksure, high-handed….' From the corner of her eye she saw him leap out of his chair, and she wheeled away round the table to dodge him, tripping over one of its ball-and-claw feet and wasting seconds as she recovered, swaying just out of his reach with a yell of, 'Arrogant puddle-head! I should never have told you how I feel, should I? I ought to have kept it to myself. No…get off! Now you're so smug with your success…get off me! I take it all back. You're horrid! And I shall not go back to Richmond with you. So there!'

But now she was trapped inside his arms, one hand closed around her chin like a goblet while he drank from her lips, silencing her protests. She struggled against him, already regretting her former urge to tell of her unexpected happiness, for they had never spoken of love, only shown it in a thousand small signs that lovers use, and now she had handed him an advantage he certainly had no need of.

Furious, and in no mood to concede more ground, she tried with all her might to hold him off, fearing that she stood little chance against his superb fitness. Losing her balance, she was pushed backwards onto the yellow silk-covered sofa with sausage-shaped bolsters that sighed as she hit them as if they'd seen this kind of thing before. She was covered by him as she fell, and it was with some difficulty that she continued to fight, and then not too convincingly.

'One can go off people, you know,' she growled.

He scooped her legs up and lay over her again, holding the wrist that came between them. 'Is that so, my beauty? That's not quite how I understood it to be. So what you told your father was not true?' His face was too close to hers for anything but the truth, and the passion that darkened his eyes told her that he knew of her love and that no protesting would convince him otherwise. 'I know what's angering you,' he whispered. 'You think your father and I had some other plan up our sleeves which you were not aware of, other than our wager, I mean. Well, we didn't, my love. That was all there was to it. I went to Paradise Road to return the phaeton, determined to make him honour the debt. Yes, I *did* know that he was still slave-trading from Liverpool because I've been up there and seen one of his ships. I *knew* he could well afford to pay. I got one of his crew drunk enough to tell me where the ship had been and what it carried, which confirmed what I suspected. I could have exposed him any time I wanted, but that was *not* what I wanted, at the time. The abolitionist society that I am a member of has an excellent network, my sweet, and news soon gets around, and there are other ways of changing men's minds without sending them all the way to Australia to do it.

'But when I saw you,' he continued, 'everything changed. Suddenly, I wanted you more than anything in the world. Even more than that kind of money. I fell instantly in love, sweetheart. Madly. Desperately.'

'Say that again,' she whispered. 'Tell me I'm not dreaming.'

'I fell in love, truly, for the first time. It was the most overpowering feeling I can ever remember. You were magnificent. Scintillating, fiery creature. Angry with men. You'd not have let me get near you if I'd not put you under some pressure. And I saw you again that day at Sheen Court, singing, and nothing else mattered but how to make you accept me. And Seton was there, looking at you like a love-struck swain, and I had to get to you before he did. We drove round Richmond and you could think of little else but the excitement of freedom, and I knew that was the way to do it, to let you fly, to give you space and my protection, and everything you want from life, music and interesting people, intelligent, kindly people. I wanted you then, and I want you near me every moment. I ache for you, Caterina.

'But I'm sorry it was all so humiliating for you. I knew I'd have to work hard to win you, sweetheart, so if I crow about it and look as if I've caught the canary, you'll have to excuse me. To hear you tell your father just now that I'm all you could wish for almost burst my heart with sinful pride. I love you, adore you, my wonderful woman. Can you forgive me for the way I captured you? Was it so very bad?'

'Very disagreeable at times…' she smiled '…and time-wasting. But very exciting, too. I have to confess…' She hesitated, overcome by memories.

'What? Confess it.'

'That I'd more or less decided to accept you, in my dreams, far too soon for decency. I've never met a man like you before. I didn't know such men existed, and I couldn't let the rest of my life go without knowing what it was like to be yours. Truly yours. I have no more conditions, my love. I simply want to be with you, no one but you. Take me home, Chase, wherever home is.'

'First thing in the morning, to freedom, to be my woman, my *prima donna,* my beautiful impulsive songbird.'

'Is that going to be enough to keep you happy, Chase?'

Studying the question in her eyes, he saw how she trod upon shaky ground. She was referring, naturally, to his past. 'I'm changed, too,' he whispered. 'I was searching for someone like you. Freedom is all very well, but I need someone special to share it with. You've seen me since we met. Have I given you the slightest reason to doubt me?'

'Not once.'

'Nor shall I ever. I have all I want.'

'I have all I want, too, beloved, except...well...perhaps we should foist a family of wicked little Bostons upon the world, as wild as their father. Shall we?'

'And as lovely and talented as their mother.'

The bolsters with the long silk tassels might have witnessed similarly loving scenes before, but these two were an exceptional pair with a love that had overcome some daunting obstacles, the narrowness of the settee being the least of them. As on the deserted moorland with only bird-calls and crickets for company, their spontaneous lovemaking was sweetened by the aroma of rain-washed earth that filled the room, banishing at last those doubts that had always kept something of her in reserve. Now, something deep within her soul opened like the last bright portal to her heart, and their union was joyful and laughing, teasing and talkative until the end, which was silent except for the breathless moans of pleasure.

As her body flew on its own soaring course, he was intense and fierce, and she was lifted and carried away into the breath-stopping vortex, clinging to him, crying for him not to let go of her.

'Never, my love,' he whispered. 'You're mine, and I love you, and I shall never let you go.'

In her overwhelming relief at having found answers

to her questions at last, it was only to be expected that there might be one which had been asked but not answered. What had he intended to do with the money he'd been so determined to win, one way or another, from her brother? Was that the way he earned his wealth? Was it put into a fund drawn on by abolitionists for the emancipation of slaves? Or was there something else?

In the room above them, Signor Cantoni had begun to pound out the exuberant rhythms of Handel's *The Arrival of the Queen of Sheba,* reducing them to helpless laughter at its suitability as well as its galloping pace.

Caterina had never travelled further north than Derbyshire, so on the next day, their journey over the border into Yorkshire, the largest and most diverse of England's counties, was for her all the more exciting because of its distance from home. So much for returning to Richmond, she thought, gleefully.

The southern part of the county harboured pockets of intense industry where valleys lay under palls of smoke punctuated by as many tall factory chimneys as church spires. Overlooking the town, they passed fields of cloth pegged onto tenter-frames, bright with new dyes. Beyond the sprawling mass below them, the hills beckoned, reminding them that there was much more to see than this. Even noisy bustling Leeds was no damper to Caterina's spirits.

After an overnight stay there, the northern route took them across the River Aire through the tiny village of Chapel Allerton to the rural retreat of the Lascelles family at Harewood House, another little pile in the country that rivalled Chatsworth for sheer volume. The son of Baron Lascelles, another friend of Sir Chase's, was eager to offer them hospitality, to show them his art collection, his books, porcelain and rare furniture that must have taken care of many thousands of pounds. Their mutual friend, Mr William Turner, had been commissioned to paint views of the mansion in its idyllic setting, though Caterina thought these were more landscape than house. She was more interested in the ceilings painted by Angelica Kauffman.

From Harewood, the pleasant spa town of Harrogate was only about seven miles away, allowing them time to rest before travelling on past Ripley Castle to Fountain's Abbey, which Mr Turner had told Caterina she must visit one day. She could hardly tear herself away from the ethereal beauty of the hallowed place, and there were tears in her eyes as she stood alone in the great ruined nave, listening to the haunting voices of unseen monks at prayer accompanied by the soft screech of pigeons' wings. They stayed overnight at nearby Ripon, all five of them attending compline together in the glorious ancient cathedral, moved by the beauty of the choir, the stained glass, the vaulted ceilings.

It was a mere nine miles through wooded valleys and over dramatic hills to the market town of Masham where they had lunch before heading ever northwards through Newton-le-Willows and Scotton, by which time Caterina was wondering out loud if they might soon be in Scotland. She had not intended any sarcasm, but her geography had come unstuck by several hundred miles. They had been moving through the dales, valleys named after the rivers that flowed through them, Airedale, Nidderdale, Uredale and now Swaledale, and the day was far advanced as Sir Chase stopped their coaches, calling for them to look ahead.

There, rising on a hilltop above the horizon on the

far side of the River Swale, a castle towered into the sky like a giant fortress with the slate-roofed town clustered around its base, a water-wheel clattering on the river, a stone bridge, a sheer wooded cliff face dwarfing them.

'Where are we?' Caterina asked.

'Home,' said Sir Chase, taking her hand. 'This is the original Richmond in the county of Richmondshire, the town after which the other Richmond in Surrey was named.'

'Another Richmond?' she breathed. 'You have a home here, too?'

'Aye. Bear with me a mile or so more, and I'll show you. It'll be hard work for the horses up the hill, so we'll take it slowly. This is the Richmond Hill of the song. Do you remember it? *"On Richmond Hill there lives a lass, more bright than Mayday morn".'* He began to sing in his rich bass, making her laugh as Signor Cantoni and Mr Pearson joined in, to the delight of the coachmen.

Leaving the picturesque limestone buildings and the castle of Richmond behind them, they saw glorious hill-sides and valleys bathed in low golden sunshine that picked out, ahead of them, a white-gold mansion belonging to every architectural style from medieval to Georgian. It was a rambling stone-built place of two and three storeys with battlements, towers, pillars and porticoes, steps and balconies, lawns, terraces and a flash of glass from the kitchen hothouses, large enough to swallow Chester Hall several times over and still leave room for Number 18 Paradise Road. Further along the road, where a farmer drove his black-faced sheep, was a white stone wall with a gate between carved posts. 'The gates to Boston Hall,' he said.

'But it's so…so *huge,'* said Caterina. 'We might never meet from one day to the next. How will I ever find you?'

'You won't have to, sweetheart. I shall never be far away from you. Like it? Think you could live here in the summer months?'

'Oh, Chase! I could live here all the year round. It's so beautiful. I had no idea you had a place like this. This is paradise. Truly paradise.'

'A fitting place, then, for Lady Boston. Come, my sweet. Let's get home.'

Named in the fourteenth century when it was little more than a manor house with a hall, the present Boston Hall had expanded with every new generation who had come from the east coast of Yorkshire where, in the thriving port of that name, merchants had made their wealth. The Bostons had added to it ever since, partly owing to some exceedingly discriminating marriages to wealthy heiresses. Miss Caterina Chester was almost the only exception to that, and her husband could not have cared less at having chosen to turn his back on a debt of twenty-thousand guineas.

The question about what he had intended to do with it was overlooked in those early days while every moment was taken up with exploring the dozens of rooms from attic and turret to food-store and cellar, from stable to ice-house and hothouse. Here was enough space to spare for every activity, and the question of which room to re-decorate first and which to make into guest rooms, where to add extra bathrooms and how to modernise the kitchens took up all of those early days.

Shopping excursions into Richmond were fun and very productive, but best of all was to ride freely over the Boston acres and to talk with the estate workers and Sir Chase. Daily, he took her out in his high curricle to teach her to drive four-in-hand, each day making new discoveries about her abilities and how to make her adored husband happier than ever.

Hours were spent with Signor Cantoni, too, for he had found a new lilt to her tone that beguiled him, and not for a moment did he regret having accepted the position of tutor when he had his own suite of rooms into which the sun flooded each morning. One morning, however, he found his beautiful pupil unusually preoccupied when they met for her daily practice. She stood by the tall window that looked out over a small Italianate lake, responding eventually to his third greeting with a stuttered one of her own, a lace handkerchief that was no longer square twisted around her fingers.

'My lady?' he said, softly. 'You are not well? Shall we give the lesson a miss?'

'Er…yes…what? Oh, I beg your pardon, signor. Miss it? No, all's well,' she said, brightly. A frown followed on, quite quickly.

'You've seen something?' he said, looking where her eyes led.

He was a close friend, an adviser, and caring. He would know what to do, or not to do. 'Yes,' she whispered. 'I have.'

'Where?' He continued to look.

'No, not out there. Just now. Someone came in.'

'In here? Who, my lady? Was it a servant?'

'I don't know…exactly…who she is. She is black-skinned, signor. A beautiful, striking young woman with the loveliest complexion like ebony, and large eyes, and she wore a bright turban to cover her hair.'

'Yes? Did she speak to you?'

'No, she didn't expect me to be here. When she saw me she stepped back again, but her little child darted forward into the room and she had to run to catch him and carry him out, wriggling. He was an adorable infant, but not as black as she.'

'A mulatto, my lady? That's what they call half-black, half-white children born of mixed parentage. Coffee-coloured. Very attractive.'

'That's it. Mixed parentage. Yes.'

'A...ah!' The sound was drawn out like a voice exercise. 'I see. And you are thinking that this lady ought to be having a white husband somewhere on the estate. Well, you could ask Sir Chase. He'll know.'

'No, *signor.* I cannot ask him.'

'May I ask why?'

'Because,' she whispered, 'he may tell me what I cannot bear to hear.'

The gentle Italian was silent, understanding her dilemma. Many men had liaisons before marriage to which wives were obliged to turn a blind eye. 'Perhaps I can find out for you,' he said, eventually. 'If you would give me permission, I would do it discreetly.'

'You are the most discreet of men, *signor.* Yes, you could do it. There would be no repercussions, but I need to know, you see.'

'Leave it to me. It may not be what you fear.'

'Thank you, *signor.*'

Later that same day, Signor Cantoni met her on the grand staircase as they went down to the dining-room and, by the absence of his usual smile, she could tell that his news was not what she had hoped to hear.

'Signor?' she said, leading him round the curve of the bannister to a seat made for two. 'Will you sit?'

His enquiries, he told her, had revealed that there was no husband, white or otherwise, but that the woman, whose name was Mara, had come to live at Boston Hall almost two years ago and had given birth seven months later to her half-caste child, Jack. No one had ever bothered to ask who the child's father was because she had lived as the slave of someone in London, which concerned no one but Mara herself and, presumably, Sir Chase. More than that no one knew, or seemed to care. They all liked her and Jack, and she lived in a small cottage on the estate, coming to the hall every day with her child to fill the house with cut flowers and to decorate the dining table in the absence of a mistress. The *signor's* informant assumed that Mara's position would be redundant, and perhaps that's why she had been seeking Sir Chase, to ask for some clarification.

The centrepieces on the dining table that evening came under closer scrutiny than ever before, and Caterina was bound to admit that whoever had arranged the assortment of flowers, fruit and leaves, shells and small ornaments from the house, had an outstanding creative flair. She could not bring herself to ask Sir Chase who was responsible, for she did not want to hear him speak the woman's name.

The food, always so succulent, tasted of nothing, and the terrible hurt that weighed like lead in her heart made it difficult for her to swallow. Afterwards, when Sir Chase asked her what had happened to her appetite, she made the excuse that her period had begun, which she had once told herself she would never do. And that night, she lay alone in her beautiful white-and-blue room with cherubs painted on the ceiling and tears washing onto the cotton pillowcase. In spite of her vow, she *was* weeping for a man she loved more than life itself. The woman was a beauty. He would see the child Jack, and he would remember what it had taken to make such a beautiful child, and she, Caterina, would have to hold her tongue and pretend not to notice any of it, even while it broke her heart in two.

Her pretence to be unwell had not been believed, as she thought it had, but Sir Chase's own observations had more to back them up when Signor Cantoni spoke some soft words to him as they wished each other a good-night on the first-floor landing after a game of billiards. What the tender-hearted and passionate Italian had to say was accepted with a frown, a nod of the head, and a word of thanks.

The door of Caterina's room opened just wide enough to allow Sir Chase's tall frame through, before closing quietly again. The white-robed figure on the bed was visible only by the light of a single candle, sitting with her knees hunched up to her chin, her arms across them with a mop of damp curls shining deep chestnut and falling untidily onto her skin. Sobbing, she did not hear him approach and, when he sat on the bed next to her and gathered her into his chest, her head fell forward as if the load of it was too great to bear.

'What is this, my darling girl? What is all this about?' he said.

The roar came from a deep wound of insecurity that still could not believe she had found the kind of love she had dreamed of, and now the anguish of reality poured forth as the dam burst in a howl of despair, for she was more sure of her disappointment than she was of him. Sob after racking sob tore words from her, so fractured that they could not be understood, her tears staining the lapels of his grey silk dressing gown with patches of black.

Stroking her hair, he rocked her like a child after a nightmare. 'Hush, my darling. Hush now. Tell me what the matter is.'

'I can't,' she wailed. 'You always tell me the truth,

and I don't think I can bear to hear it. I love you too much, Chase.'

Waiting a moment longer for the terrible sobbing to slow, he held her damp head in the crook of his shoulder, wiping her eyes with the sheet. 'The truth,' he said, 'is what you shall have, nevertheless, because I would not insult you with anything less. Listen to this, and then let's see who needs your tears most. Will you hear me, sweetheart?'

'Yes. It's best to know, I suppose.'

'Oh, much the best. Well, the story goes like this. About two years ago I was walking home one evening from a Royal Society meeting in London with some friends. There was a scream from further up the street, and some shouts, and a woman came hurtling round the corner as if demons were after her, and she crashed straight into me without looking. She was torn and very distressed, weeping, bleeding, and terrified. Two young men were chasing after her but, as soon as they saw the woman with us, they tried to run off. My friends chased them, caught them and dragged them back. They were as drunk as lords, abusive and unrepentant. The woman was the servant of a friend of theirs. They named him, a man I know, and they had decided to torment her because she had a dignity they found inappropriate in a woman with black skin.'

'This is the lady called Mara? The lady I saw today?'

'Yes, her name is Mara, and those two had assaulted her, very seriously. She had been a virgin, but not any more. One of the two, an eighteen-year-old, was Harry Chester, whose face I searched for in London's gaming dens until I found him again this year. He didn't remember me, but then, he doesn't appear to remember much, does he, except how to squander his father's money?'

'*Harry?* Oh…oh no! He *assaulted* her?'

'He told me so himself, quite proud of it, he was. "She was nothing," he boasted. Just a black slave. Worthless. We let them go and we carried her to Half-moon Street where my housekeeper treated her. I went to Mara's owner the next day and paid him for her. Then, when she'd recovered enough to travel, I brought her up here in my coach and gave her the use of the woodman's old cottage. They've all looked after her. They're a good crowd up here. When I came up a few months later, I could see the result of that night's work. Your brutish brother had fathered a child on her. That winter, she gave birth to Jack. He's just over a year old now. A lovely lad. Your nephew, sweetheart. I'm sorry, I didn't want to shock you. I would have told you, eventually, when we'd settled in. But you saw her. I should have asked her to stay out of the way for a while. She's an employee like all the others. No more, no less.'

The sobs subsided as she listened to the appalling story, hardly able to believe that any member of her own family could have behaved with such barbarity, especially towards a woman. She *was* shocked, but who would not be?

'Chase, I'm so…so *very* sorry. So sorry. The poor woman. Will she recover, do you think?'

'She's very quiet, very spiritual and dignified, and I'm sure she's happier here among friends than she was in London. But as for recovering, I don't know. She will talk to me, but there is no man in her life. Shall I find another place for her, sweetheart? I will, if her being here upsets you.'

'No…oh, no, Chase, absolutely not. She must stay, and I will find lovely things for her to do, creative things that will help her. And Jack must be sent to school when he's old enough. We must do all we can for them.'

'Although I think,' said Sir Chase, kissing her swollen eyelids, 'that neither of them need ever know that you are related to Jack's father. That would serve no useful purpose. But now you will understand why I was hell-bent on relieving your brother of so much money. Which member of the Chester family it came from I didn't much care as long as I could use it to help Jack and his mother.'

'Yes, my darling. I do understand, and I think what you did was right, and honourable, and very proper, and I am shamed by my brother more than I can say. But I can try to make it up to them by kindness instead of money. What a pity you were not able to win it, after all. It would have kept them in luxury for life.'

'No, my love. I won what I wanted. It turned out perfectly in the end.'

'I was jealous. I am not proud of my thoughts, dearest one.'

Tipping her backwards, he loomed over her, studying her tear-ravaged face. 'Do you know,' he said, trying to remain serious, 'that this is the first time you've ever shown me how jealous you can be? Everything else, but not jealousy. I was beginning to wonder if you ever would, but now I know. You went off like a little fire-cracker, didn't you? Eh? I'm quite flattered, to tell you the truth.'

'Then you had better watch your step, Chase Boston, had you not? I tried to tell myself that I must not care so much if my husband reverts to his old habits, but…oh…the pain of it,' she whispered. 'Even without any evidence at all, the pain was terrible, Chase. I love you so very much.'

His lovemaking was exquisitely tender, and for Caterina there was the added piquancy of the fear that her jealous response had caused. Though it had been fleeting and soon dealt with, the pain was still vivid in her memory, her tears still close to the surface, her heart torn by the shocking behaviour and callousness of the two men in her family. Like father, like son, she thought. Never had she felt so alienated from them, so glad to be well out of their orbit.

She did not reach a climax, as she'd always done before, nor did either of them strive towards it, for her energy had been spent, and what she needed was his reassuring closeness to every surface of her body, the security of his arms, his adoring endearing words of love.

Afterwards, they lay talking about Chase's involvement with the Slave Emancipation Society, how he had made enquiries about Harry, visited Liverpool docks with friends to find out more about his drunken boasts, and had there seen one of her father's ships with its cargo of sugar, tobacco and raw cotton.

Guessing was one thing, but proving it was another, and when a voyage of the triangle could sometimes take as long as two years to complete, one had to play a waiting game, though there were some abolitionists who believed that arson was a swifter punishment for law-breakers than a trial and deportment. It was then that Caterina began to wonder how she could be involved, too, as a kind of atonement for her family's shortcomings.

The answer to this came on the following evening when Sir Chase, Caterina and Signor Cantoni paid a visit to the well-known Theatre Royal in Richmond. Expecting that the standard of acting might be comparable to that of Brighton, Caterina was relieved to find that she was much mistaken. The shower of calling-cards left at Boston Hall since their arrival had come mostly from patrons of the theatre, eager to be among the first to visit the new Lady Boston, reports of whose amazing singing voice had preceded her.

For the event, she had dressed in one of her loveliest gowns of aquamarine and silver tissue over a deeper silk that shimmered like water as she moved. Her beautiful emerald ring was now augmented by a fabulous matching necklace, earrings and bracelet, with ribbons binding her bodice and hair in the Grecian manner. Here was a chance to wear the white silk stockings given to her by the Tolbys, the white satin slippers with *diamanté* buckles bought in London, the long silk stole bought here in Richmond only two days ago. The proprietor of the shop was also the patron who supplied the theatre with its excellent costumes, and his name-dropping had sent ripples through his customers for the next few days.

Consequently, the theatre was not only full to capacity a good half-hour before the first of the season's performances of *Othello,* but the whole of Richmond's high society had taken the expensive boxes all except one, the one next to the Mayor's Box, which overlapped the stage itself.

So when Sir Chase's coach arrived there was already a small crowd of people outside, good-naturedly craning their necks to catch a glimpse of the vision in aquamarine and jewels with her two handsome escorts.

'Who are they waiting for?' Caterina asked the welcoming manager.

'For you, my lady,' he replied.

She laughed. 'Oh no. For the Mayor and his lady, surely?'

'No, I assure you. Word of your presence in Richmond has got around.'

She smiled at Signor Cantoni, sharing the joke with the lift of an eyebrow. Provincial they may be up here in the northern counties, but they certainly knew how to make one feel welcome. She could not have anticipated, either, the smiles, bows, curtsies and handshakes issuing from all sides of the trio as if they were royalty, nor could she have known that the colours she had chosen to wear were as close as one could get to the colour scheme of the auditorium. Everywhere, on every surface, the greeny-blue was reflected in three different tones highlighted with gold; even the ceiling was a rectangle of blue-and-white painted clouds.

As they entered their box, the be-wigged Mayor and his elderly wife followed close behind, smiling in triumph and drawing their attention to the crowd on the benches below, in the boxes round the room, and in the gallery above. Like the surge of the tide, the audience rose to its feet, applauding and whistling their delight.

'What a wonderful welcome they give you,' Caterina said to the mayor's wife, above the din. 'And for Sir Chase, too. I had no idea he was so popular.'

The mayor's wife twinkled. 'Listen to them, Lady Boston. I think you'll find it's you they're eager to see more of.'

Puzzled, she turned to the sea of faces, then across at the waving occupants of the boxes. 'Paradise Lady!' they were calling. 'Songbird! Lady Boston…the Paradise Bird…wow! What a stunner…well done, Sir Chase!'

They were calling for her by name, by a flattering sobriquet with a saucy ring to it, whistling, clapping, and a loud bellow of, 'Gi' us a song then, m'lady!'

Laughter and cheers covered her from all sides like a soft blanket of adoration, and she knew as she had never known before that she was at home, not away from it. Holding Chase by the hand, she felt the warm squeeze as he shared her pride, then her hand was lifted to his lips while the audience applauded the gallant gesture. Their eyes met in shared amusement at the neck-breaking speed of their progress, recalling their fights and her attempts at avoidance, the obstacles, the balking and the impulsive, passionate loving.

The wonderful experience of that evening, however, was a catalyst for an idea that began to form in Caterina's mind during the performance, for it was obvious that she had a large and unexpected following of enthusiasts. During the interval, Sir Chase had introduced many who had left their calling-cards and who wanted to know when she would be giving her first recital, a question that was asked again and again of them, of Signor Cantoni, too.

'With a place as large as this,' she said to her husband that same night, 'we could hold a series of charity concerts each year, as they do in Ham House, and Syon, and Marble Hill. Nobody in Surrey minds paying handsomely for an evening of music, and it's a chance to dress up and gossip, and just think of the money we could raise once a month.'

'What charity did you have in mind, Paradise Lady?' he said, going to stand behind her to look at their reflections in the mirror. He pulled gently at the ribbons still binding her hair, releasing layer upon layer of red-brown curls.

She turned to him, holding out her arms as he knelt to her level. She enclosed his head and shoulders, admiring the noble beauty of his brow and the thick spring of hair that defined his chiselled features. 'Do you need to ask?' she whispered. 'Your society, for slaves, for their freedom. I've been given my freedom, but I cannot begin to share their sorrows. It hardly bears thinking about. If I can earn money by singing, then it makes sense for us to contribute to our own cause rather than other people's, and here we have every facility for indoor *and* outdoor concerts, as well as a list of patrons eager to attend. Signor Cantoni would love to be the music director, and there's sure to be an orchestra locally just waiting for a chance to perform. What do you say, darling? Shall we give it a try?'

Lifting his head, he smiled into her dreaming eyes and saw how the eyelids drooped with fatigue. 'I say, my beautiful girl, that you are the most tender-hearted and generous creature I know, the most talented and the loveliest…'

'Stop, Chase. That's not what I'm asking you.'

'And the most enchanting songbird, and it's no wonder they want more of you. So do I. But I've got you in my arms, as I've wanted to all evening, and I don't think I can wait any longer. Shall we discuss it tomorrow, my sweet?'

'Only if you promise to agree,' she whispered, watching as his fingers eased her chemise off one shoulder. The lace frill rested upon her breast, teasing him with the sight of her half-exposed voluptuousness.

His mouth tasted the sweetness of her skin, nudging the frill downwards until it dropped onto her lap, allowing him access to the full curve beneath the breast, the darker ring around its peak, the proud inviting nipple like a small ripe hazelnut, and the soft slope above. 'Peerless woman,' he rumbled, deep with passion, 'did you or did you not promise me obedience in all things and at all times?'

Her fingers smoothed his bare shoulder. 'Yes, husband. I believe I did say something to that effect, foolishly, once.'

'Then will you leave these matters until a more convenient time, wife? Or shall I be obliged to claim a husband's rights while you're still negotiating?'

'Er...yes,' she whispered as he pushed the lace off her other shoulder.

'Yes to which?' he murmured, lapping at her skin.

'Just yes, my love. Yes to anything.'

Swinging easily to his feet, he placed his hands beneath her back and knees, lifting her into his arms, pausing as his eyes travelled from breasts to face and back again. 'That's another thing I love about you,' he said. 'Your wonderfully quixotic change of mind. You used not to have the knack of it.'

'It must be something in the air,' she sighed, dropping her head into the angle of his neck.

Epilogue

Only a month later, Sir Chase and Lady Boston gave the first of their musical evenings for charity, which soon became so successful that each month was a sell-out, guests coming from miles around to stay with friends in the area.

Signor Cantoni had far more to do in his new role than ever he could have foreseen, and his popularity was well-deserved. He and the beautiful Mara formed a close bond which was a delight to see, quiet, unobtrusive, utterly devoted, a perfect friendship that never went quite as far as marriage, though everyone had hopes.

To Caterina, Mara became a special kind of friend, more than a servant but never a rival in any sense. Nor did Mara ever discover Caterina's relationship to her son, never having discovered the full name of his father. Jack himself grew to be a fine lad who, by the age of four, was showing a musical talent that Caterina and Sir Chase did all they could to encourage.

Stephen Chester and his rapidly expanding family moved back up to Chester Hall in Buxton, but Caterina and her husband had little to do with them, or Harry, for she realised that, after all she knew about them, the distance between them was about right.

Sara and her adoring Constantine were regular visitors to Boston Hall, and also to Number 18 Paradise Road in the other Richmond, when the Bostons were at home there. It was one of Caterina's joys that she was able to restore the elegant house to its former serenity as it had been when she and Aunt Amelie had lived there. Readers may be interested to know that Numbers 18-24 Paradise Road in Richmond, Surrey, is now the UK headquarters of Harlequin, Mills & Boon, publishers of this story.

Seton, Lord Rayne, went slightly downhill for a while until he discovered another wonderful woman, though it may be more accurate to say that she discovered him. That story will have to be looked into more closely, perhaps.

But Caterina *did* produce those children who loved, as infants, to bang drums and pipe pipes and then to sit with Signor Cantoni for fun on the piano. Duets, trios, quartets and even a children's orchestra then became part of the charity concert programme, comprising the talented sons and daughters of the Richmond set.

On sale 3rd August 2007

Regency

MARIANNE AND THE MARQUIS

by Anne Herries

Surrounded by danger, Marianne trusted the enigmatic Mr Beck – until he was revealed as a marquis! He would never marry the daughter of a country vicar. But he paid Marianne such flattering attention…

WARRIOR OR WIFE

by Lyn Randal

Leda was once the beloved daughter of a Roman senator. Exiled from the riches of her birth, she sold herself into gladiatorial slavery. Donatus is determined to right the wrong he did her and reclaim his bride!

THE MATCHMAKER

by Lisa Plumley

Molly knew that she'd be a success if only someone would take her seriously. But who'd ever have thought it would be the arrogant Marcus Copeland? And was his proposition strictly business – or secret pleasure?

Available at WHSmith, Tesco, ASDA, and all good bookshops

www.millsandboon.co.uk

0607/41/MB094

A compelling North-East saga in the bestselling tradition of Catherine Cookson

Born the day of the great mining disaster at Jane Pit, Merry Trent is brought up by her only surviving relative, her feisty grandmother Peggy, and lives in stricken poverty. Times are hard, and when an unwelcome visit from the ruthless mining agent, Miles Gallagher, leaves her pregnant, she tells no-one.

When Merry begins training as an apprentice nurse she attracts the attention of dashing young doctor Tom Gallagher, Miles' son, and Merry falls pregnant again. She loses her job and accommodation at the hospital, and her future looks bleak as she faces a tough choice: a marriage of convenience, or destitution and the workhouse…

Available 18th May 2007

www.millsandboon.co.uk